The Morningside

"The dreamlike novel draws on elements of folklore and fairy tales for a narrative set eerily close to present day that explores environmental collapse and human resilience."
—*Time*

"The textures of *The Morningside*—a familiar city, a familiar crisis, a familiar complacency—make this future feel closer, shot through with an almost excruciating intimacy. Here, storytelling is not a way of relating to a mythical past but of growing up in the long middest."
—*The New Yorker*

"By weaving in folklore and ample wonder, [Téa] Obreht gives her climate fiction ancient roots, forcing us to reckon with the ruined world that future generations will inherit, while reminding us that even in the face of catastrophe, there's solace to be found in art."
—*The New York Times*

"[*The Morningside*] is delicately and truthfully done; Obreht deals in big, topical and often brutal themes without ever sacrificing the artistry of her storytelling to preachiness or brute allegory. . . . Obreht is a novelist of great skill and warmth, for whom the ancient forms of storytelling—folktales, myths and legends—retain all their capacity to explain and mystify, soothe and terrify."
—*The Guardian*

"A touching, inventive novel about belonging and loss."
—*People*

"A beautiful examination of displacement, identity, and the effects of unchecked political power, enriched with touches of magical realism and dystopia."
—*Bustle*

"Obreht has a visceral sense of the saving power of stories for people propelled into a perilous world." —*The Washington Post*

"This touching and inventive novel follows a young woman searching for meaning and belonging, both through her loving aunt's stories and the enigmatic resident of the building's penthouse suite." —*Oprah Daily*

"An astounding rethink of the mother-daughter narrative." —*Real Simple*

"Try to read ten pages of this book and resist its fairy dust. . . . Obreht is a pure, natural storyteller with a direct hotline to the collective unconsciousness." —*The Minnesota Star Tribune*

"Obreht is offering a cautionary vision of what our future might look like, but she's also asking questions that are as old as storytelling. What do we want to tell ourselves about ourselves? What do we try to hide from ourselves? And what's the cost of our lives?" —*Kirkus Reviews* (starred review)

"A bewitchingly atmospheric, psychologically lush, and deeply knowing tale of ancient sorrows and coalescing crises, courage and fortitude." —*Booklist* (starred review)

"Satisfyingly unsettling . . . *The Morningside* soars in its depiction of an alternative world frighteningly similar to our own. Whether or not they ever face forcible displacement in their life, everyone at some point must confront their past. Obreht addresses this truism with startling freshness in this entertaining work." —*BookPage*

"Well wrought, charming, and quietly bent . . . This book is pure unpredictable but organically and esthetically coherent pleasure from start to finish." —*Locus*

"Enthralling . . . Obreht draws upon plausible dystopian and post-apocalyptic futures and strong elements from Serbian folktales, as well as magical realism. The result is a strange, almost dreamlike novel, distinctive for its memorable characters and beautiful writing."
—Library Journal

"Striking . . . Readers will once again be beguiled by Obreht's lyrical imagination."
—Publishers Weekly

"Obreht is an expert and generous storyteller, infusing *The Morningside* with the pleasures of folklore and fairy tale while simultaneously diving deep into the silences and irreconcilable contradictions in the stories we inherit about the past."
—Karen Russell, author of *Orange World and Other Stories*

"Imagine a Ballardian dystopia injected with a double dose of magic realism, so that the pages seem to glow. An ideal novel in which all is invented and everything is true . . . I loved it."
—Ed Park, author of *Same Bed Different Dreams*

"Fresh and immensely gripping, *The Morningside* is a rich saga of migration and the search for belonging, bravely imagining our capacity for survival and love in an uncertain future. . . . A stunning achievement."
—Claire Vaye Watkins, author of
I Love You but I've Chosen Darkness

"*The Morningside* is like nothing I've read—at once playful and profound, harrowing and tender, a sparklingly original story of coming of age in a broken world."
—Karen Thompson Walker, author of *The Dreamers*

By Téa Obreht

The Tiger's Wife
Inland
The Morningside

The Morningside

The Morningside

A Novel

Téa Obreht

Random House
New York

Published in the United States by Random House, an imprint and division of Penguin Random House LLC, New York.

RANDOM HOUSE and the HOUSE colophon are registered trademarks of Penguin Random House LLC.

RANDOM HOUSE BOOK CLUB and colophon are trademarks of Penguin Random House LLC.

Originally published in hardcover in the United States by Random House, an imprint and division of Penguin Random House LLC, in 2024.

LIBRARY OF CONGRESS CATALOGING-IN-PUBLICATION DATA
Names: Obreht, Téa, author.
Title: The morningside: a novel / Téa Obreht.
Description: First Edition. | New York: Random House [2024]
Identifiers: LCCN 2023011845 (print) | LCCN 2023011846 (ebook) |
ISBN 9781984855527 (Paperback) | ISBN 9781984855510 (Ebook)
Subjects: LCGFT: Novels.
Classification: LCC PS3615.B73 M67 2024 (print) | LCC PS3615.B73 (ebook)
| DDC 813/.6—dc23/eng/20230313
LC record available at https://lccn.loc.gov/2023011845
LC ebook record available at https://lccn.loc.gov/2023011846
International edition ISBN 978-0-593-73269-4

Printed in the United States of America on acid-free paper

randomhousebooks.com
randomhousebookclub.com

2 4 6 8 9 7 5 3 1

Book design by Virginia Norey
Map © Jeffrey L. Ward

For Dan and Nela

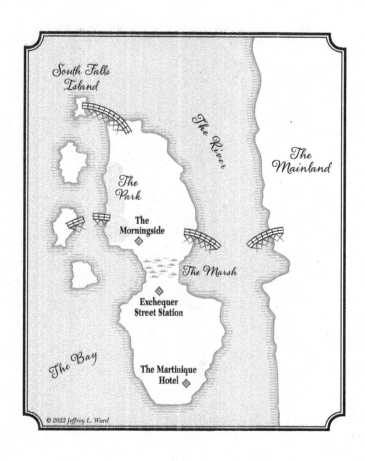

South Falls Island

The River

The Mainland

The Park

The Morningside

The Marsh

Exchequer Street Station

The Bay

The Martinique Hotel

© 2023 Jeffrey L. Ward

The Morningside

An old familiar dread was waiting for me this morning. I couldn't tell where it came from. It hadn't followed me out of a dream—at least not one I could remember—but when I got up, there it was in everything. The airless heat of the motel room. The halo of sunlight around the window shades. The vacant smile of the girl at the front desk when she took the key from my hand.

I thought it might stay behind when I left the motel, but it hitched a ride through the desert with me. Just sitting there. Tightening the world. It knew me so well.

When I got to the train station, I finally gave in and did what I knew the feeling was after me to do: I looked up my mother. I hadn't done it in a long time because the suspense made me sick, even though what I imagined I would read was always worse than what was actually posted. It didn't feel like the kind of morning for bad news: quiet, unusually free of wildfire smoke, blue, and windless. The train was late, the platform mostly empty. A few passengers had drifted out of the station and were standing in the sun as they looked down the track. The handful of others, like me, were clearly there to meet someone. It was the calmest I'd felt all week, so I thumbed my mother's name into the search bar. There was the brief nervousness that always stopped my breath before the forums loaded. The dread of something having changed, some new, poisonous derangement. Usually, there was nothing. Hadn't been for years.

Today was different. A new picture had been added to the Belen case file. It was not, as I always feared it would be, a police snapshot of Mila's corpse. It was a Polaroid taken almost sixteen years before, the day we arrived in Island City. In the picture, my mother and I are backlit by the vanishing sun, standing side by side on Morningside Street. Our suitcases aren't quite out of view. We're smiling halfheartedly, hovering just far enough away from each other to make a comfortable embrace impossible. My mother looks worn and flustered, standing there in an old dress of mine that is clearly too long for her. I'm the tallest eleven-year-old you've ever seen: gangly, shapeless. I've got my arm some of the way around my mother's shoulders, and am obviously smiling just to oblige the person behind the camera: my aunt Ena, whom I haven't yet hugged hello.

I remembered the moment the picture was taken, and vaguely remembered seeing the finished result pinned up on our fridge, until it disappeared under months of Repopulation Program leaflets. I hadn't seen it since we escaped, and hadn't thought about it in years. But here it was, after all this time. Who had put it up? And how the hell had they gotten hold of it? And when? Here I'd been going about my life, thinking this memory and this picture were back in the past somewhere, invulnerable to even the kinds of things I was afraid of—and yet, for some unknown while, strangers had been peering at it on their cursory journey through the handful of forums still devoted to the question of my mother's criminality.

It didn't take me long to feel dizzy enough to faint. When the vendor walked by, I got a bottle of water from him and drank the whole thing in one tilt.

Then it got worse. In the background of the photo, way up the sloping street behind us, I recognized the unmistakable form of Bezi Duras. She was just starting up the hill, and her three dogs—rangy silhouettes, black as the gaps between stars—were out ahead of her. Whatever I remembered of this photo, Bezi Duras certainly wasn't part of it. Neither were the dogs. How funny, I thought. Here I'd had a very different, very specific memory of the first time I saw her, and all the while, this picture had been out there, confirming an entirely incompatible truth. Some stranger, whose name I did not know and face I would never see, had held all of us together in the palm of their hand: Bezi, my mother, me. Even Ena, offscreen. The only person absent from the scene, fittingly enough, was Mila.

Of course, also fittingly enough, she was the only person the people commenting on the picture really cared about. They couldn't put any of it together. The furthest they could get with it was "Isn't this the woman from the Belen case?," which earned them a smattering of replies from strangers.

For the first time in years, I thought about adding my two cents. What harm would it do to chime in? To write something like "You don't have the first clue." There were plenty of anonymous comments. Nothing would set mine apart. Nothing would point back to me.

But then the loudspeaker crackled to life, announcing the coming train, and I x-ed out of the forum, stood, and went forward with my little sign.

BOOK I

Ena

Long ago, before the desert, when my mother and I first arrived in Island City, we moved to a tower called the Morningside, where my aunt had already been serving as superintendent for about ten years.

The Morningside had been the jewel of an upper-city neighborhood called Battle Hill for more than a century. Save for the descendants of a handful of its original residents, however, the tower was, and looked, deserted. It reared above the park and the surrounding townhomes with just a few lighted windows skittering up its black edifice like notes of an unfinished song, here-and-there brightness all the way to the thirty-third floor, where Bezi Duras's penthouse windows blazed, day and night, in all directions.

By the time we arrived, most people, especially those for whom such towers were intended, had fled the privation and the rot and the rising tide and gone upriver to scattered little freshwater townships. Those holding fast in the city belonged to one of two groups: people like my aunt and my mother and me, refuge seekers recruited from abroad by the federal Repopulation Program to move in and sway the balance against total urban abandonment, or the stalwart handful of locals hanging on in their shrinking neighborhoods, convinced that once the right person was voted into the mayor's office and the tide pumps got working again, things would at least go back to the way they had always been.

The Morningside had changed hands a number of times and was then in the care of a man named Popovich. He was from Back Home, in the old country, which was how my aunt had come to work for him.

Ena was our only living relative—or so I assumed, because she was the only one my mother ever talked about, the one in whose direction we were always moving as we ticked around the world. As a result, she had come to occupy valuable real estate in my imagination. This was helped by the fact that my mother, who never volunteered intelligence of any kind, had given me very little from which to assemble my mental prototype of her. There were no pictures of Ena, no stories. I wasn't even sure if she was my mother's aunt, or mine, or just a sort of general aunt, related by blood to nobody. The only time I'd spoken to her, when we called from Paraiso to share the good news that our Repopulation papers had finally come through, my mother had waited until the line began to ring before whispering, "Remember, her wife just died, so don't forget to mention Beanie," before thrusting the receiver into my hand. I'd never even heard of the wife, this "Beanie" person, until that very moment.

For eight long years I'd been conjuring Ena out of nothing—and I'd come up with a version of her that really suited me: a tall, flowing, vulpine sort of person, generous and chuckling and mantled in benevolence. Imagine my disappointment when she turned out to be short, loud, and incredibly ill-practiced at speaking to eleven-year-old nieces.

"My God, Silvia" was the first thing she said to me face-to-

face, standing out there by the Morningside gate with her camera while my mother and I dragged our suitcases up the hill.
"Are we going to have enough rations for you?"

It was impossible to tell whether she felt I should have more
or less than I was already getting. Something about her tone
implied that she might be able to secure a grander breakfast
than I was used to, the kind I'd only ever read about—pastries
and jam, maybe even eggs. But, of course, Island City was ad-
hering to its own version of Posterity measures, and breakfast
here was a roll of the dice, just as it was in every other place
we'd ever lived. Sometimes it was government tea and canned
mush. Sometimes a loaf of bread and a suspect egg to share
between two or three or four people. Whatever your ration
card happened to say when it refreshed in the morning—
assuming your local convenience store could even fulfill the
request.

Ena lived in the battered little two-bedroom superintendent's suite on the tenth floor of the Morningside. The place
was furnished with scrounged items: a haphazardly reuphol-
stered sofa, a small dining table surrounded by chairs in different states of refurbishment, a jungle of ferns and ivies Ena had
found abandoned on the sidewalk and nursed back to abundance. The bay, gray and brackish, filled the view from our window. On low-tide days you could see the old freeway, which
had once run just west of the building. Every now and again, a
barge would get stuck between the submerged guardrails, and
the whole neighborhood would descend to the waterline to
watch its rescue, reminding you that the city was not as empty
as it seemed.

My mother and I shared a cot in the room that had served as
Beanie's study. Our first night under that greening roof, I lay
awake, watching unfamiliar lights rove the ceiling. You could

have fit our whole Paraiso flat in just this room, but that small-
ness had felt safe. Upstairs, downstairs, all around us, neighbors had been laughing and quarreling, playing music, tromping
up and down the ancient, echoing stairs. But here, the only
noise seemed to come from the occasional lighthouse horn,
and a strange clatter and screech that periodically sounded
through the window. My mother didn't seem to hear it, which
made things worse.

I hadn't felt the urge to make a protection for us in a long
time. I was proud of that—not just because I had followed
through on my decision to leave all that behind in Paraiso, but
because doing so meant that I had managed to conceal the
habit from my mother. For years, I had lived in fear that she
would find the talismans I'd hidden around our flat, mistake
them for trash, and throw them away without my knowledge,
thus nullifying their effect. Or, worse, confront me about them.

"What the hell is this?" she would say.

I, having imagined this precise moment, would be ready.
"Looks like your old perfume bottle."

"What's it doing behind the stove?"

"I have no idea."

"I could have sworn I threw it out years ago."

"Huh."

That was meant to be my innocent, ignorant closer—because
what else was there to say? "You actually *did* throw it out,
Mama, but I dug it out of the trash because you really loved
that perfume, and Signora Tesseretti said that I need at least
three meaningful objects to make a good protection"?

Anyway, that was all behind me now. The Morningside could
be as looming and empty and laden with unfamiliar noises as it
liked. I didn't have three items to make a protection with anymore. I had deliberately thrown away the fragment of a photo-

graph of a person I suspected might be my father, breaking the necessary triad. All I had left were a pair of scissors and the perfume bottle my mother had continued to spray in the vicinity of her neck long after it was empty. And I was determined that nothing would compel me to use them.

Besides, Ena was a kind of protection in and of herself. There was nothing she couldn't explain or abate. When I asked her about the clattering and shrieking the next morning, she pointed out a huge nest that crowned the roof of a neighboring townhouse.

Rook cranes had begun migrating through the city only about ten years before, so they were still a novelty—though to even more recent newcomers like us, they seemed as much a fixture of its rooftops as the water towers where they made their nests. We had a few breeding pairs up-island, but their big rookery was sixty blocks south, in what had come to be known as the Marsh, that impassible waistline of the island that separated its upper and lower reaches, newly narrowed by the river on one side and the bay on the other. Callers to the Drowned City Dispatch radio station were equally divided between the opinion that Island City must honor its place on the birds' migratory route and the belief that the whole flock should be exterminated. Ena leaned toward the latter view—though, in truth, she would probably have felt differently had the birds just bypassed the surfaces she was responsible for maintaining.

Anything that hindered Ena's work was a liability. She was getting too old to serve as superintendent, and was keenly aware of it. She was prideful about her endurance, her mind stretched by the constant tally of what she had done, was doing, and had yet to do. On matters not pertaining to the Morningside, she cultivated a cool neutrality. Had she spent the past few years fervently praying that my mother and I would number among the lucky few accepted by the Repopulation Program? Not really—but she was glad we had made it. Did she have a lot of optimism about the Posterity Initiative—did she believe that ration cards and tidal mitigation and everyone pulling together would actually work, and that we would, as promised, be rewarded with a new townhouse on South Falls Island for doing our part to revive the city? Perhaps. She would believe it when she saw it. For now, she ate breakfast by the pale light of five A.M., leaning over the sink, locked in a one-sided argument with those callers to the Drowned City Dispatch whose opinions enraged her the most. To supplement our rations, she foraged in the park at the bottom of our street, returning with bags full of nameless greens, which she boiled, pinned between flat disks of dough, and stacked in the back of the freezer. She smelled of metal and soap. Her right thumb stuck out from the rest of her hand at an odd angle, and when she felt like fucking with me, she pretended she'd just broken it anew.

There were plenty of opportunities to break thumbs and other appendages all over the Morningside. In its time, the building had been an architectural wonder. Thirty-three stories of pale Malta limestone. Six opulent units per floor. A library. A basement pool designed by the great mosaic artist Flynn Vethers. A stunning penthouse, served by a private elevator. Beyond the courtyard, the lobby doors opened into a huge, glass-enclosed entrance hall with a black spiral staircase leading up to the lounge, which in the old days had boasted a glittering bar, the site of glamorous parties immortalized in the photographs around the door.

But the building was more than a hundred years old. Mighty forces were at work on it. The Board of Occupants had an annual appointment with the engineering firm of Mishkin &

Mishkin, whose findings were always the same: things were stable for now, but the Morningside had not been built to withstand hurricanes, nor a soil base that was disintegrating, however gradually, into the bay. We weren't looking at an Exchequer Street situation just yet; a total collapse wasn't imminent. But cracks were beginning to form. These days, the elevator got stuck at least once a week. You did not want to be aboard when it did, Ena told us during our introductory tour. Minds had been lost this way. Fingers, too—not so much in the elevator as in the ill-advised attempts to climb out of it via the emergency hatch. A teenaged boy had been crushed, twenty years before, in just such an effort. He now lived on the eighth floor, occasionally appearing in the hallway outfitted in the same clothes he'd been wearing the day of his demise.

"Don't talk nonsense," my mother said, jerking her head in my direction.

"Why? He's harmless!" Ena grabbed my shoulder and stared reassuringly into my face. "Harmless!"

The same could not be said of the building's other quirks. The windows were difficult to open, and if offended could come crashing down onto your hands like guillotines. The mezzanine carpet, red as a tongue, had a tendency to pull itself into folds underfoot. Sometimes you went into the breaker room and felt a charge, and you wouldn't know what to make of it— you couldn't tell if a wire had come loose or if the building just needed a minute to pull itself together. In such instances it was advisable to wait before touching anything, to listen for the exhalation of those dense, rust-streaked basement walls.

"Write that down," Ena said, so my mother—rolling her eyes at me—did.

There were exactly three reliable things at the Morningside. The first was Sanitation. No matter how bad things got, Sanitation was right on schedule. They did get stalled in disputes with the city, though, so if more than a week went by between pick-ups, it was necessary to start up the rusted little car Ena kept in the sub-basement garage and drive the trash over to the land-fill, six bags at a time, until the sidewalk in front of the building was clear.

The second was Bezi Duras. She was from Back Home, too, but had come to Island City years ago, well before the war, and so could scarcely line up five words of Ours, and then only in a disgraceful accent. She lived in the penthouse, with its private elevator. You could rely on her to be on time and polite, and to never, ever summon you for help. "In ten years I haven't been up there," Ena said. "If she needs something done, she gets her own people to do it."

The third were the gawkers. Only a few varieties of thistle persisted in the courtyard flower beds now, but the Morning-side had once been renowned for its gardens. They had been impressive enough to attract the admiration of passersby, who would stick their heads through the main gate whenever it opened to admit a car. People still wanted this kind of access. Students from the old university down the street were always asking to be let in to photograph the gargoyles or to peruse the library collection, or to sketch the lobby. Ena no longer had patience for any of these characters. She kept blurry printouts of the most persistent ones taped above the blank screens in the security shed: a studious-looking wisp of a white girl with a nose ring; a broad-shouldered, soft-faced Black man with glasses and a receding hairline. We were to memorize their faces and refuse them entry, no questions asked. "This one," she said, tapping the man's picture. "This one is relentless. He tries at least once a month."

"Tries what?" I asked.

"Oh, you know. To get in. To poke around."

"Is that wrong?"

"This isn't like Paraiso, Sil. You have to watch out for people here. Thieves and shifters."

"Is he a thief?"

"Everybody is."

The people who weren't thieves and shifters were janglers, a term Ena and my mother used to denote the kind of person who wore all their jewelry at once. Of these, the Morningside admittedly boasted a few. Their defects of character sprang, in Ena's opinion, from a fatal combination of wealth and age. They weren't about to let a few hurricanes and a submerged industrial district stand between them and the prosperity their grandparents had so doggedly eked out. "So they pretend things are just like they were forty years ago, and they throw their little tantrums. Leaving out trash, letting their dogs shit in the hallways, complaining about the water and the heat and the noise."

Most of these specimens spoke to you without eye contact, and often without bothering to form full sentences. Like Mrs. Gaspard, the Board's cadaverous president, who, upon being introduced to us in the lobby, had only one question: "And how much did the Board have to shell out to get you here?"

"Not a cent, Mrs. Gaspard!" Ena said cheerfully. "Repopulation Program! Credits!"

"Ah," said Mrs. Gaspard. "God bless the credits."

"She's the worst of the bunch," Ena told us.

By all rights, that should have been Bezi Duras, with that penthouse on the thirty-third floor all to herself. Ena was still forming an opinion about her, but if a person had made no strides toward proving they weren't a jangler in ten years, then perhaps it was safe to default to the assumption that a jangler was exactly what they were. Many signs bore this out. Bezi Duras's wealth was one. Her obstinate solitude was another. And then there were the dogs. Bezi Duras owned three behemoth hounds. She indulged them in better food than the rest of us had gotten in a long time, and they slept all day in the sun upstairs.

"But I don't want you to get the wrong idea about the residents. There's decent enough folks, too." Mrs. Sayez in 16A, for instance, was a darling. She was the Repopulation Program coordinator for the upper city—a fact she kept repeating while she squeezed my mother's hands in the hallway outside her apartment.

"How's the tour?" she asked.

"Very wonderful," my mother managed. "Thank you."

"It's a bit overwhelming, I'm sure, but this really is one of the finest old buildings in the whole city, and I'm so glad you get a flavor of how it used to be."

"Beautiful," my mother said. "Beautiful."

"Do you have everything you need?"

"We are so happy. Thank you."

"I'm delighted to hear it." Mrs. Sayez patted my mother's hand. "Oh! Here." Her momentary dive back into her apartment offered a glimpse of corridor wallpapered in brilliant marigold. "Can you read English?" she asked. I could, and said so. "And your mother, can she?"

"Of course," I lied.

"That's just wonderful—isn't it? You already know the language, *and* you have your aunt to make you feel at home. Here." She put a stack of cards into my hand. "The Repopulation Program is always eager to hear your thoughts. How you're feeling, what might make you feel more at home. Every few weeks, make sure to fill one of these out and drop it in the mail.

Don't worry about postage—they're already stamped. And answer truthfully—but don't forget to have fun!" She turned to my mother. "It's meant to be fun."

Each card asked the same three questions, spaced neatly down the page and presented in unobtrusive capital letters: WHAT IS YOUR LEVEL OF SATISFACTION WITH YOUR NEW HOME? WHAT DO YOU LIKE MOST ABOUT YOUR NEW HOME? WHAT WOULD MAKE YOUR NEW HOME EVEN BETTER?

"What are those?" my mother asked as soon as we'd moved down the hall.

"Fun cards," I said stupidly. It wasn't difficult to imagine the effect this barrage of intrusions would have on my mother.

"But these are questions—look, these are question marks."

"Right."

"What are they asking?"

"Just how we're settling in. Things like that." I tried smiling. "Light and easy."

Ena must have known that I was twisting the truth, but she didn't betray me. Perhaps she, too, sensed that heading off my mother was the right thing to do. The last question on the fun cards had brought me to a quandary, however—one I had been contemplating since the beginning of the tour.

"Are there any other kids in this building?" I asked Ena.

"There used to be," she said. "But all the families went upriver, you know?" Halfway down the service stairs, it occurred to her that this was not what I wanted to hear. A squeeze of the arm was waiting for me when I caught up with her. "But that just means you'll have the place all to yourself. Want to see the playroom?"

This was the final stop on our tour. Seeing it, I wondered whether Ena knew anything about kids at all. It was a room for the very young. It smelled faintly of early childhood pastimes—

watercolors, chalk, glue—but was empty save for a mural of a painted woodland, a wraparound scene of forest animals at a party. A prim, worried doe was arriving late to the festivities. The sound of her footsteps had drawn the attention of a badger, who occupied the seat farthest to the left, with his back to the viewer. The act of turning his head to look at her had caused him to knock over a glass of what must have been wine onto the white tablecloth. All around sat a host of woodland friendlies engaged in various little confabs and misdeeds, though they were clearly meant to be paying attention to the wild boar, who stood at the head of the table and was in the middle of holding forth, tusks agape, a wineglass tilting perilously from his hairy trotter. A feast had been laid at the center of the table. Its particulars were familiar to me only because the books I'd grown up reading had a tendency to dwell on dazzling suppers. The bright yellow orbs spilling out of an upturned basket were almost certainly quinces. The huge, round, layered thing was surely some sort of cake. The cross-cut wheel off to the side was cheese, obviously, orange and full of holes, from one of which protruded the face of a mouse who, for some reason, had not been invited to the party—perhaps because, of all the creatures on display, he was the only one not wearing any clothes. In the very middle of it all sat a glistening red-and-white hunk, rimmed by a crown of bones.

"What's that?" I asked, already suspecting the answer.

Ena looked. "That's meat."

THE BASEMENT LAUNDRY VENTED DIRECTLY INTO the playroom, so it is impossible to recall that decadent yet horror-provoking mural without likewise remembering the floral burn of the ancient machines. Their rumble was the bass line of the adjoining superintendent's office, that place of shadow and hum, where the pipe-laden ceiling pressed down and unseen water rushed back and forth overhead in the flickering gloom. There, under a deluge of mail and toolboxes, sat Ena's desk, and on it, her little radio, tuned to the Drowned City Dispatch all day long, like every other radio in town.

It was common in those days for people to call in to the Dispatch for just about anything. The Dispatcher mainly urged them to stick to stories about Island City, as it was now or as they remembered it—but once they were on the air, callers did whatever they liked. They'd share grievances about their neighbors. They'd get sentimental about past loves. They'd play a game we affectionately called Ration Roulette, where they'd list the most useless combinations of items they'd been assigned for the week: beets and baking powder; kerosene and parsnips; tinfoil and matches and half a packet of almonds. For the most part, the Dispatcher let them get on with it. He had a gravelly, coursing voice and a breezy manner. He didn't talk about himself, and hardly ever participated in the kind of reminiscing he asked others to do. Sometimes people would call in because they thought they'd finally figured out his true identity—he was their neighbor, they said, or their mail carrier, or that guy who used to sell books on the east side of the park—to which he would always say, "Hey, you're right!," though they never were.

The week we moved in with Ena, a starfall was observed above the outer bay. It was reported to the Dispatch by the crew of a patrol boat, who mistook it for a new phenomenon. Then somebody called in with a correction: it was, in fact, a recurring celestial event that happened every hundred and forty years. By the following evening, it was all anybody could talk about. It bled out of the radio into the corner stores and funding offices, into snippets of conversation you passed in the street. The cover of every newspaper was suddenly overtaken by the same hazy picture of night above the skyline. The Dispatcher encouraged experts to call in and debate whether such a subtle fizz of light could have been visible to the naked eye even as recently as ten years ago.

Most agreed that no, it could not.

"So perhaps," the Dispatcher said, "just perhaps, this means that some measure of light pollution might finally be receding?"

Yes, they told him. This starfall could, in fact, be the long-awaited sign—the Big One, the Real One, a clear indication that Posterity measures were working and that things were changing for the better at last.

But then a few weeks passed with no governmental acknowledgment of the phenomenon. People stopped calling in about it. The starfall did not bear out, and we went back to waiting for the next omen.

There was no dearth of them back then. In every corner of the city, some phenomenon akin to a miracle promised to portend the long-awaited return of better days. Some, like the starfall, were momentous. Others were just eerie: the discovery by a father and son, for instance, of football-sized goldfish in the sewer drain outside their building.

Sooner or later, one of these near miracles would be the right one. And when it manifested, people said, they would buy the biggest loaf of bread or the biggest bottle of champagne they could find. They would rip up their old ration cards and stop watching the sky for signs. They would dance on piers and bridges, on boat decks and rooftops, surrounded by loved ones and the crash of music from competing parties. With fireworks overhead. Always fireworks.

"I have a lot of reservations about whether this can or will ever happen," the Dispatcher would say. "But if it does? My friends, if it does, we will be the luckiest people in the world."

We would have stuck it out on our flooded streets and disregarded the panic-mongering of naysayers to help reclaim Island City from the tide. We would find ourselves back in the Island City of before. The city as it had always been, and still was, under or above water: the city of fanfare and electric autumns, of lamplit streets and music and dazzling marquees, of lovers tangling furtively in windows, of lush parks, of townhomes glowing warmly on a moonless night. The ensuing party would be magnificent. And if you doubted it, all you had to do was look to the Dancing Girl billboard for reassurance. Every neighborhood had one. Battle Hill's, at the crossroads of Moritz and Pine, just a few blocks south of the Morningside, was a shapely, dark-haired figure in a blazing yellow dress. The billboard had her in profile, waltzing with a lamp in the foreground of faceless, silhouetted revelers, all of them packed into the living room of one of those turn-of-the-century townhouses. Something about the billboard made you feel that it was the Dancing Girl's own, perhaps newly acquired, perhaps one of those South Falls Island places that were promised to the likes of us. Tables around the room exploded with colorful fare. You had to stand right under the billboard to see the details: sprays of zigzag fish bones, fireworks of bonbons, coupes filled to the brim. Framing the dance floor was a huge window, beyond which lay the distant and unmistakable down-island skyline and a thin, cheerful stripe of the coming dawn. Disregarded in the only unoccupied corner of this blissful scene lay a folded-up umbrella. But not just any umbrella: the unmistakable emblem of the Posterity Initiative. The umbrella under which we had all been living: folded up, unnecessary now that we had come through the fire. No coincidence that it and the girl's dress were the same shade of yellow. You toiled in faith under it, the billboard seemed to say. Now wear it in celebration.

To the girl's right were tastefully emblazoned the names of the billboard's sponsors: the Island City Repopulation Program and the National Bureau of Posterity. To her left, underscoring all of this, was the ruling mantra of our time: WE'RE NEARLY THERE.

Belief in the sign and the party was the city's lifeblood. The sight of that Dancing Girl chipped away at your doubts. No one was immune to her thrall—not even my mother.

MAYBE YOU'VE NEVER HEARD OF MY MOTHER. OR maybe you followed the Belen case and formed an opinion of her years ago. Maybe you've seen her face, that unflattering picture from her Repopulation file that ended up all over the news. How sinister she must seem to you, the shock of hair clouding her forehead, the bloodshot eyes which, in that one picture, admittedly look a little crazy.

My mother was a small, sinewy, dark-haired woman. In another life she might have been a jockey, but in this one she'd been a mechanic, a carpenter, and, for a little while one unfortunate summer, a hoof scraper.

She was an agile, quick-thinking person. Unafraid of things that could befall her body. Exceedingly adept at languages, except for English, which she considered messy. She hated a mess. She hated ignorance, too—or, rather, hated finding it in herself about something she felt she should already know. She hated inconsistencies in people and stories alike. She hated rudeness, and strangers who acted too familiar, and friends who turned out to care less about you than you cared about them. But she liked animals. And keeping busy. And she loved me.

Rules made up her world, and mine. Never ask a question in writing, for instance, if you could ask it in person—words committed to paper could haunt you forever. Don't keep pictures or records for more than a year. If you have to think about whether the information you're revealing might be compromising to someone, then shut your mouth. Speak Our language only at home, only with family—which, until we moved in with Ena, meant only with my mother herself. Don't reveal where you're from. If asked, name only the place you'd most recently called home—which, until we moved to Island City, had been Paraiso. If pressed, stick to this answer. Say you don't remember anything before that.

I had spent years unwinding a knot of theories about my mother's commitment to obscuring our origins. At first, a sinister family history had seemed the most plausible explanation. A militant grandparent. A disgraced uncle. As I got older, I convinced myself we must be some sort of royalty, hunted from city to city, hiding from faceless usurpers. Setting aside my mother's aptitude for manual labor, and the fact that she occasionally mentioned veterinary school, it seemed to make sense. It would certainly explain why we had no records, no pictures of my mother's childhood, nor mine, nor of any relatives living or dead, including my unmentioned and unmentionable father.

Ena, on the other hand, kept the past in full, abundant view. Pictures, cards, pamphlets. I'd never known a home so crowded with information. Most of it was about Beanie. Her radiation appointment schedule was still pinned to the wall. Her hairwash was still in the bathroom. Her watercolors were still spread out on the hall console. You got the sense, looking around, that she had just stepped out and was due back any second. Ena even spoke about her in the present tense. I didn't know much about love, but this felt like it to me. A persistent keeping-around of the object of your affection. A surrounding of the self.

In countless photos obscuring the fridge door, Beanie was a small, alert-looking woman who seemed vulnerable to sunburn. It was clear that she and Ena had traveled for leisure a great deal back in the before-time. Here they were in front of some ancient, sun-bleached temple. Here in a hot spring.

"Where's this?" I asked Ena about a week after we'd moved in, pointing to a photo of Beanie holding a smug piglet in the foreground of some sun-scorched hills.

"You don't remember?" She sounded hurt. "That's Baba's farm."

While I reeled from the revelation that we were farm people—not only *not* royalty but not even city folk!—Ena described juniper trees, a little red-door garage topped with a sprawling balcony. The balcony was overgrown year-round with grapevines, she said, and when you stood up there you could reach out and pluck the dusty green orbs right off the stem and put them in your mouth one by one. "Remember?" she said, but I could barely remember Paraiso, let alone someplace that preceded the whole string of homes that brought us to this moment of painful revelation. "There was a huge old olive tree in the foreyard," Ena went on. "We put a swing up for you when you were little. I think there must be a picture of it somewhere—all of us sitting around and you in the swing. Remember?"

When she was unable to locate this photograph, I felt cheated. How strange to hear her talking about memories of which I was part, but which were not part of me. There I was, apparently, wandering all over that sunlit hillside, swinging from the olive tree, eating grapes, hugging piglets, in *her* memory, but somehow not in my own. How unjust.

"Can we go back there?" I asked.

"I wish we could, Sil," Ena said. "But it's gone."

On this terminal point, her view of the past converged with my mother's. The notion of home being "gone" had been instilled in me for as long as I could remember. And because I'd never seen pictures of that home, its goneness had always felt rather abstract. Yes, the fact that it had been there one day and not the next was essentially tragic. But never having seen it, I could only imagine both the vacancy and what had preceded it. Photographs of the real thing, however, obliterated that imaginary space.

From the little I'd been able to eke out from my mother, I knew that where home had once been there now remained only a ragged palisade. Dust eddies and roasted fields, tracts of coastline bristling with the ruins of old houses as far as the eye could see. This displacement of earth, which had been threatening for decades, had caused the displacement of people—thousands of families, my mother intimated, including our own. It had turned something into nothing. Had turned somebodies into nobodies. Had turned my mother into the kind of person who would abandon everything and take a one-year-old by the hand and set off on foot with no plan.

What I'm saying is, seeing the picture of the farm there put into sharp focus how little of the layout of the past I really knew. After a lifetime of reserved curiosity and hazy projections, I wanted to know more. And this desire of mine immediately became the principal point of conflict between Ena, who was keen to reminisce about it, and my mother, who was not.

"Do *you* remember the farm?" I asked my mother one night,

not long afterward. We were lying face-to-face in our rough little cot in Beanie's office. I was hoping that our proximity, the presence of Ena in the next room, the fact that we were here, at last, in Island City, after all this time, might somehow combine to draw out a conversation that, in my experience, only ever lasted a moment or two.

"I remember this and that," my mother said.

"Was it like Ena says?"

"Well. Yes. Sometimes."

"And—?"

"Oh, I don't know, Sil. We spent a lot of time waiting for rain. When it came, the floods would carry people off. Houses, too."

"But there *were* grapevines and piglets?"

"Don't put so much stock in your aunt's version of things." My mother swept the hair off my face. "She was lucky enough to leave home before she had to. While it was still green."

"What does that mean?"

"Before everything went to hell."

"How did it go to hell?"

"You know. The droughts. The slide."

"But it wasn't *just* that."

"Well, then came the war. You know that."

"But what about before? What about the good things?"

My mother rarely bothered to hide it when she had reached the limits of her patience. "I'm very tired, Sil." She rolled over and looked up at the ceiling. "No matter how your aunt makes it seem, it was a very hard place to grow up. I didn't want that for you. I was glad for a reason to leave."

But this, according to Ena, was an outrageous misrepresentation of the truth. "She *loved* that farm! Where'd you think she learned so much about animals? Always with her hands in some critter's mouth. Always some half-dead thing under one arm, and can we keep it. Hell, who do you think ran the place after I left?" I was marched back over to the fridge and made to wait until a picture proving my mother's mendacity could be found. "See that? That's your mother with the dog." It certainly seemed to be. "And here she is again, pregnant with you. And you see where she's standing? Follow me." From a box in the hallway, Ena lifted a stack of little Polaroids and riffled through them until she found a faded image of a girl holding a baby. "Now, that's *me,* holding your mother, right in front of the very same gate. See that? That's about two months after my sister abandoned your mother. Just left her there, for *us* to raise, me and your great-grandmother. She couldn't have been more than two months old, your mother, pink little thing, and as small to a regular-sized baby as she is to a regular-sized person now. My sister gave her to me and said, *Here, hold this, I'll be right back.* And then she turned around and walked down the drive and out the gate and down the road like she was on her way to the store, and we never saw her again."

"That's *crazy,*" I said, dizzy from the intake of so much volunteered intelligence.

"But true. Just ask your mother."

It took me a week just to summon the courage. "Did your mother leave you with Ena and Baba when you were just a baby?"

"Of course not," my mother said. "What did I tell you about your aunt?"

Words were exchanged about the telling of this story. My mother and Ena raised their voices about it, but always behind closed doors, so there was no way for me to determine whether Ena was being berated for telling me truths or for spreading lies. The standoff's unintended result was that Ena became more determined than ever to supply knowledge she felt I'd been unjustly denied. How my cunning Baba once tricked a local bigwig into laying the foundations for our house. Or how our cove came to be called Needle Bay thanks to the efforts of a neighbor who, for many decades, had tossed every sea urchin that snagged in his net back into the water, until the seafloor was littered with them, and their offspring, and their offspring's offspring, wavering black spines in the millions.

"For the love of God," my mother said, "stop filling her head with this nonsense."

But it was not nonsense—and any insinuation that it might be was met by the immediate producement of evidence to the contrary. In this case, a newspaper clipping—in Ours—of one swimmer's harrowing account of how attempting to traverse this bristling minefield nearly cost him his life.

The more my mother protested, the more Ena dug in. If the past had previously felt like a forbidden room, briefly glimpsed as my mother was shutting its door, here was Ena, holding the door wide. I could see all of it, any part, and linger as long as I liked. Whenever my mother was called away on some errand in the building, out came one of Ena's huge family scrapbooks. Here was a picture of my great-grandmother's house: faded white, shutters thrown wide, stifling on summer evenings and so close to the sea that you could hear the surf sighing over even the roar of the cicadas. Here was the old bougainvillea that grew huge and bright as fire against the southern wall. Here was my hawk-nosed great-grandmother, Baba to family and strangers alike, scowling out from the depths of a patio chair.

"What's that?" I asked, pointing to the wooden instrument tucked under her chin.

"A fiddle." Ena leafed into the future until she reached a

photo of Baba, laughing over a bonfire, flanked on all sides by blurry revelers. "She never turned down a chance to play. Sometimes a wedding party would come down the street at three, four, five in the morning, and she would leap out of bed in her nightgown and start playing for them. When her strings broke, she would pluck two or three hairs out of her head, string her violin with them, and just keep right on going."

"That's not possible," I said—but my protestation was silenced by the retrieval of yet another album, wherein lay taped a length of white hair thick as a knife's edge. "Pluck that," Ena said. "See if it sings."

These jaunts through the past rarely progressed without interruption. I would raise the impossibility of some stated fact, and Ena would build a case for the truth of it. Here, for instance, was a picture of the wild fox my mother had caught in the hills one winter; and here it was again, sitting tame on the kitchen floor, begging for scraps.

"She never told me about this fox."

"You know those little bumps all over her left hand?" I nodded—I knew them well. "Where do you think she got them? Do you know how sharp fox teeth are?"

This was part of Ena's magic. Familiarities you had come to take for granted were transformed by the act of her storytelling. Her version of things became the only one. She could change the reality of something you thought you'd known all your life.

In due course, Ena's stories moved away from Baba's house, with its stony little beach, down the street, along a shoreline of sun-whitened buildings. Here was a picture of the little stall where the neighborhood children would get honeycomb. Here was the pine grove, the monastery, the churchyard where, on blue winter nights, the terrified children would wait for their ancestors' ghosts. And here was a picture of the village from above: sea, roofs, monastery. The acres and acres of my great-grandmother's orchard: plum and pear trees, apricot and fig, mile upon shadow-twisted mile of the sweetest fruit you could ever imagine, right to the very foot of Modra Gora, the mountain where the Vila lived.

"What's a vila?" I said.

"Ah." The Vila was a spirit of the mountain. Not every mountain had a Vila; but every Vila had a mountain, some high place from which she could observe her lands and tend her gardens without interference. The Vila of Modra Gora was known for her fruit trees, from which my great-grandmother's orchards were descended. Everything south of the stone wall of ancient Modra Gora—apparent in Ena's photographs only as a thin, ragged line—belonged to my baba. Everything north of it, up the slope of the mountain, belonged to the Vila. Pickers and children were cautioned to take great care during harvest time, because the Vila was notoriously protective of this boundary but also couldn't resist her proclivity for mischief. Her three sons, who roamed the mountain in whatever form pleased her most—weasels, foxes, crows—would lure guileless pickers over the boundary wall, so that they could mistakenly harvest her fruit and then have to make restitution for the offense.

"She sounds unstable."

"Oh," Ena said. "You have no idea."

Forever and a while ago, an old king decided he would build his castle on the eastern shore of the river that drained into Needle Bay. So he went to Modra Gora, as was the custom, to ask the Vila for permission to build. She was in her orchard, as always. Her three sons, crows on this occasion, were perched up a tree. She was less than pleased to see the king—she had been living in that mountain for more than a thousand years already without encroachment from people and was not about to share her shoreline now. "Do you know why, Sil?"

"People bring drought," I said.

That's right—and they have since the beginning of time. Still, an eon of solitude will wear on just about anybody, Ena said. And the king flattered the Vila with gifts and didn't try to steal any of her plums. So she gave her blessing on the condition that the castle and its town be confined to the eastern side of the river, a good distance from her mountain. The king took this in his stride and, like all builders, said, "I can make adjustments later," and then went home and built his castle.

The town around it prospered and grew, and the king and his children rejoiced. But it wasn't long before houses started cropping up on the river's western shore, so the king thought he'd better build a bridge. Masons from all over the land vied for the chance to build it; one by one they came and presented their plans to the king, and one by one he hired them. But one by one, their bridges collapsed. The king consulted with the witch who lived nearby, and she asked him whether he had recently made a pact that he had broken—and then he remembered.

"The Vila," I said.

Well, sure enough, it was the Vila herself preventing the building of the bridge. Every time the workers began, she would wake up and see their bridge and the new houses and paved streets coming her way; and every night, she would scream in a fury so vast that the bridge would crumble to dust. And thus it went on, for three years, until the king finally paid her another visit.

"Took him long enough," I said.

"Well—few things take longer than a man owning up to a mistake."

On his knees, the king made his case to the Vila. Couldn't she see how necessary it was to build the bridge? How cramped the little town was becoming? "We agreed that you would occupy the farther shore," she told him. "You've already broken your word." But the king took offense to this. If he had broken his word, it was only because of how successful the town had become! People from all over the land were flocking there; they wanted guild jobs and clean water and fish to eat.

This was the wrong tack to take with the Vila.

"Obviously. Why would she want *more* people coming?"

Well, she didn't. And to make sure the king appreciated the full weight of his request, here's what she said: "No matter how many times you try and build that bridge, it will fall. Unless you make this sacrifice to me: choose a woman from your town to be bricked up, alive, in the bridge's foundations."

"That's horrible," I said.

"Isn't it?"

"It's the worst thing I've ever heard."

Well, the king thought so too. It didn't seem right to pluck a random life from among his subjects and end it. After all, it was his broken promise that had led to this mess. If such a sacrifice must be made, he told the Vila, let it come at a cost to his own family. His wife had died many years before, but all three of his sons were married, and it was from among these women that the tribute must issue.

"That's very equitable," I said.

"Well, hold on."

The king told his sons about the plan—but he would not put the burden of choosing which of them would be widowed upon the boys themselves. Instead, he would let fate decide. He

charged them to tell their wives *nothing* of the Vila's terms; and
the next day, whichever young wife arrived first to bring the
workmen their lunch would be given up. Fate would have chosen her. What could be fairer than that? All the young princes
agreed to these terms and went home with heavy hearts.
Well—you can guess what happened.

"Somebody talked."

"They certainly did."

The eldest brother was a good man but a big drunk. Sitting
by the fire that night, watching his wife sing to their young
sons, he drank and drank, and then wept like a child. When she
asked him what the matter was, he couldn't stop himself. He
begged her, on pain of death, not to take the workmen their
lunch the following day. What a ridiculous request, she said,
and mocked him. But, being a good wife, she obeyed.

"One down," I said. "Two to go."

Well, the second brother lasted a little longer than the first,
probably because he didn't have a problem with the drink. He
spent all night with his wife, and in the morning, he was suddenly overcome with guilt and pulled her back into bed. Don't
go out, he said. Spend the day with me.

"It's always the youngest who does the right thing," I said.

"Are you going to interrupt whenever you think you know
what happens?"

"I'm not."

"Because if so, I can just stop now."

"No, no. Don't."

Yes, it would ordinarily have been the third son who kept
faith with his father. But the third son of this particular king
was a weaselly little bastard who didn't give a damn and had a
real chip on his shoulder about the fact that he wasn't going to
get any inheritance anyway. He told his wife outright: "My

brothers have always had everything—they're not going to take you, too." And he bade her stay at home.

So it was the king's own daughter, the princess, who brought the workmen their lunch that day. The king had gone down to the river to await whichever of his sons' wives would appear. When he saw his own child coming over the hill and understood the depth of his sons' betrayal, he wept. Without doubt, his daughter was his favorite. Though she would never inherit his kingdom or carry his name to honor in battle, he loved her above the rest.

Through tears, the king found his way up Modra Gora. There he again fell to his knees before the Vila. "Please," he said. "My daughter. Take someone else instead."

But the Vila only shrugged. "A deal's a deal."

And so it was.

True to his word, the king ordered his daughter bricked up in the foundation of the bridge. The princess understood why it had to be done, but she pleaded for her life all the same. She was a new mother, you understand, and wanted to see her little daughter grow up.

"I hate this story," I said.

To stop the breaking of his own heart, the king made his daughter one concession. He had the workmen build a window through which she could peer out from the foundation of the bridge and see her little girl playing on the riverbank. Until the child was about two, the princess could put her breast to the window to nurse her. The Vila let the bridge stand. And sure enough, as the king had foreseen, people from all over the land flocked to the western shore and built houses and farms—and as the years passed, fewer and fewer of them remembered the Vila, and the bridge, and why sometimes on cold winter nights the river ran thick with salt.

"Tears?" I said.

"Of course."

I thought about it. "And it's all gone?"

"All of it. The town, the bridge, the mountain. Washed away in the slide."

"And the Vila? What happened to her?"

Aunt Ena closed the album. "What happens to any woman who gets to be a certain age? She becomes comfortable in her ways and gets strange looks when she leaves the house." I got the sense that she had said this more for her own amusement than my edification. I frowned. "Nobody knows. As the world breaks, the Vile move on. There must be hundreds of them drifting along just like the rest of us."

I sat with this for a bit. "And my grandmother's orchards?"

"Gone."

"I wish I could remember them."

Ena squeezed my shoulder. She led me to the kitchen, and from the bottom refrigerator shelf, she excavated a bundle tightly wound in brown paper. Inside was a jar, mostly empty save for a thick crystallized layer of some purplish substance at the very, very bottom.

"Jam," Ena said. "From your grandmother's figs."

I peered down at it, this precious stuff, soil and water and sunlight and the fruit they had borne, all concentrated into half an ounce of brittle darkness at the bottom of a jar.

Ena nudged me. "Let's have some."

"No! Really?"

"Only because you didn't ask."

She doled out a bit for me and a bit for herself on the tip of a spoon. It was dry and waxy at first, but after a while of warming on the tongue, it gave up a faint and distant sweetness that grew and spread.

"Breathe in over it," Ena said, while I stood there, not daring to swallow for fear of losing the taste. "Good stuff, right?" She watched me closely. "Does it make you remember anything?"

Because it made me think of sunlight, I said, "I think so."

Ena nodded. "It helps, doesn't it?"

WE'D BEEN LIVING WITH ENA FOR ABOUT TWO months when my mother reached out to the school to see about enrollment. My name was put on a wait list, where it was preceded, my mother was made to understand, by the names of thirty-nine individuals *not* in the Repopulation Program. A number of factors could still alter my place on the list: my willingness to take certain supplementary aptitude tests, for instance; or my fellow wait listers' willingness to do the same; or, more important, their parents' willingness to grease regulatory palms with something other than the Repopulation credits on which my mother and I depended. In any case, there was no point in holding out hope that I would start before next fall. This was disappointing news to everyone, especially my friendless self.

Gloomily, I pulled Mrs. Sayez's fun cards out from under my side of the mattress. WHAT IS YOUR LEVEL OF SATISFACTION WITH YOUR NEW HOME? WHAT DO YOU LIKE MOST ABOUT YOUR NEW HOME? WHAT WOULD MAKE YOUR NEW HOME EVEN BETTER? The answers—or at least those my mother would expect me to give if I made the indefensible mistake of putting pen to paper in this context—were quite obvious. High.

Everything. Nothing. But would it really be so terrible if, in response to the final question, I instead wrote: *The opportunity to attend one of your fine institutions of learning*? What would happen if I dropped the card in the mailbox the next time I was hauling the trash cans in off the street? In my mother's version of the world, uniformed men would presumably appear in the doorway. They would sit me down in one of the Morningside's several cold storage units and press me until I turned blue. Why had I answered the question this way? Was I dissatisfied with my present situation? How about the Repopulation Program—did I feel it wasn't doing right by me? And why had I left the other two questions blank? What would my response have been if I'd had the integrity to answer them? And so on.

But what if, instead of this scenario, my answer was simply filed alongside hundreds of others and studied as part of the Repopulation Program's efforts to improve their work? It might not happen in time to help me—but it might help some other schoolworthy newcomer down the road.

To PASS THE time, I made myself useful around the Morningside. Ena insisted that I should never be observed doing work, especially by the janglers, and *especially* by members of the building's Board. Jobs suited to me were the kind that could be accomplished in secret, in solitude, like going around to all the empty apartments and checking them for signs of what Ena called "disruption." You would be forgiven for assuming, as I did, that vacancy was deadening. But no—old buildings are full of life, full of movement and crisis. Radiators leak. Pipes burst. Mice chew through plaster and wire. When such things happened in occupied apartments, residents were there to sound the alarm. But disruptions in vacant units could go unnoticed for weeks, sometimes months, often to great detriment. It was my responsibility to investigate and ensure that stillness reigned as it should.

I would usually find the units in good order: clean, softly lit, quiet save for the squeak of my sneakers on the ancient varnished floors. The disruptions I uncovered tended to be small. A window left inexplicably open. A ceiling fixture that had fallen, after years of apparent stability, and now lay shattered on the floor. The desiccated corpse of a bat that in life had found its way in through some mysterious opening, which would then have to be located and sealed.

The most persistent disruptions were caused by the birds. Rook cranes wily enough to nest, unobserved, for a week or a month on a balcony would leave behind spoil heaps of feathers, twigs, and partially digested prey. Disposal of these piles required gloves and a mask, and my mother had forbidden me from touching them. But they were irresistible. Apparently, such a heap somewhere down-island had once produced a human rib bone, leading to brief hysteria on the Dispatch. But all I ever found were frog carcasses and fish spines—shining silver needles that barbed your fingers if you were careless picking them up.

It was during the covert investigation of one such heap that my life rerouted. I was on a balcony on the thirty-second floor, crouching against the barricade overlooking the shaft that ran up and down between the penthouse tower and the east wing of the Morningside. The spoil heap before me had yielded a few predictable disappointments: rat teeth and fur. From where I crouched, I could make out where runoff from the gargoyles overhead had begun darkening the walls with skeins of something slippery and probably living. I was sure someone would look out and spot me. But the windows facing the shaft belonged mostly to back bedrooms, and apart from the occasional outline of a painting or mirror on some distant wall, or shadowy movement signifying some resident crossing a curtained room, there was little to see. I had just begun to poke around in the pile when my gaze sailed across the shaft and into the window one floor up and across.

A woman stood there, in the penthouse, dressing or undressing—but in any case, naked from the waist up. Her head was out of sight above the blinds, but I knew it must be Bezi Duras. On either side of the huge blue pendant lying flat against her sternum, where her breasts should have been, grinned two long, ragged scars.

They were in view for only a moment. She turned away from the window and then a silk white shirt dropped over what I could see of her back, and it was over. She did not reappear. She did not look down and see me. But just the same, it seemed necessary to crawl off the balcony and retreat to the cool darkness of the empty apartment, where I stood for a long time, measuring by the beats of my heart when it might be safe to move again.

Hours later, still flushed, I picked through my rations in silence. My mother's hand was bone cold against my cheek. "You're burning up." Her lips dropped to my forehead and rested there. "What's the matter?"

"Nothing," I lied, and I took care that night to keep my wakeful tossing from exposing my torment.

What *was* the matter? This was hardly the first time I had seen something I shouldn't have. Back in Paraiso, through the window across the street, I had borne frequent witness to the passions of Signora Tesseretti, who had a habit of entertaining other men while her husband was at work. I immediately reported these sightings to my mother, whose outward acknowledgment of my innocence in spying such antics was always accompanied by a small spark of blame. True, she said, I would not have seen anything if our neighbor had been more discreet. But perhaps I would have seen *even less* if I had been less curious, more honest, more wholesome in my impulses.

This trespass against Bezi Duras felt particularly devastating. There was nothing illicit about it. Though it embarrassed me to see her naked, I hadn't intended for it to happen. She had merely been getting dressed. Also, while the neighbor in Paraiso had been engaged in something morally questionable, there was no doubt—in my mother's assessment of the situation, anyway—that she'd been having a very good time doing it. Here, on the other hand, was a thing that could not be considered good, no matter how you tilted the prism. Something had happened to Bezi Duras. Some violence. Somebody—or something—had hurt her horribly. Horribly enough to leave massive purple wounds. These wounds were kept hidden, a secret known only to Bezi herself. And by showing up at the wrong place at the wrong time, I had robbed her of her solitude in that secret. Worse still: Bezi Duras hadn't seen me. She had no idea, as she knotted her hair and leaned toward her mirror, that not fifteen feet below her the girl gathering up bucket and rags and retreating into the cool sanctum of 32F had intruded on her greatest vulnerability.

It must have been Bezi's ignorance of the truth that brought me this deep sense of shame. To harbor such knowledge in and of itself felt wrong. Yet at the same time, I was suddenly the only person responsible for it. If I told nobody, nobody would know. I had the power right then and there to carry her secret with me in silence forever—and for some reason, this was even more unbearable. But to whom could I unburden myself? Certainly not to my mother. She would ask questions. She would want to know why I'd been out there on the balcony, and even if I lied, she would guess that I had been doing something I shouldn't have, and then she'd go up to 32F and discover that I'd been digging around in a spoil heap—which, by virtue of its being forbidden, would cast a shadow over the whole rest of my story. Suddenly, every inch of the event would be subjected to the blinding spotlight of my mother's suspicion. Where exactly had I been crouching when I looked up and saw Bezi Duras? Had I stayed there when I realized she was naked, or had I done the polite thing and turned away from this vulnerable and unsuspecting stranger? Had I been observed in my transgression? Had Bezi Duras said anything to me since then, intimated in any way that she had seen me, and that my mother and Ena were thus implicated in my wrongdoing?

Absolution lay on the far side of a vast chasm of unknowns. There would be too many questions to get around, too many opportunities to further enervate my already exhausted mother.

I was doomed, then, to carry this terrible knowledge around in silence. What did that say about me? A better daughter would surely have come clean, withstood her punishment, and gone up to the penthouse to apologize.

This daughter, however, folded to her old impulses and snuck a pair of scissors under the living room sofa and her mother's empty perfume bottle under the kitchen sink. But that only added to my misery. The protection was half-baked, and I knew it. Without a third talisman, the items were useless, nothing more than a reminder of my failure to rid myself of the habit I'd sworn would not follow me out of Paraiso.

Well into the following week, I had trouble breathing, trouble swallowing. Meals wouldn't go down. Air wouldn't come up. I must have dropped a couple of pounds, because my beleaguered mother dragged me to some seedy medic. I was surprised when he said I had a cold, and not an actual stone lodged in my throat.

This might have gone on for months. Me, ghouling around in a half-nourished state, while the scissors and the perfume bottle languished in useless malignancy in their respective hiding places.

But things came to a head one evening not long afterward. I was in the courtyard running out the hose for Ena while she power-sprayed the flagstones. Overhead, wisps of cloud turned from October yellow to nightfall gray. I heard Ena mutter, "Here she comes," and sure enough, here she came: Bezi Duras was leaving the little back alley that led to her private elevator. She was an immensely tall woman, taller than I'd expected, thin and long-necked, standing ramrod straight despite the bulk of a backpack slung between her slim shoulders. Her pale hair was drawn up in a bun at the nape of her neck. The dogs massed around her waist. Ena had made them sound like big, lavish nuisances. Spoiled and unruly. Maybe a little overweight. Nothing could have been further from the truth. They looked like they were made of soot and steel wool. As though they'd started out as gaunt shadows long ago and somehow assembled themselves over the years from leaves and bits of darkness they'd rolled in along the way. Wiry, black, wolfish things with diamond-hard eyes. They were not so much leashed as chained to Bezi, all three of them clipped into a belt that was cinched around one of the same white blouses I had seen her pulling over her scars the week before.

Ena called out, "Good evening!" in English.

Bezi Duras turned around. "Good evening."

Ena's thick-gloved finger swung obtrusively in my direction. "This is my niece, Silvia."

There was Bezi Duras. Looking at Ena. Then looking at me.

Smiling only with her mouth. I made the mistake of meeting her gaze. If her voice had erupted in my head, I would not have been surprised. It seemed already present in everything, an oceanic boom all around me. She knew. She knew I was hiding something. In fact, there might be nothing Bezi Duras did not know. That my mother was a foundling. That I had failed to kick the habit of laying out protections. That a man I'd never seen before had pulled down his pants in front of me in a Paraiso alleyway, and that I had run away shouting, as well as a thousand other secrets I had willed myself to forget, all the little sins that had scattered into the unlit corners of my heart: That I used to cry myself to sleep, praying for my father's return. That I knew the taste of flesh because I had once eaten meat—inadvertently, when a patron of the hotel where my mother worked had offered me a bite of it as I passed her table, and I (three or so, underfoot) had leaned in and gummed it off the end of her fork without a second thought, to the horror of my mother, who was watching from the corner, or so she kept telling me, because I had no memory of this event, though my mother had relived it often enough for me to form a kind of half reel of it, all in the third person.

All this knowledge Bezi Duras carried through the main gate and out into the street, where the dogs hauled her up the darkening hill and out of sight.

Ena turned to me. "Why didn't you say good evening— what's the matter with you?"

What a question. Maddening, unanswerable. I sat down on the stairs and heaved a sigh that was meant to convey just how burdened I was with things that could not be shared. Ena's elbow dug into my arm. "What's wrong?"

"Nothing," I said. "Nothing."

She must have decided that some ordinary niece nonsense

was behind all this. She went on watering while I sat uselessly there, willing myself to honesty. Why was it so difficult to admit?

"I know something about Bezi Duras."

"What?"

"I don't know how to tell you."

Ena shut off the water. "What is it?"

"I'm not sure I can say."

"Is it something bad?"

"I don't know."

"Something dangerous?"

"I don't think so."

"It's about the dogs, isn't it?"

I frowned. "No."

"You've figured it out, haven't you?"

"No, it's about her—about Bezi."

"Oh. Well, what is it?"

"Promise you won't tell Mama."

Ena raised her hand solemnly.

"Bezi Duras hasn't got any breasts."

"What do you mean?"

"She has these scars." I showed her on myself, clear across one side and then the other. "I think someone really hurt her."

"How do you know that?"

"I saw her changing in the window. I didn't mean to."

"And that's all?"

"That's all."

Ena looked—what? Disappointed? Relieved? "She was probably just sick, is all."

"Cancer," I said somberly.

"Most people get it."

"Why did they cut off her breasts?"

"So it wouldn't spread. God, Sil, you ridiculous girl. You gave me a fright."

"I'm sorry." It didn't seem like she was going to berate me further. "I just felt bad for knowing something like that about her without her meaning me to. I needed to *say* it."

"Don't worry, I won't tell anyone."

"Thanks."

She lowered the nozzle of the hose again and sent the water hissing into the grooves between the pavers. She looked relieved. Why? What had she thought I had figured out?

"What did you mean about the dogs?"

"I can't hear you, Sil."

"The dogs! What did you mean? What did you think I'd figured out?"

"Nothing."

It was my turn to be incredulous. "Ena!" I got up and went to her. "What is it? Tell me!"

"I might," she said. "But not today."

"Oh, Ena. Come on. Please."

She shut the water off again and looked at me. "Think about it," she said.

I wanted to, desperately. But I didn't even know where to begin.

"Have I ever been up to Bezi's place?" Ena asked. "No. Have you? No. Have you ever seen those dogs during the day? No. Matter of fact, I bet you've never seen dogs that look like that anywhere. Not even in a picture book."

She was right, I hadn't. "What does it all mean?"

"Isn't it obvious? They're not dogs."

"*Wolves*," I said breathlessly. Of course.

But this revelation, and my triumph at having stumbled upon it so quickly, only caused her to look at me with disgust. "No," she said. "For God's sake. *People*."

"People," I repeated.

"Men. They're men during the day and dogs at night."

I blinked. "What are you saying?"

"Come on, Sil."

"How do you know this?"

"It's obvious if you know the signs."

"What signs?"

Wearily, she bent down and started coiling up the hose. "I'll tell you more some other time."

"Why not now?"

"I'm tired, Sil."

It was exactly the kind of answer my mother would give to shut me down. The moment was over. Whatever measure of worth Ena had been looking for in that brief stretch when she'd been almost ready to talk had come up short. I returned to my seat on the stairs and waited until the sting was out of my eyes.

"I told you *my* secret," I finally said.

"So? Did I ask you to?"

"No."

"So leave it alone."

"Until when?"

"Until the time is right. You can't just force these things, Sil. You have to drift into them, and you're not ready. There's a world underneath the world. You can't ask and ask and ask to see it. Otherwise, these glimpses of it, they turn bad."

I didn't know what that meant, but I resolved to ask and ask and ask no more. To drift onward in silence and wait for Ena to bring it up herself when the time was right—which I hoped would be soon enough. But then we were running late to dinner, and afterward Ena fell asleep on the couch. And the following morning a pipe burst in a bathroom on the fourteenth floor and Ena spent the whole afternoon opening up the wall and holding the light up for my mother and setting up fans to blow the moisture out. Two days later, in the stairwell between the sixteenth and seventeenth floors, Ena stooped to secure a shoelace, and died. It was instantaneous, the coroner told us, an aneurysm that had probably been crouching in her for years.

Nobody seemed to notice that the person now emptying the trash and crawling under their sinks at two in the morning was my toothpick of a mother, and not the robust older woman they'd been seeing for years. I presume this transfer of power was on the books in a basement management office someplace, but frankly, it may not have been. It wouldn't surprise me to learn that my mother just kept on filing Ena's credits because nobody knew, or bothered to verify, that they were not the same person: not the bank, not the security office, and certainly not the handful of Morningside residents who sent a wreath to Ena's funeral without bothering to check the spelling of her name. Nothing to do but lay her down on Fells Island, where the grave trenches stretched one after the other like stitches in the earth.

My mother waited a week before moving her things into Ena's room. I sat at the end of our cot and watched her pack for the journey across the hall. It was a somber occasion: the first time we would be sleeping apart since before I could remember. Something about it felt even more terminal than Ena's death. As if somebody were going into all the rooms of my life and turning the lights out one by one.

"Aren't you worried Ena's going to show up tonight and ask what you're doing in her bed?" I asked.

My mother laughed. "No."

"You seem really sure."

"Even if something like that *could* happen—and, Sil, it can't—I don't think Ena would make for a petty ghost."

"Tell me something about her from when you were little."

My mother gave this earnest thought. "I guess I was surprised after all this time to realize how short she actually was. She always seemed very tall to me. I felt safe around her."

"Me, too. I felt safe, too."

"You still feel safe, right?"

In truth, I did not. I'd spent my life convinced that my mother and I were more or less alone in the world—but Ena's death made it clear that there had always been a third. She'd been there, in the distance, invisible but real. Now it really *was* just the two of us, and it felt different. Lonely and peripheral. We were so very small, my mother and I, in this old apartment, in this drafty building with its unshared secrets, in this strange and unknowable city. But I couldn't find the words for any of that, so I just said: "Of course."

She tried to move my hair out of my face. "Maybe we'll make this place feel a bit more like our own—what do you think?"

"But it's not," I said. "It's Ena and Beanie's."

"I know, my heart. But they're gone." She looked wearily around the room. "We'll put some of their things away next week. Maybe that will help?"

There it was. My mother couldn't even wait until Ena was cold in the ground before she started slamming the doors to all the spaces of the past where I had only just gained admittance.

I left her to her mercenary designs and went to the kitchen, and stood before the cheerful refrigerator with its collage of Ena and Beanie's life. Already everything I knew about them was beginning to fade. Why hadn't I paid more attention to Ena's stories? My ribs were so tight I thought they might pulverize my heart. How little it had taken to rob these memories of meaning. And now my mother would deal the final blow, turning them into dust, as she did everything.

Then came my initiation into the overwhelming freedom of sleeping by myself. I could toe my socks off under the covers and breathe as loudly and roll around as expansively as I liked. And I did, all night long, while my runaway brain found things to count: the pleats in the curtains, the whoosh of passing cars, the racket of cranes on the nearby roof. Maybe my mother couldn't imagine Ena taking umbrage at the obliteration of her entire life story—but I certainly could. She would appear, hand in hand with Beanie, at the foot of my bed, and probably say something like "After everything I did, everything I told you, what did *you* do but just sit there and let your mother sweep it all away?"

A few hours after the light under my mother's door had gone out, I found myself stealing into the kitchen again. There was the jam jar, back of the fridge, still in its brown paper wrapping. It just about fit under the slats of my bed. My only intention was to put it there for safekeeping, out of my marauding mother's reach. But within the hour, I was touching it with my mind in that warm, comforting way. There it was, waiting for me at the end of my circuit of objects—the bottle, the scissors, the jar, one two three, one two three, one two three—a familiar and fitting embrace.

BOOK II

Bezi Duras

NOT LONG AFTER ENA DIED, MY MOTHER BROUGHT
me down to an abandoned storefront at the end of our block. It
had once been a café named Tufaah. I could see the name
printed on a menu that lay open on a bench near enough to the
window to be visible through the gaps in the newspapers covering the glass. Half the tables in there were overturned. The rest
looked like they'd been abandoned mid-meal. The vines drap-
ing down from the big chandelier above the marble bar weren't
real, so they were the only thing with any color in the place,
bright and green forever, thriving in the dark.

"What do these say?" my mother asked of the deluge of
handbills rustling around the door. I started reading them to
her: pest control adverts and town hall invitations. "Do any of
them say if it's for sale?"

I looked again. They didn't.

"Sil," she said, standing on tiptoe to peer inside again. "We're
going to buy this place."

My mother talked about Tufaah as though our eventual celebration there were a foregone conclusion. She imagined its
doors flung wide to the evening, its lights smearing the sidewalk. I had never known her to make plans of any kind. Plans

required belief. You had to believe that you could lay out steps toward an outcome of your choosing. My mother knew better than that. The pronouncement of intent, the hubris of self-determination—these did not fit her notion of the universe. On the few occasions when she had been forced to plan something more consequential than dinner, she had set a limited horizon. Get from Vesvere to Safar, but plan no further. Get from Safar to Paraiso, and leave it at that. She hadn't even planned our move to Island City; she'd merely accepted the opportunity to apply to the Repopulation Program when it came.

But from the moment she wiped the grime off Tufaah's dark window, things changed. She started to plan. She tried to hide it, of course. To moat it with *maybe*s. Maybe things would go the way they were supposed to, for once. Maybe, by next year, we really *would* have a new little place of our own on South Falls Island. The Repopulation Program insisted that its restoration of historic townhomes was right on schedule—maybe that was true. She had been skeptical of their enthusiastic claims that such a place would come to us free of charge, earned only by our willingness to move here and give things a shot. But—maybe it was true. And if it was, maybe we'd be able to put some money aside. And maybe, if *that* happened, we would have enough to buy Tufaah. Not right away, of course, but soon. Maybe she would track down the owner. Make him an offer. So that maybe, when the sign came—the Real One, the Big One—we would be ready to welcome the faceless revelers of Battle Hill into a party of our very own.

She released these visions into the air as though we were somehow out of earshot of the jealous, vengeful forces that had shadowed her all her life. When I pointed this out, she laughed.

"Well, Sil," she said. "In some places, you can be certain of things. And in some places, you can't. And we came here so we could have some certainty."

Certainty in those days was confined to two blocks in each direction and the thirty-three floors of the Morningside. We were certain, within a reasonable margin of error, of when the elevator would malfunction, and when the intractable Mrs. Golub would call the police on a neighbor for some imagined slight. We were certain that pack rats were raiding apartments in the east wing, and that we would find their middens in the most unexpected places.

And I, of course, was certain that Bezi Duras was up there on the thirty-third floor, guarding her secrets.

NOT LONG AFTER we buried Ena, I gave up hoping that my aunt would reappear, like the specter of the disaffected teenager, in the hallway, or in the mirror, or in a sliver of pale light the curtains trapped. Clearly, whatever obligation she felt to honor her promise about Bezi Duras was not enough to keep her spirit around. She had no unfinished business. She was gone.

This realization should have tamped down my curiosity about Bezi and the dogs—but it did the opposite. With me as its only keeper, her vague revelation had little to do but foment. It boiled there, a secret on top of a secret, all I had left of Ena, tantalizingly out of reach. Reliving our conversation over and over, I felt the truth move away from me. What had Ena actually claimed to know? How certain had she *actually* been of the dogs' predicament—and did she think it a predicament at all, or just a fact of their existence? Had she said that Bezi Duras had turned the men into dogs? Or that something—or someone—had turned them on her behalf? Was she their caretaker or their captor? Had Ena ever acknowledged the existence of proof, or her possession of it? Or had she merely evaded the question, saying she would tell me "more" when the time was right, without ever intending to do so?

If only I'd known that evening in the courtyard would be my last opportunity to ask Ena what she meant. If only I'd pressed her a little more gently. Perhaps she would have decided that the time to tell me was already right, and I would not now be roaming the hallways of the Morningside with this unfinished feeling, hoping to bump into Bezi Duras—or else, hoping not to bump into her, because to face her again would mean having all *my* secrets excised by her terrifying stare.

Secret wounds, I thought, and men turned into beasts. How were the two connected?

Ena knew.

And now I probably never would.

WHAT DID I KNOW ABOUT DOGS? THEY HAD NOT featured much in my upbringing. I'd seen them, of course, living as they did on the outskirts of various towns. Milling around the dumpsters after dark. Ducking the occasional projectile. Grinning at you, long-tongued, if you were fool enough to sit outside with that rare bit of special-occasion cheese that might come your way. Sometimes they were almost tame, belonging abstractly to some party that put them to use—hunters or farmers, people who saw to it that they were regularly fed. But even these specimens were part of that cosmos of dangers I'd been raised to avoid—strange men, sheds, cellars, woods, fast-moving bodies of water.

"What do you know about dogs?" I asked my mother one evening. She was humming a shapeless tune over the stove, and I thought she might be enough at ease to miss the question's red flags.

"Dogs?" She thought about it. "They have strong skulls and weak stomachs." The benignity of my question failed. "Why?"

I shrugged.

"We're not getting a dog," she said.

"I know. I just see them around. They're different here than in Paraiso."

"Well, they're spoiled here. They're allowed indoors. Let up into their people's beds." A disgusting mistake, clearly. She went on stirring the pot, but with one eye on me.

"Why do they have weak stomachs?"

"Because they're scavengers, and they get into a lot of dangerous things, which they have to be able to throw back up quickly."

"What do they get into?"

"Anything you can think of." She said I wouldn't believe the things she had pulled out of dogs' stomachs in her two short years at veterinary school. Plastic bags. Shell casings. And, once, a whole road flare, striker to end.

Did it help to contemplate Bezi Duras's dogs with eyes freshened by this knowledge? Not really. They hadn't seemed especially ordinary to begin with. I didn't really believe their stomachs would disgorge something as prosaic as a plastic bag, or a toy tank, or anything that hadn't once been filled with blood.

Perhaps the answer I was looking for lay in Bezi Duras's comings and goings. But I couldn't keep tabs on her from our apartment. The penthouse elevator doors could only be staked out from two positions: the little park across the street, which patrol officers were constantly sweeping for new encampments, or our very own courtyard, where I had a credible reason to linger but would be visible to every occupant of a south-facing apartment. The latter felt like the safer option, and it was the one I tried. But the courtyard was so sparse, and needed so little tending, that I ran out of plausible excuses for being there after an hour or two of work. You could only oil the gate or water the thistles for so long. Two days into my vigil,

Mrs. Golub flung open her window way up on the eighteenth floor. "I see you down there, you little urchin!" she roared. "Stop lurking!"

And that was that—at least for a little while.

About a week later, I happened to find myself in a vacant studio, 16F, holding the ladder for my mother while she changed the lightbulbs. From where I stood, sighing my boredom in the direction of the window, I saw the back-alley gate open and Bezi Duras's twilit form round the corner below in the wake of the dogs. They slipped from streetlamp to streetlamp and vanished over the hill.

It felt providential, seeing them like that. One two three, one two three.

From that day, 16F became my base of operations. My mother was reliably busy in the evenings, called away to those final little inconveniences that might bloom into disaster if allowed to persist overnight: a clogged sink, a suspicious stain spreading on the ceiling. From the studio's window, I had a clear sight line to the stretch of Morningside Street that Bezi Duras and the dogs traversed on their way north, toward the unknown reaches of the upper city.

It took me a few weeks to deepen my knowledge of several crucial details.

First of all, when Ena had said you could rely on Bezi Duras, she really meant it. Bezi was a creature of habit. She always wore the same clothes: black pants, a white blouse. She always took the exact same route. If she had daytime errands to run, she always left the house at one-thirty, always alone, and she always returned before three o'clock.

The dogs only ever accompanied her in the evenings. This was certainly one of the signs Ena had been talking about. It was completely at odds with the lifestyle of the neighborhood's

other canines, who, according to my observations, went out
with their people two, often three times a day. The patch of
dead grass in front of the old townhome across the street could
attest to the volume of their traffic. But Bezi Duras's dogs never
ventured outside before the sun went down.

Then there was the fact that Ena had never set foot in Bezi's
place. Ten years of hauling trash and mending curtains and
silencing the building's notoriously boisterous radiators—but
never on the thirty-third floor. Wasn't that odd? Even suspicious? It made sense if you allowed for the fact that Bezi
Duras needed a place for those dogs to be men during the
day. She couldn't have the building staff coming up there, seeing unaccounted-for people, growing suspicious, et cetera—
especially staff who hailed from Back Home and might have
enough knowledge to put the whole thing together.

But here was the real clincher: though the actual hour of
sunset might deviate as the autumn went on, the timing of the
quartet's magic-hour exit always changed to match it. It held
true week after week after week: as the days grew shorter, Bezi
and the dogs appeared earlier and earlier, rounding the corner
just after the sun had dipped below the buildings across the
river. It was a subtle sign, one I liked to think not just anybody
would have noticed, but a compelling one nonetheless. If Bezi
Duras reliably clung to routine in every other aspect of her life,
then surely her evening walk should be as bound to the clock as
her other errands were. If she always headed to the store at
one-thirty, and returned without fail by three, would she not be
the kind of person who would fasten her final walk of the day to
a particular hour—say, seven or eight o'clock—rather than the
arbitrary and ever-changing schedule of the setting sun?

Something else must be precipitating her movement into

the street for this nightly ritual. And it obviously had nothing to do with any man-made measure of time.

I was pleased with my little tally of signs. They would stand up to Ena's scrutiny. But Ena, I occasionally reminded myself, was not the one I had set out to convince. I was gathering evidence so that my mother could join me in this strange and powerful secret. And whenever I imagined sharing what I had learned with her—sitting her down at the dining table to tell her that the lady on thirty-three was some manner of enchantress holding three men captive in canine form—my whole heart shuddered. Even if she was amused rather than furious, my mother would pick me apart. Had I ever seen the dogs turn into men? What evidence did I have that any transformations were taking place at all? Wasn't I putting too much stock in the fact that I had never seen them come back? No, you couldn't go more than six blocks in any direction from the Morningside without running into the tide, but wasn't it possible that Bezi was visiting friends or family within that radius? There was so much unaccounted for.

Sometimes, I imagined myself calling the Dispatch for a bit of help filling in the gaps. "Hey, Dispatcher, I love your station—I listen to it all day, every day, no surprise. There's something strange going on with a woman in my building who has these three huge dogs. I'm dying to know where she goes and what she does, but I can't follow her without my mother noticing. Can anyone tell me anything about them?" Then the calls would come from along Bezi Duras's route: *Yes, I've seen them on my corner. I see them in the park every day.* There would be something delicious about it, gloriously communal, the calls pouring in while I stuck pin after pin into the ratty map of the city that hung above Ena's desk. But, of course, this was an impossible fantasy. Even if Bezi didn't hear that particular broadcast, somebody in the building would. They would recognize the subject of inquiry. They might even realize who was asking the questions. And then they would tell Bezi, or they would tell my mother, and it was hard to know which would be worse for me.

ONE AFTERNOON, FILLED with unreasonable courage, I let myself into the penthouse elevator courtyard. It was nothing extravagant, just a little rotunda of the same pale stone that made up the rest of the building, surrounded by a low wall. The elevator was a brutalist sort of structure, with no buttons on the panel, just a round depression in the metal that looked like it might take a key. If so, it must be unlike any I'd ever seen: the keyway was not a narrow slot, but a circle about half an inch in diameter, with a crown of little mazelike depressions all around it.

As I stood there, the door let out a high, solitary chime.

I bolted.

There was a lesson here, one two three, I thought later on from the safety of my bed. I must not force my way into more knowledge. When the time was right, the knowledge would present itself, just as Ena said.

And a few weeks later, it did. I was helping my mother set rat traps in the basement when Mr. Ellers startled us. He was a frail-looking foreigner who lived alone in 17D. He looked translucent, and was so thin he seemed to be held upright entirely by the structure of his suits. It was impossible to tell whether he used sentence fragments because he didn't have enough English or because he assumed we didn't have enough

English. He had a tendency to greet me with exclamations of "Running!" devoid of context, unadorned with directives that might have introduced some sense to the matter. Like: "Stop running!" Or: "No running!" Or even: "Let's go running!"

That particular day, he led with "Locked out." He blinked at my mother and tilted his wrist slightly. "No key."

My mother went to a locker in the back of her office that I had always assumed was just another storage place for endless boxes of paper. But I'd been mistaken. Behind the door was a safe. And in the safe was an enormous ring of keys.

My mother hefted it out. "You're in 17D?" she asked Ellers.

"Yes." Ellers went on standing there while she parsed through the ring once, and then again. I, too, stood there, probably with my mouth agape. It had never occurred to me that, of course, my mother would have access to spare keys for every single unit in the building. Or perhaps it had—but it had never occurred to me to consider this in a material sense, as a cache kept in a specific place, accessible by specific means and for designated reasons.

"No 17D," my mother finally said. She glowered at him. "You leave key with us for sure?"

"Yes," Ellers said, persevering through his inner battle with her question. "I'm sure I gave a spare."

She rummaged through the keys again. "I don't see—can you find?" She slung the whole ring in his direction. He just about managed to catch it.

"How rude!" he stammered. "We *pay* you!"

In wordless fury, my mother led him up to the seventeenth floor, with me trailing along. I was angry on her behalf, and a little embarrassed of her, too—but these feelings were diluted by the mesmerizing spectacle of the keys rotating through her hands while she tried them against the lock of 17D. Key after key after key. Barrel and dimple and double-sided, twice, maybe three times as many as there could possibly be doors at the Morningside. Some of them looked a hundred years old. The penthouse elevator key must be somewhere among them—just as Ellers's was.

A few days later, after Bezi Duras had left with the dogs, I returned to the little courtyard to take another look at the elevator panel. Sure enough, I'd remembered the most important detail: the keyhole was a moated depression with a sequence of elaborate grooves, mazelike, finely drawn.

I tried to hold the image of it in my mind while I waited for the right time to strike. Weeks passed. I became my mother's tireless helper, washing mopheads, clearing debris, even sweeping out the carcasses of the monstrous bugs that perished belly-up in the corners.

"You're really working hard," my mother told me.

"I'm bored," I said, and this was not untrue—we were in the third month of waiting to hear back from the school.

Screwing up her courage, my mother called the school once again and struggled through a gauntlet of impatient operators until she was directed to the Repopulation representative. The news was not good. They were "full, ma'am—completely full." There were some virtual courses I could take while I crawled up the wait list, and they would be happy to share the syllabus so I could catch up on my own for the rest of the year.

"You know how much schoolbooks cost?" my mother said.

They knew. They invited her to a district meeting for parents navigating the Repopulation Program, and while she was out, I seized my chance, helped myself to her tool bag, and opened the safe. The knowledge that the ferry schedule and the maze of down-island streets and the meeting itself would keep her busy for at least three hours didn't stop my hands from shaking as I stood in the dark penthouse courtyard with a flashlight between my teeth, going through her keys, checking them one by one against the elevator panel's stupefying port.

It must have taken me twenty minutes to get through the entire loop just once. No match.

I stepped back and gazed up the edifice in the swimming orange light of the streetlamps. Maybe there was another way. A breaker box or a maintenance panel, some mechanism to get the thing going in case of an emergency. I began feeling along the wall. Back and forth, nothing, nothing, nothing—until my fingertips finally hit a little metal door hidden in the bushes. I crouched down and unlatched it. There was a panel inside, teeming with levers and buttons. Did I feel brave enough to try one? What if I got it wrong, and instead of the door opening, it became permanently jammed? Perhaps that might be an opportunity to have my mother ride to the rescue when Bezi Duras returned. And then what? A drawn-out investigation of what had malfunctioned, and the inevitable discovery that the panel had been tampered with. My sticky, incriminating fingerprints all over the gleaming metal. My guilty face. One two three.

In the time I'd been crouching half-in, half-out of the bushes, a face had appeared at the low wall that bordered the alley. I didn't notice until I heard a voice behind me say, "Back again snooping."

I scrambled to my feet. A portly-looking man, Black and bespectacled, was leaning over the wall on rolled-up sleeves. Something about him felt familiar despite the flat cap shadowing his features, but I couldn't quite place it.

"I'm not snooping," I said.

"Oh, you are," he insisted. "This is—what? The third time I've seen you out here?"

"Sounds like you're the one snooping."

"I'm just walking by," he said. "Minding my own business. Staying out of places I don't belong. Unlike you."

That stung. "I belong!" I held up the keys with my steadier hand. "You see these? I work in this building."

"You *work*? In this building?" He took off his hat and raised an eyebrow. "I should call social services."

"What? Why?" I had never heard of them.

"You're what, ten? Twelve? I don't know where you're from, Snoopy, but we have laws in this country against child labor."

"I'm not child labor," I said. "I'm helping my mother."

I had the sudden, violent impression that I'd done terrible harm by sticking around to argue instead of just begging ignorance and retreating. Here I was, thinking I was being so careful—when in fact I had failed to notice the nosy stranger monitoring me. I was going to get stung for my thieving and my lies, and so was my poor mother.

"What exactly are you helping your mother do? Break into Bezi Duras's penthouse?"

"What?" I cried. "Of course not!" Then it hit me. Who he was. His hair was cropped shorter. His widow's peak was more pronounced now, and there was more white in his beard, but it was definitely him. "I know you," I said. "My aunt, she has your picture on the wall. In the security shed!"

"I don't know what you're talking about."

"Yes you do—you're always taking pictures of the courtyard. I know your glasses. *You're* the snoop! Snoop!" I yelled preposterously after him, even after he'd disappeared. "Snoop!"

I'm not going to list the ways a nighttime interaction with a grown stranger could have turned ugly for an eleven-year-old girl. I'll tell you up front: This is not that kind of story. He was not that kind of stranger.

WHEN MY MOTHER came home that evening, I was already waiting for her at the dining table. Our rations were warming on the stove. The keys were back in their usual spot. I was flushed with panic and disappointment and rebuke, and I felt certain she would notice. But she seemed too dejected to even look at me. "I think you'll have to start following the curriculum on your own," she said.

"What did you find out?" I asked.

She sat down and began rubbing the arches of her feet. "They say the wait list is six months backed up. But some of the other parents there—well. Maybe I misunderstood."

"What did they say?"

"They were all speaking so fast."

"What did they say, Mama?"

"I think they said they've been waiting for years."

"Years? How many years?"

"The most I think was two."

"Two *years*?" Panic lanced through me.

"I probably misunderstood."

"In two years I'll be an ogre," I told her.

She smiled at me. "You're a bit of an ogre already."

I was in no mood to joke around. "You would be, too, if you were me."

FORTUNATELY, A DISTRACTION materialized. Welcome for me, but less so for my mother, who noticed one morning that

the trash cans we had hauled out to the curb the previous evening had not been emptied—at least, not into the garbage
truck that usually rumbled past the Morningside in the pre-
dawn hours on its way to the Marsh. Instead, their contents
were scattered down the block. Receipts and wrappers lay everywhere. To make matters worse, a light rain had fallen sometime after the cans had gone over, and debris had found its way
into the gutter and traveled as far as the front door of Tufaah all
the way down at the end of the block. It took us most of the
morning to gather up all that trash. Harder still was storing it
until the next pickup, while the residents kept hurling fresh
bags down the chute. On Friday, we hauled all of it out again—
and on Saturday, to my mother's fury and my dismay, we were
met with a similar scene. Cans upended, and a cascade of
windblown detritus.

My mother suffered this as a personal humiliation—first,
because not a single resident departing the building that day
was able to refrain from commenting on it. Not directly to her,
of course, but rather loudly into the air, as though some watching force shared their frustration with the ruined aesthetic of
the block. "Oh my goodness—what's *become* of the place?"
And second, because she was certain that people whose faces
she couldn't see, in the Morningside and the surrounding
buildings alike, were watching her go up and down the block
with her picker for a second time that week, and speculating
wildly about her incompetence. I stood behind the gate and
watched her, overhearing snippets of the tirade that unfurled
under her breath, until she suddenly stopped.

She came back to the gate and stuck whatever was in her
tongs through the bars to me. "Do you know what this is?"
Whatever it was stank greasily. She didn't wait for me to guess.

"It's a chicken bone." Her face was an unusual combination of pale and red. "Somebody," she said, "is eating *meat*."

All her rage at the mess now had the added weight of this gruesome discovery. Somebody in the building—perhaps more than one somebody—was accepting government rations while willfully breaching not only Posterity Initiative protocols but the far, far older edicts by which we had all agreed to live. The hypocrisy of it. The injustice. She might expect it in Paraiso, or Back Home. But here? Here?

By the time the trash collectors returned on Tuesday, she had an earful for them.

"Lady," the binman said. "If it's not in the cans, we can't pick it up."

"What you mean?" my mother cried, pointing. "Cans!"

The binman with whom she was dealing had a grizzled but patient face. He set one foot down off the back of the truck so he could stand closer to her. "Cans tip over," he said, tilting his hand from vertical to horizontal. "Spill everywhere. Can't pick up."

My mother was furious. She had taken great care to rest the cans against each other so that the weight of one wouldn't topple the others. For a day or two, she raged about the trash collectors, their mendacity, the fact that they were probably laughing at her behind her back. Then she changed her tune. "I bet it's those goddamn kids kicking them over at night," she said, failing to specify what goddamn kids she was talking about. Save for a little white girl in a green coat tottering down the street behind her mother, I hadn't seen any in weeks.

I was conscripted into helping her uncover the responsible party—an effort that found us in the little alley between the Morningside's outer wall and the adjacent building one night,

sharing an overturned milk crate while we waited for the cul-
prits to show themselves.

Around four in the morning, a fat gray creature came am-
bling down the sidewalk from the direction of the park. We
spotted it at the exact same moment, the only movement on
the entire street. My mother gripped my arm.

"What is it?" I said.

"Raccoon."

Neither of us had seen one before. We watched it knock the
bricks off a trash can, lift the lid, and lower itself inside. It did
this with a kind of smug certainty—the bent elbows and the
little black hands making the animal look as though it were eas-
ing itself into a bath. It was only in there for a few minutes,
rocking the can from side to side. With every soft grunt and
jettisoned bit of debris, I saw my mother's resolve to kill it
erode. Eventually, the raccoon knocked over the can, rolled
out, and moved on to the next one. When it had leveled them
all, it clambered up the wall and went back the way it had
come.

"Can you believe it?" my mother said.

I couldn't remember seeing her so—what? Moved? Enchanted? We went along the curb, righting the trash cans. My
mother started smiling giddily. She went out into the middle of
the street and stood with her hands on her hips, looking up the
hill. "You know, sometimes I think people are right."

"About what?"

"Maybe things *are* getting a little bit better."

She turned and looked down the street, and that was when
her face changed. "Look," she said.

A light was on at Tufaah, burning between the gaps in the
sheets of newspaper. In three seconds, my mother was at the
bottom of the block, pressing her face to the window.

"What do you see?" I called after her. She didn't answer me. "Mama? What do you see?"

"Not much. It's hard to tell if anything's different—come take a look."

But I didn't dare. That light inside felt like a living thing, glaring out at us. I didn't want to meet its eye. My mother, on the other hand, went on looking straight at it. "I wonder if someone's inside?" She came around to the door and, before I could stop her, pounded on it.

"What are you doing?" I cried.

"Mrs. al-Abdi!" my mother called through the door.

"Who the hell is that?"

"The woman who owns the place." My mother stepped back and looked up at the darkened windows of the apartments above the café. "Mrs. Safiya al-Abdi?"

"Please stop shouting!" My hands were sweating. When had she found out who the owner was? How long had she been sitting on that information? And whatever her designs on the place, why did she think roaring its owner's name up at the windows in the middle of the night would make them manifest?

From up the street, in the direction of the Morningside, there came a crash and a bellow. We got back to find Bezi Duras trying to extract herself from the tree bed just outside the gate. Her dogs had treed our raccoon and were whining balefully up at it. From where we stood, we could see it glowering back down at them from among the branches, its masked face full of triumph and scorn. My terror on its behalf evaporated: Bezi Duras was smiling.

"Well how about this," she said. "I haven't seen a raccoon in a long, long time."

"How lucky!" my mother exclaimed.

How lucky indeed. Lucky the Raccoon—the unwitting revelator of the timeline of Bezi's return. She was rumpled and hoarse, but still as elegant as ever, kicking the dirt off her shoes. I hadn't heard her voice since before Ena died, and I had forgotten how it sounded. Something about my pursuit of her had created distance between me and my fear of her—but all it took for it to come rushing back was one moment face-to-face. She looked at me and smiled and my insides dented.

My mother and I walked Bezi Duras back to the courtyard, and she let herself through the gate. I watched her remove the key from her pocket and twist it in the lock. The elevator opened, and she beckoned the dogs inside and vanished.

IT WAS OBVIOUS THAT MY MOTHER WOULD HAVE TO rethink her plan to terminate the raccoon, and sure enough, a few days later, she went out to find the means to trap it. She returned huffing and red-faced, and if I hadn't known better I would have thought she'd been crying.

"I need your help," she said from the doorway. "Right now."

She led me down the street and two blocks over to Ricky's, a tiny, half-subterranean establishment that reeked of bleach and camphor. The proprietor, Ricky, was leaning over the counter with the bald dome of his head in both hands. When he saw me, his face welled with hope.

"Ah," he said. "You must be the interpreter."

"Sure." I hesitated. "What's going on?"

"Tell this idiot that I'm trying to catch a raccoon," my mother said, in Ours.

"Please explain to your mother: we don't sell whatever it is she thinks we sell here."

The problem, it seemed, was that she had gotten mixed up en route to Ricky's and upon arrival asked for "mild" traps. This had led Ricky to present her with a substance for mildew removal—and when that turned out to be the wrong item, he had brought her mild soap, followed by mild detergent, all of which had only served to infuriate her further.

"Tell him: *humane*," she said to me in Ours. "I'm looking for a *humane* trap." She turned all her fury in his direction one last time. "Mild catch. No kill!"

"My mother wants a *humane* trap," I explained. "A big one."

Ricky brightened. He took my mother's arm and led her around back. There he presented her with everything he had to offer: plastic mouse boxes, snares, and even one cruelly smiling leg trap. "What does Mama want?" he asked me.

"That one," I said, pointing to the most benign-seeming of his cages, and removing myself before I started thinking too explicitly about the capabilities of all the rest. I drifted along the aisles, skimming the ironically bright labels of his sundries— water-purification tablets, security cameras, emergency kits— until I got to the far end of the store, where, under the distinct impression that I was being watched, I peered through a row of canned pumpkin and into the face of the spectacled stranger from last week.

"Hey there, Snoopy," he said.

The intervening days had muddled my memory of him. First of all, he was older than I'd initially thought. Streaks of white had begun to spider into his hair and beard. He wore slim, mustard-yellow glasses and a linen coat of a creamy salmon color. Once upon a time, the outfit had been perfectly tailored, even glamorous. Everything about the way it held together now was meant to tilt at the notion that this might still be the case.

"Any luck?" he was asking me.

"Luck?"

"Getting into the elevator."

It was terrifying to have my efforts so bluntly revealed within earshot of my mother. A quick glance around the corner confirmed that she was still in the back, reviewing Ricky's animal-control wall with scathing gestures.

"Snoopy?"

"Yes."

" 'Yes'—you've been up to the penthouse?"

"Yes," I lied, resolving that this was the fastest way to bring the matter to an end. "Yes, I have."

His eyebrows shot up with so much force his glasses tilted. "How'd you manage that?"

"I don't know—I just did, all right?"

My chiropteran mother, picking up on my voice in distant discourse with a stranger's, started looking around.

The stranger, meanwhile, made the disastrous decision to join me on my side of the shelf. "Snoopy," he said. "You're lying."

"I'm not. Why would I lie? Why do you care? Stop following me."

"Calm down," he said. "I'm not following you. What's it like up there?"

"Fine."

"Fine?"

"Nice."

"Snoopy." He grinned. "Come on, now. Do you want help? Getting up there?"

This was when my mother came bristling around the corner and set herself between us like a furious little drone. "Can I help you?" she said. "Who are you, sir? You want talk to me? Or are you just talk to little girls?"

It was a preposterous question, one that came from so deep

within some vortex of her horrors about the nature of men that she didn't even realize the absurdity of it. I was a full head and shoulders taller than my tiny mother—little girl, indeed.

The stranger was unfazed. "Hello, ma'am. My name is Lewis May." He held out a hand and stood there with it extended until my mother grew uncomfortable enough to shake it. "I was only telling your daughter: when you catch a raccoon, you must take it far, *far* away."

He was talking to her in that slightly elevated volume that people use to address the very old. This didn't escape my mother's notice. Her scowl deepened. "Oh yes?" she said.

"Oh yes! *Far* away. Or it will come right back. Isn't that right, Ricky?"

"It certainly is." Ricky had come around the side and was observing us. "But honestly, May, I don't know that there's any far away far *enough*—you sure you don't want some poison, Mama?"

"No poison," I said miserably.

"You know where you should take it," Ricky said brightly. "Sorey Park."

"Or the eastern edge of the Marsh," May put in. "It'll be happy there."

My mother, flustered at this incomprehensible barrage of suggestions, went on scowling. "That is all?"

"That is all." May looked at me. "This is Battle Hill. We look out for each other."

After the door closed behind him, she swung around to me. "Who the hell is that?"

"I have no idea." One two three.

But she didn't buy that. Did he live in the neighborhood? Had he approached me before today? Had he ever attempted

to get me to follow him somewhere? He looked familiar—
where had she seen him before? I parried her questions as best
I could, and settled into the lie that I thought he might work at
the funding office a few blocks over—which would have been
a mistake, had I not known that the language barrier would
prove too insurmountable for her to verify that I wasn't telling
the truth.

After a few days, her questions slowed to a trickle. Whatever
course of action she had imagined herself pursuing to root this
person out of my life was slowly fading from her bank of priorities. Meanwhile, May's offer of help burned in the back of
my mind. What kind of help could he offer? And why was he so
willing to offer it? This seemed like the kind of obstacle that
might be placed before a person to determine whether they
were ready to receive insight or were still the same old stub-
born self that had been unworthy of it. On the one hand, an
intercession from a stranger might happen because your patience had earned it. On the other, it might present a false turn
at the crossroads. "Do you want help?" the stranger had said.
Did I want it? Of course. So, the right answer, according to
everything I understood about the exchange rate of the universe, was obviously: "No."

And yet.

Finally, I relented and made my way to the courtyard again
after more than a week of avoiding it. May showed up within
the hour.

"You've been hiding," he said.

I shrugged. "Just busy."

"I've got better things to do than lurk around out here, wondering if you'll show up."

"You obviously don't."

He hoisted himself up onto the wall, swung his feet over, and sat looking down at me. "What's your interest in Bezi Duras?"

"Why do you care?"

"I thought you wanted my help."

"I don't know," I snapped. "I don't know what you're going to ask me to do in return."

"Don't be disgusting," he said. He was frowning. "What does your mother do at the Morningside?"

"She's the super."

"What happened to that old one—Eba?"

"Ena." I felt myself grow hot. "My aunt. She's dead."

He was silent long enough for me to believe he was giving this earnest thought. "I'm sorry. She was a nice lady."

"No, she wasn't. You're not doing her any favors by lying about her. But she was my aunt, and I love her."

"That's fair." He sat with this for a minute. "Well, we're a long line of garbage rustlers and can clangers, then, Snoopy. Who do you think held that job before Ena?"

"Let me guess."

"None other than yours truly."

"What a coincidence."

"Isn't it just?"

"You dress very fancy for a super."

"I was a writer in a past life."

"Why should I believe anything you say? I don't even know you."

He pushed up his glasses and squinted across the courtyard at me. "How's old Mrs. Golub doing? She still letting her dog take those curly little shits all over the hallway?"

It was hard to remain expressionless. I'd picked up so many of those very shits, often in full view of Mrs. Golub, who had a knack for emerging from her apartment at the exact moment I was bending down to remove them. She would sweep her trembling little one-eyed mutt into her arms, looking at me with bitter disappointment—as though I were the one who had just taken a shit on the floor.

"All right." I shrugged. "So you know the name of somebody who lives in the building. So what? That doesn't mean or prove anything. Mrs. Golub takes that dog everywhere she goes. You could've seen it out here in the street. Wouldn't take much to figure out how incontinent it is."

"How do I know her name, then?"

"I don't know. You could've introduced yourself in the neighborhood."

May burst out laughing. "Snoopy—can you imagine Mrs. Golub giving her name to a stranger? Let alone a Black man?" I could not. He raised a palmful of fingers and began knocking them down, one by one: "Mrs. Golub lives in 18F. She used to chair the Board of Occupants. At least once a week, she'll ask if you can hear the clanging in her walls. If she hasn't gone out and left the stove on and then come roaring back because the dog is going to be burned to a cinder, she will soon." He searched the recesses of his mind for a reason to knock his pinkie down. "The dog's name is Cleo." Full fist. "But that's all right, Snoopy. You don't have to believe me. I promise you this, though: you're never going to find the key to Bezi Duras's elevator down in the basement."

"Why not?"

"Because Bezi Duras never let one be kept down there again after her last one walked off."

"Is that right?"

"That's right."

"How did the last one walk off?"

"With me."

He took a key out of his breast pocket and held it up. It was impossible to see, from this distance, whether it was *the* key or not—and it vanished just as quickly as it had appeared.

With it went any hope that May's offer of help might be vague or useless-sounding enough to resist. One two three. "I guess you're going to offer it to me in exchange for something."

"Maybe. I haven't decided if you're worth my time, or if you're even going to be able to do what I need you to do."

This was the moment to walk away. I let it pass. "What do you want?" I said.

"When I left the Morningside, my departure was"—he took a few seconds to find the right word—"abrupt. Some of my things got left behind. I'd like to get them back."

"What things?"

"Personal correspondence, mostly."

"What, you mean—your mail?"

May nodded. "Especially some letters that may have been delivered after I was already gone."

"Where would they be?"

"I used to live in 16D," he said.

Rage shot into me. "I knew you were lying. The super's apartment is on the *tenth* floor."

He shrugged. "Not back in my day. They wanted the upper floors to look more occupied."

"I know 16D. That place has been empty for years. There's nothing of yours, nothing of anybody's in there."

"Well, no, not *in* the unit itself. But what about the mailbox downstairs? Look—I moved out. Mail didn't start arriving to my new address until several months later. I've been gone ten years, and some letters still don't make it to my new place, even now. All I'm asking you to do is check—just *look*. And if you can do that, I don't see any reason why I should hold on to this key any longer."

"Even if I don't find anything?"

He shrugged.

I had the sense that he was waiting for me to indicate that I might allow myself to be swayed, even if I wasn't feeling it at this very moment. As for me, I knew I shouldn't ask him any more questions, since I had no intention of entertaining his request. And yet: "Why'd you steal it?"

"I liked going up when Bezi wasn't home and looking at her paintings."

"Paintings?"

"Bezi Duras is a painter. A real big deal." Then it dawned on him: "Wait. Why do *you* want to go up there, Snoopy—if not to look at the paintings?"

I shrugged.

"Do we have a deal?"

"Maybe."

I DIDN'T DO much over the next week besides think about his proposition. What needed squaring most was my own not-insignificant conviction that the whole venture was premised on a lie. Apartment 16D was a huge west-facing two-bedroom right on the corner of Park Place, with a seasonal view of the flooded freeway through old, stately sycamores. I couldn't imagine that any super, ever, would have been permitted to oc-cupy it—especially by Popovich. Still, May had only told me to think about it, and there was plenty of time to do that while I sat chaperoning the raccoon trap.

I let myself linger in my mother's office one evening. The radio was on, the Dispatcher in the process of trying to interrupt a man who was in his eleventh minute of extolling the virtues of the old charbroiler he had owned, once upon a time.

("That smell, Dispatcher."

"I know, friend. I know."

"Sometimes I wake up and I swear I can still smell the steak."

"You don't have to tell me, friend.")

Ena's old desk was like some archaeological dig—as the layers receded away from the present, you could glean all kinds of things about the organizational proclivities of superintendents past. My mother was at the very top: fastidiously neat stacks of paper, everything sitting at right angles, and a labeling system that would have earned the admiration of the public library. Just below that was Ena's work: boxes overstuffed with papers and bags stacked in the corners and under the desk. Most of them seemed unlikely to yield anything but old rags and odds and ends she'd bought two of and discarded one; broken bathroom fixtures; a plunger minus its inner suction cup. When eventually I did excavate a bag labeled "Mail," it contained a hodgepodge of unrecognizable names. There was only one thing for 16D in there: a promotional flyer for recording equipment addressed to one LAMB OSMOND. "Studio-quality sound," it promised, "right in the comfort of your own home." It was dated twelve years back, to right around the time mail should have been arriving for May, which made me feel both vindicated and nervous. Who the hell was Lamb Osmond?

Reluctantly, I went looking for the answer in the mailbox of 16D. It turned out to be crammed full of letters. A few were the kind of junk mail I had heard persisted in the past. The rest were handwritten, stained with rust, torn by the weight of years and years of letters pressing down on them, and all addressed to Lamb Osmond. I thought about sneaking them into my room so I could go through them in peace—but how would I explain their presence if my mother happened to find them? And why would I take the risk, when not a single envelope was actually addressed to Lewis May? I jammed them back into the box, locked it, and replaced the key.

"Who's the mail addressed to?" I asked May when he showed up that evening. "Just in case I decide to look for it, I mean."

He grinned. "You've already looked."

"I have not. And I won't if you don't start being more honest."

He settled himself on the wall and crossed his legs. "Most of the letters will be for Lamb Osmond."

"And what did you say your name is?"

He hesitated. "Lewis Allen May."

"See why that's a problem?"

"L.A.M. Osmond. Lewis Allen May Osmond. Lamb, for short."

"That's not how you spell 'lamb.'"

"It's an endearment, Snoopy. My mother used to call me that. Osmond was my grandfather's name."

"Sure."

"It was. Frank Gareth Osmond. My mother's father."

"None of that explains why you'd be receiving mail under Lamb Osmond when you already have a name of your own, Lewis Allen May. If that even *is* your name."

"Plenty of people go by more than one name."

"Suspicious people."

"I'm not a suspicious person."

"You sure seem like one."

He could tell now, if he'd been unable to tell before, that there was a lot riding on this name business. All his glibness faded. He took his time. "Tell you what," he said. "I can prove it." He edged along the wall until he was a good deal closer to me. "There's a fireplace in the living room in 16D. Right? Right?" This seemed like a detail Ena wouldn't admit to knowing, so I didn't either. "Well," May said, "there is. If you sit down on the hearthstone and feel around with your feet, one of the tiles will give. And if you turn it over, you'll find a little inscription. 'Lamb Osmond wrote *Nothing Fades* here.'"

I stared at him. "That doesn't prove you're Lamb Osmond. All that proves is that you know what's written under Lamb Osmond's hearthstone."

"Would anyone but Lamb Osmond know what's written under his hearthstone?"

"I don't know." My thoughts felt slow and stuck together. "Maybe he asked you to help him loosen it so he could turn it over. Or maybe you were fixing it after he moved out."

"But it isn't fixed, Snoopy. It's still loose." He could see that I wasn't convinced. "What are you worried about?"

I shrugged. "That you're asking me to steal someone else's letters."

"Trust me, Snoopy. Everything in that mailbox belongs to me."

I still couldn't convince myself that he was telling the truth. Or, perhaps, I was too convinced, and ashamed at being won over so easily. Ena—or perhaps any person grown-up enough to warrant involvement in this kind of decision—would have asked him better questions. She would have seen the holes in his story. Perhaps this was why he'd had no luck with my sensible panopticon of an aunt, and had resorted instead to bribing an eleven-year-old with promises of a secret key.

Doubt grew around me and hardened. Imagine having to explain to my mother why I had participated in a series of misdeeds premised on lies. Why the pilfering of keys and the sneaking around? Why the thieving of mail that wasn't mine to open and did not even bear the name of the person on whose behalf I was stealing it? Hadn't she raised me to be better, smarter, more sensible, than this? It was in my mind to give up on the whole endeavor—and I might have done so.

But then, later that week, I ran into Bezi Duras. I was coming back from Ricky's when Bezi Duras turned the corner. I jumped aside. She didn't see me. She was past me in a flash, but not before I noticed that her shirt and boots were splashed with paint. Royal blue and a strange electric green, so pale it was almost yellow. Right there, made brilliant in the sunlight on all her plain clothes.

I stood staring up the slope after her.

Paint. Wouldn't paint announce itself this way on the body of a painter? Wouldn't it hitch a ride away from the easel, ending up where it didn't belong? Wouldn't it stain her nail beds, speckle her eyelashes, brighten in rivulets the ends of her hair? And if May was telling the truth about *this*—this granular evidence, this vital thing I had missed about Bezi because I was too busy studying the dogs when I should have been studying her—couldn't he be telling the truth about the letters?

So I let myself into 16D. After all, why not? I'd never have to admit it to May if I didn't want to. I stood in the great room, one two three, with the evening light melting in and tried to picture him living in here all those years ago. His slim glasses on the bathroom vanity. His suits hanging in the closet. His books piled on the mantel. I climbed up onto the hearth and stood there. The fireplace was empty, tiled in white, soot-covered. The little whirlwind that lives in every chimney pulled and pushed, as though it couldn't quite decide what to do with me.

I sat on the hearthstone and felt around with my sneaker until I felt one of the tiles give a little. It was a huge slab, three feet by one. I had very little faith in my ability to move it, but a crowbar did the trick in the end, when I eventually returned a few days later to give it another, more committed try. The lip of the tile came right up and sat suspended in the air before grating ruinously back down. I waited to see if the noise would bring anybody to the door, but no one came.

When I finally managed to get enough leverage under it, I found the promised words. "Lamb Osmond wrote *Nothing Fades* here." The inscription was followed by a ragged abstract of what I took to be a rook crane standing on one leg.

The next time I saw May, I had pen and paper waiting in my pocket. "There's something else under that hearthstone," I said. "Can you remember what it is?"

He frowned. For the first time since we'd met, he didn't look smug.

"I don't think so," he said.

"It's a picture of something. Remember?" He went on looking at me. I held out the pen and paper. "It's a—a bird."

His whole face lit up. "Ah! Snoopy—yes, of course."

His reproduction was close. Very close. I had the sense not to reveal whether he had passed my fiendishly clever test, though I could tell he was beginning to get a bit irritated with me. Was it reasonable to push him further? And, if so, how? I couldn't think of anything else to ask him. Everything he'd said thus far had been some form of true. Would that have been enough for a grown-up? Or would a grown-up have denied him the letters on the simple, irrefutable grounds that they did not bear his name?

We were both equally surprised, I think, when I showed up the following evening with a box of Lamb Osmond's mail in my hands.

"Snoopy! You did it." He sounded moved, which took me by

surprise. I had been imagining a more formal and dignified exchange, not unlike a briefcase trade in some old film—that's why I'd gone to the trouble of putting all the messy envelopes into a single container. But May got down on his hands and knees right there, in Bezi Duras's courtyard, and started in on the box, thumbing through fistfuls of paper before reaching in for more. "This is wonderful," he said. Indignity upon indignity: at some point, he began to cry—or, rather, his glasses fogged up, mortifying me.

My embarrassment turned to unease. He was taking forever. I could picture it all unraveling so clearly: Bezi Duras would pick tonight to return early from her walk, and she'd find us there in this absurd tableau, a stranger blubbering into a box of crusty old mail, and me standing there with my arms crossed, muttering, "One two three" under my breath.

May finally remembered I was there. He grabbed my wrist. "Snoopy," he said. "Thank you."

"You're welcome." What else was there to say to a grown man in such a state?

He went on riffling through the box. As he came within sight of the bottom, his whole being started to slump.

"Is there more?" he said over his shoulder.

"No."

"This is everything out of the mailbox?"

"And the basement."

He paused a moment to compose himself. "Anywhere you can think that a stray letter might be?"

"It's not there, is it? Whatever you were hoping to find?"

"Doesn't look like it, no."

"Sorry."

He shook his head. "Ah, Snoopy." He forced his face into a smile. "You know, sometimes you're so far away from what you once were, you need the slightest little reminder that your past was real?" He waved a slip of paper at me—an old ration card dated twelve years back, the year I was born.

I squinted at it. "Think you still might be able to collect that soap and coffee?" I said.

He laughed a little. "Maybe, Snoopy. Maybe." He took forever to stand up. "Well, fuck. It was worth a try. Thanks for this. I won't forget it."

A MORE TECHNOLOGICALLY LITERATE PERSON would, by then, already have sought out what might be found on Lamb Osmond. And in so doing, they would already have known that once upon a time, the twenty-year-old Lewis Allen May had packed his bags and ditched the flat, green brilliance of the wind farm where he'd grown up, leaving behind a poetry-loving librarian mother and a stoic father of ordinary emotional capabilities, and returned to that same Island City his grand-parents had abandoned to seek his fortune as a writer.

The city had fallen several times by then, but it had always come back. It couldn't help itself, revived by the fire it kept managing to stoke in its most recent newcomers. May felt like he knew it through and through. He'd heard his grandfather's stories and read about it all his life, and he knew that he had the necessary fire in him. He hadn't been prepared for how fast the city was emptying, though, or how tired it felt. He hadn't been prepared for the size of the trash beaches mid-island. Or how indifferent the up-island girls would be: somber, about their own ways, wiping down tables in tea shops inherited from great-grandfolk, the tea itself long gone, its memory kept alive only in pictures on the wall. He sought out his grandfather's little antiques store on a quiet block, boarded up like all the other houses around it. Cracks in the foundations. Fire escapes dangling uselessly.

The Repopulation Program was just getting off the ground. Talking about it in company was the fastest way to pick a fight with almost anyone. The white tower people up- and down-island were all for it—it was a way for the administration to cover the climate debts it owed around the world without raising taxes. Plus, Repopulation awardees were exhausted and grateful. They took a rosy view of what they found when they arrived, unlike the people of the outer islands, who had nothing but centuries of complaints and questions. Why had the administration waited so long to offer new housing as an incentive to stay? Why hadn't new houses been built in time to keep people like May's grandparents from leaving in the first place, instead of letting their trains stall and their shops sit empty and their neighborhoods crumble into the bay?

May knew. He'd known it all his life. What he didn't know was why the city would invite more people in when it couldn't even make someone who loved it so much, and knew so much about it, welcome.

Of the three books he wrote in those hazy early years, two were published, both under the name Lamb Osmond, one to modest acclaim—which May had leveraged to a part-time position at the university up-island.

He was determined to drudge alongside other lecturers in his department until his literary luck bloomed. In his youth, he had imagined himself the kind of person who would thrive in the limelight—but during the couple of instances where the opportunity presented itself to test this belief, he had found the public eye uncomfortably penetrating. He needed a beta blocker just to introduce the readers at a charity event down-island. He started to think he might be fine with staying unseen.

And unseen he was—by the literati, and often by reviewers, but not, to his surprise, by the great poet Benjamin Bowen, whose university office shared a wall with May's own. May's mother was an ardent fan of Bowen's, and May had grown up reading his poetry. He did not expect to see the legendary, bull-necked lothario refilling water bottles at the corridor fountain or sleeping off his fifth divorce on the same old office sofa where he had spent so many nights after the previous four. Nor would he have thought him capable of taking a genuine interest in an underling. But Bowen surprised him by seeking out and reading all of May's books—even the one already out of print. "You've got some real sand," he shouted after May one morning. "That scene with the turbines!" And there, under the blinding hallway lights of the fifth floor, within earshot of every open classroom, Benjamin Bowen whistled.

Whether or not this remark had been facetiously intoned, May couldn't decide. He let his misgivings fade as Bowen began inviting him out: to coffee at first, then chess games in the park, then a succession of literary parties, often held in the dimly lit penthouse apartment of some admirer of Bowen's or another, usually an older man with a suspiciously amassed fortune and an effusive, inebriated wife. Every now and again, after such an event, Bowen would lead May farther up-island, to some crumbling turn-of-the-century fortress, where they would burst, unannounced, into the abode of a literary giant May hadn't realized was still alive: Stuart Levshin ("still eats meat," Bowen warned), Paul Brightwood ("pervert"), and eventually, even Fazal Khan ("you've never met someone so much up his own ass, but he does serve good wine").

May wasn't really sure how he had ended up there. It felt

most of the time like a life that had befallen somebody else. Perhaps if he laughed very quietly and sat off to the side, no one would remember that he had no stories of the city to share with these lions, who in their twilight seemed to have nothing *but* stories: of their youth, of their time on the stages of theaters and music halls, of the half-remembered parties at which they were honored, of freezing walks home arm in arm on those incredibly rare nights when all three or four of them struck out with the intended recipients of their romantic overtures. In their company, May finally understood the difference between people who were *from* the city and people who were *of* it—people whose presence in its history had left as much of an imprint on the city as it had on them. It lived in their work and their minds in its most formidable iteration. And in return, it had allowed them to see it as it really was—stark and unpredictable, eternal; uncorrupted by changes great and small, by the creeping tide and the doom it portended, or the steady exodus of what the great writers deemed "weak leavers," who didn't want to endure Posterity measures.

Did his stomach dip a little at the thought of admitting to his mother, that adamant and lifelong fan of Bowen's, that another Black writer did not feature in the great poet's roster of friends? Certainly. He didn't want to hurt her. He didn't want her to feel differently about the hand-scrawled lines from "Fortune's Favor" that had been taped to the freezer door since before he was born.

Six months after May's admission to this fellowship of reminiscence, Death met Benjamin Bowen in his kitchen by means of pulmonary embolism. May was surprised to find himself named to the pallbearing party. He couldn't figure out how he'd become such a part of the great poet's inner circle—but then, a man of Bowen's age and stature, he reasoned, was likely to feel quite apart from ordinary people. It made sense that he would want the solace of knowing the roster of his send-off, lest it turn out to be sparsely attended.

This theory disintegrated at the viewing, during which May was forced to stand for twenty-five minutes in a line that stretched around the block. Later, following the hearse that carried Benjamin Bowen's coffin on the procession route across the bridge and down the city streets, he was astounded to see every sidewalk crammed with people holding signs of farewell. Poor May began to feel a tightening in his chest; the pain persisted throughout the services and the reception, and was only amplified by the presence of more than a thousand mourners—among them, the mayor—who fogged up the church with their sobbing. The pain in May's chest grew quite acute. It was grief, he told himself that night, unable to sleep. "Just grief, right?" he asked the doctor when he went to make sure it wasn't something else.

It was a panic attack, the doctor told him, smiling up from her notes. Had he found himself under any acute stress these past few weeks?

The acute stress was this: witnessing Bowen's send-off had forced May to imagine his own. In the brief instant when his brain had fastened onto a vision of himself lying in a coffin, he had been unable to picture the occupant of the role he himself had played for Bowen. He couldn't think of a single person he might nominate to bear his pall. And when he tried to populate the streets of his mind with mourners and well-wishers, he couldn't actually picture any of the people from the university, or from the literary parties, standing there to see him off.

No. No, they wouldn't be there, he realized—and his chest seized up again. He didn't really know any of them, and they didn't know him. And he couldn't rely on his readers, either.

His work, though well received, was neither fashionable nor popular. He was not the figurehead of a movement, nor the spokesman of a cultural turn. He didn't even understand his students, who only ever reached out to him when they needed references for residencies with which he was unfamiliar. He was a young Black man who had written a few books in a city he had always fantasized about but didn't really know, alone in his profession, solitary even in crowded rooms. And he was not *of* this city—he wasn't even from it. He was on track to go off entirely alone.

This was the state of mind May was struggling under when the Exchequer Street train station collapsed. We needn't dwell on the details. You probably remember most of it: the sinkhole and the rubble, and how the word "pancake" suddenly became a verb. As in: the train station "just pancaked." The footage of weeping people swarming the highway, and the fires, and the rescue teams. The inquest, which took three years, and the endless lawsuits and the eventual reconfiguration of building codes that finally forced the administration to admit that much of the city's down-island reach was landfill, and therefore essentially a sinkhole—a fact borne out by the subsequent flooding, not to mention the collapse of other buildings throughout the growing tidal zone.

Before all that, however, May was just another dizzy bystander leaning over the highway rail, watching the dust twist out across the bay. He was there when the choppers came to sweep the debris. He was there, too, when they started pulling bodies out of the rubble. Newscasters were frantically doing the math: six trains had been entering or exiting the station at the moment of collapse. Any of the people aboard—not to mention the two hundred or so in the station itself—might still be down there. Might still be alive.

May was in attendance for twenty-nine of the thirty days of rescue efforts. The first half of this time he spent among the news crews, where he could drift from group to group, catching little snippets of information before they were polished for official release. But this felt too peripheral. He began spending time in the Martinique Hotel bar, just outside the containment zone, where the victims' families congregated every evening to pray and share stories about the loved ones they hoped were trapped, unharmed, somewhere below. When eventually asked if he was waiting for someone to be found, he said yes. And when they asked him to share details about his missing person, he found himself inventing a character that very much resembled Benjamin Bowen.

The news crews plaguing the families were relentless. He managed to avoid most of them, but at long last he was cornered by a blustering redhead in an ill-fitting suit, who shoved a microphone under his chin. "And you, sir? Who are you praying for?"

May stuttered, "My grandfather."

"Is there anything you want our viewers to know about him?"

What to say? "He's a poet."

The clip was still in its first rotation when his mother called him. She sounded beside herself. "Was that you on TV tonight, Lewis, or am I just losing my mind?"

"No, no," he lied. "It's just some guy who looks a lot like me." And then, to comfort her: "You're not the only person who called thinking it's me."

His mother bought this, but the rescue coordinators who tracked May down the following day did not. They had seen his interview and wanted him to provide the full name of this poet grandfather for their ever-changing tally of the missing. May couldn't very well say "Benjamin Bowen," so he made up a

name: James Fahey. He improvised the spelling as he went,
and didn't think of the name again until it showed up on the list
of the presumed dead a month later when the rescue efforts
were finally suspended.

If only he had known what that "James Fahey" would lead
to—would he still have done it? I don't know. Probably. When
he first told me this story, many years after I gave him the box
of letters in Bezi Duras's courtyard, he claimed otherwise. But
as the years went on, and we revisited the story, he went back
and forth. What he kept coming back to was that after the collapse, there was a growing sense in him that he had, against all
odds, ended up at the center of a turning point in the city's history. One of *those* moments, the kind to which only people like
Benjamin Bowen and his friends could lay claim. Yes, it was a
horror, the beginning of some kind of end. But it was going to
be part of the city's history forever. And he, Lewis Allen May,
was part of it. And it was better to be part of something—
however tragic—than part of nothing at all.

Anyway, May stuck to the James Fahey ruse as operations
shifted from rescue to recovery. He visited the collapse site
often while the thinning crews continued to push the rubble
around and send small teams down to retrieve the bodies one
by one. He saw them lifted out, plastic-wrapped, usually in the
still hour of three in the morning, carted off to the morgue up-
island to await identification. But even that close, he didn't feel
quite close enough. He'd never know which of the red-eyed
mourners from the hotel would be summoned to identify whatever lay in those big yellow bags. Who was getting that call at
three or four in the morning? *Come on down as soon as you
can, please, we think we have your father, your sister, your
friend.* Every so often, May had to remind himself that such a
call would never be made to him. There *was* no James Fahey.

Despite having been right at the center of it all from the very first day, he would have to wait—like some outsider—to find out what had happened down there in the station. He would never hear a word of condolence, never receive a scrap of paper or an article of clothing. The tragedy had turned from national to private grief, and there was no place for him in it anymore. He was a spectator, adjacent to but not of it. How could he explain that his heartbreak felt much closer than this?

So when the rescue crews laid out a reclamation area where families could collect the belongings of their dead, he made sure he was one of the first to arrive. In a garishly flowered backpack, he found balled-up socks and a copy of Benjamin Bowen's *Moonlight*. It felt like a sign. He took the backpack home and read the collection again, trying to piece together what he could about its original owner. He didn't know her name. She had been gifted the book by someone named Soraya, who referred to her as "wondergirl." Among the meaningless margin scribbles—grocery lists, addresses—were interspersed lines of what May guessed was her own poetry. It wasn't half-bad. In fact, he suspected Benjamin Bowen would rate it quite highly. At least the parts of it that didn't tend toward the political. ("Social change is up to time," Bowen had said. "Very little of it is up to people.") Wondergirl clearly did not share this view. May imagined her as a young woman, similar to himself—a person looking for answers in letters, with a deep love of, and a desire to understand, the city to which she had given her entire heart. Only where he had blindly accepted its wonders, she had trained a keen eye on its shortcomings. The way it failed its poor. The way it pushed its most vulnerable, back and back, all the way to its outer margins, to the places that were already flooding. He had wanted to write about its hidden truths, the resilience of its people this way. How terrible that wondergirl had died, and he had not. All that promise snuffed out by chance.

The short story he eventually wrote about a disaffected young poet falling in love with the memory of a girl whose backpack he steals from the scene of a hit-and-run was his best-received work. When he called to share the news that *The Islander* magazine had selected it to appear in one of its final print issues, his mother wept, and proudly drove into the nearest town with a bookstore to buy ten copies. There it was: "Wonder Girl," by Lamb Osmond.

The story was short-listed for two prizes and won a third. Its most significant gain was his invitation to a series of festivals and panels he had previously attended only as an audience member. He couldn't believe that people were willing to put him up and pay him to read aloud from his work. And this was the headspace in which he found himself when a fine-boned, middle-aged woman wearing a teal shalwar kameez stood up during the question-and-answer session and said, "Mr. Osmond—I wanted to ask about your use of language."

"Of course," he said, feeling a great, dumb rush of warmth toward this stranger, who had come all this way to see him on a high-tide evening with a gently folded copy of the magazine in her hand.

"I'm a great admirer of your prose—particularly the passages you use to describe city life." She flipped to his story, adjusted the microphone, and, to his agony, read out a few sentences. A handful of people behind her clapped.

"You don't have to do that." May himself wasn't sure whether he was addressing the woman or the source of the applause. "Thank you so much."

"Just a minute," the woman said, and kept going. She read two lines, three, four. He sat there, half-listening, grateful for her enthusiasm, yet desperate to catch the moderator's eye so that they could bring an end to this excruciating interlude. Something about the tone of the woman's voice seemed to grow harder and more deliberate. He wasn't sure exactly when he began to feel chastised—probably around the same time the people in the row in front of the woman started turning back to get a look at her, one by one. She did eventually stop. The face that emerged from behind her glasses when she finally lowered the magazine was full of rage and pain. "These words, Mr. Osmond—they're so very apt."

By that point, beta blocker be damned, his palms were sweating. "Thank you."

"Are they really yours?"

"I'm sorry?"

"Are they entirely yours?"

"What do you mean?"

"It's a very simple question. Are these words your own? Or did you take them from a dead author whose work you found or stole or I don't know what?"

"Ma'am," he said. "I don't know *what* you're talking about."

"Think carefully, Mr. Osmond—this would've been around the same time you made up a missing person so you could infiltrate the Exchequer tragedy."

"Of course not!" He started to protest, to tell her she was wrong—and then all the blood left his brain. She *wasn't* wrong. Not really. He'd just forgotten the truth. He'd forgotten James Fahey and the real wondergirl. He had lived so long with those words from the margins of *Moonlight* that he had forgotten where they came from. Here he was onstage, caught out—and for things he himself had put out of his mind, little land mines of terrible judgment he'd left somewhere back in the barren hills of the past.

Wonder Girl—the real wondergirl—had a name, the woman told him. It was Maryam Handak. She had a mother, too, obviously: the kind of mother who served as first reader for Maryam's poetry. The kind of first reader who subscribed to *The Islander*, and who had, upon first reading May's story, suffered a strange spell of vertigo. She had called up her surviving daughter—Soraya from the inscription, Soraya who was the only person who called Maryam "wondergirl"—and together they had read the story again and concluded that so many coincidental similarities to Maryam's unpublished poems were simply not possible.

With their grief blown open, mother and daughter had steadily worked their way through every forum, every interview, to learn what they could about Lamb Osmond. They had found an obscure interview in the neighborhood newspaper where he talked about the difficulties of finding inspiration in tragedy. They had dredged up the news clip of him laying claim to a missing relative named James Fahey. They had crosschecked his records and discovered that his maternal grandfather, Frank Gareth Osmond, had in fact died years before May was even born. They had learned that, in fact, nobody named James Fahey had swiped their subway pass through any turnstile's reader the day the train station came down. They didn't know *how* he had gotten his hands on Maryam's works in progress—but the fact of his presence, amid a cloud of lies, at the site of the tragedy that claimed her life was no coincidence.

"You stole her work," Ailin Handak shot at him, waving that folded-up copy of *The Islander*. "You stole her life."

By morning, a clip of this confrontation had gone viral. May woke up to find himself assailed in fifteen languages across all major platforms. He was a fraud, a thief of lives, a sick man. What was wrong with him? Wasn't he ashamed to have reaped the tragedies of others for his own benefit? His girlfriend at the time said: *Apologize, wait it out, come back.* And he meant to. He sat in silence meaning to, and simultaneously waiting for some appropriate opportunity to launch himself over to the side of the angels. Once in a while, he was able to convince himself that his return to letters would be met not with insurmountable derision but with understanding and compassion. Maybe even some enthusiasm—after all, he himself had written the story, out of a well of feeling that Maryam Handak's work had brought up in him.

But by that point, he could no longer trust his own judgment. The things he was able to tell himself privately—"I was young, I was foolish, I have grown"—fell apart in the mental debates to which he subjected himself whenever he entertained the thought of reemergence. So one year went by. And then another. He sat there revisiting the reviews of his work, reading the notes of the personally bereaved and the derisions of the proximally affronted. Absorbing the sting of true heartbreak, learning afresh the depth of his ethical breaches. Every time he looked up his own name, he was confronted by not only all the things he had done but all the things he had been accused of both doing and being. There were so many opinions about who he was. The past was so immense. Overcoming it would be a true feat. And perhaps he might have done it if he'd started when it was still in balance—while the future held as much possibility. But he had let so much time go by. He had let them reduce his course load until his university job was no longer enough to pay the bills. He had taken to sleeping through the days and staying up all night. His girlfriend had suggested they part company until he found a way to distance himself from constantly checking the forums. To this end, May had taken to roaming the neighborhood, bumming cigarettes from the superintendents who gathered at the end of the block to gossip and occasionally helping one or two of them out, mostly just to keep his hands busy and his mind occupied. One of them, Joe Zbegic, was down a partner due to funding shortages. He needed help, so May helped him until the day he retired, and then he moved into Joe Zbegic's place at the Morningside and kept right on working.

One day, he had simply stopped showing up for the one remaining class he was still supposedly teaching. And now the Posterity Initiative had radically reconfigured the city's priorities. The moment for redemption had passed him by. The years went on, and the past continued to get bigger, and the future continued to constrict.

When Popovich replaced him with Ena at the Morningside, May moved into a basement studio down the street. He withdrew into himself. He had written, by his own count, no less than thirty letters to Ailin and Soraya Handak, attempting to explain and apologize for intruding on their grief, for taking Maryam's unattributed words, for making himself part of their lives and Maryam's death. Neither of them had ever responded. He had learned to live with their silence. But every now and again, he sat up in bed and thought about his old mailbox at the Morningside. What if one of them *had* written to him—and what if that letter was sitting, unopened, unnoticed, in that rusty old mailbox marked 16D? What if he was as unaware of his redemption as he had been of his impending downfall? What if his life was continuing along its course without the necessary information?

When those thoughts crushed him, usually around two or three in the morning, he would put on his coat and walk over to the Morningside. He had tried again and again to convince

Ena to let him in, or to at least check the mailbox on his behalf, to no avail. And then I came along.

IT WOULD BE another few years before May told me the balance of this story. When he finally did, I fell over myself to tell him that I was sure Ena didn't mean anything by it, that other people's vulnerability made her stone-hearted. It wasn't true, and he knew it. "Sure, Snoopy," he said, "vulnerability," and I was ashamed.

I'd like to tell you that in that moment, in the courtyard, I felt moved by how slow and quiet he'd gotten, by the sight of this grown person unable to hide his disappointment, the weight of all his years of expectation eradicated in a few minutes by a box of tattered mail. But in truth, I was irritated. It was interminable, his rummaging. His crying, too. When he got up to leave, I braced myself in horror for the inevitable revelation that I had been duped after all: there was no key, never had been, and whatever fantasies I had been entertaining about gaining access to that elevator were a production of my own mind, a lie I had held close in order to make myself believe I was doing the right thing when every sign had pointed me away from the whole endeavor.

"Aren't you forgetting something?" I said desperately.

He turned. "Oh—of course. Here, Snoopy." He took a handkerchief from his pocket and held it out to me. It was an act of absolute faith to stand there and resist unfolding it until he had disappeared over the wall.

There in my hand, after all this time, was the key to Bezi Duras's place.

HAVING THOUGHT FOR SO LONG OF LITTLE BUT THE
penthouse key, I now found myself having to decide when and
how to use it. Because I hadn't allowed myself to imagine the
moment of acquisition, let alone what might follow, this was
not as straightforward as I thought it would be. Standing in the
courtyard with it in my hand, I realized for the first time that it
would be *possible* to sail right on over to the elevator and up to
the thirty-third floor, right then and there. For weeks and
weeks, I'd been working my way to this moment, and now here
it was. With enough courage and a turn of the wrist, I could be
in the next phase of it. But maybe this was too fast. Maybe I
wasn't ready after all. It would doom me to be careless and
impatient now. I ran upstairs, past my half-asleep mother, and
slid the key under my mattress, where, I assumed, the powers
of the jam jar could at least surround it a little, and maybe even
give me the courage to use it.

For most of the night, I lay awake, willing myself to change
my mind: "You still have time, you still have time, go now,
there's plenty of time." But my heart was beating too fast. What
a tremendous undertaking it would be to get up, get dressed,
sneak out, down the stairs, into the courtyard, into the elevator,

then all the way back unseen. Something would obviously go wrong.

My reasons for wanting to access the penthouse, which I had considered in only vague terms, now demanded a real reckoning. Why was I doing this? To honor Ena, of course. I wanted to know what she knew, to prove to her inevitably watching spirit that I had been ready to see the world beneath the world after all. Well—if that was the full extent of my aims, then I should wait for Bezi Duras's next sunset exit with the dogs and let myself upstairs the minute my mother's attention was diverted, and it would just be me and Bezi's things and the little clues to the enchanted truth that she had inadvertently left lying around. I could snoop around the place knowing I'd be long gone by the time Bezi got back. It was a simple plan, clean and manageable and almost certain not to go wrong if the fates were in my favor, which they would be if the time was right.

But there was more to it than that, wasn't there? It wasn't enough just to know that Ena had been telling the truth. It had been wonderful to stand, however briefly, in the lighted rooms of Ena's heart and know things as she knew them. But she was dead now. And were you really part of something if you were part of it alone?

That must be why I'd been wondering whether my revelations would pass muster with my mother. All this while, I had known that I would eventually have to invite her into my knowledge. And my mother would not come willingly. She would rage. She would scoff. She would want proof.

So there would be no point in my going upstairs while Bezi and the dogs were out. I would have to do it during one of Bezi's daytime errands, while the dogs were men. I would have to be able to say I had seen them with my own eyes. One two three.

I tried to calm myself down. There was no rush. Before any of that happened, I had to find out if the key actually worked. If it did, I could plan my next steps. If not, I could go back to berating myself for handing over my collateral to May without waiting to see if our trade was legitimate.

And so, on an unremarkable Wednesday when the air was clear and the weather good, I waited for Bezi Duras to disappear on her errands, let myself into her courtyard, and plunged that hard-won key into the port.

The elevator doors slid open. The car looked exactly like the one in the main tower. Dark-paneled, clean. Tinged with that faint metallic smell that pervades all elevators of a certain vintage.

I only meant to step inside for a moment. Just to see what it felt like to stand there under its single bulb. But then the doors closed behind me, and the car began to climb.

The immediate thrill of this was brief. I realized I was now heading into a situation for which I was completely unprepared. Where would the elevator doors open? Into an access hallway? Or just straight into the penthouse itself? Why hadn't I thought to ask May whether the dogs would be just outside, waiting for me the moment the elevator doors opened? One two three.

It was one thing to climb thirty-plus stories in the main building—the fortress of the Morningside, its warm, humming density, pressing in all around you. There were plenty of reassurances to interrupt the dark anxiety of the ride: little darts of pressure between floors, signs of life where the rising car bypassed light and sound and murmuring residents waiting to catch it on the way back down. Plenty of opportunities to hit the button for an upcoming floor and get off there. But this—there was no way off this, no detour. No way down till you reached the top. Too thin. Thin of air, thin of substance. The higher I went, the thinner it all felt. How could something so fragile, so rattletrap, support the mass of all three dogs at once?

There was an unnerving thump as I passed the counterweight on its long journey to the ground. The car began to lose momentum. I hit the button to go back down. No matter what happened next, I would crush myself into the very back of the compartment, unseen as a shadow, silent as death, until the doors closed again. And then I would be carried back to the courtyard, and all would be well.

But then—the sky. The doors rolled open and all around me, the sky spread out, blinding, filled with bolls of summer clouds.

What had I imagined I would find when I finally reached the top? Certainly not a rooftop garden. Certainly not a warm veil of silence, disturbed only by the wind and the soft rustle of short, twisted trees that stretched away in unbroken rows toward the penthouse, a pale little temple at the far end of the roof.

Then the elevator doors rumbled shut, and my wilding heart and I were ground-bound.

LATER, I SET about trying to untangle the knot of shock and disappointment that had followed me back from the penthouse. Why had I assumed the elevator would open straight into Bezi Duras's apartment? Because May had talked about the paintings. He'd stolen the key all those years ago so he could go up here and look at them—which had led me to assume that the elevator would open into a place where paintings were kept. A hallway, a gallery, some indoor space. So yes, though May had told the truth about the key summoning the elevator, he had lied about the rest.

May hadn't stopped by the courtyard since our exchange of letters and key, so I had little hope of unloading my frustrations on him. Imagine my surprise when, a week or so after my heart-stopping excursion to the roof, I ran into him on my way back from Ricky's. I was just starting up Battle Hill with a bag in each hand when I saw him turn the corner on the opposite sidewalk, salmon coat flaring out behind him. All that old anger flattened my airway, and without further thought I lurched onto McCobb Street after him. I dodged a bicycle and a skirling van and was charging May's side with one of my bags before he'd even had a chance to look up and see what all the honking was about.

The bag—which had been threatening to rupture since Ricky's—burst. Toilet rolls bounced in every direction. I yelled, "Thief, liar!" while trying to get enough of a purchase on my surviving bag to take another meaningful swing at May, on whom it was just beginning to dawn that the assault was coming from below eye level. "Snoopy?" He tried to grab my arm. "Jesus!" Seeing that the street was empty, and that the only witnesses to this event were the drivers I had just enraged during my lunatic dash across the street, he shoved me in the chest and sent me sprawling. "What's the matter with you?"

I couldn't even cry. I was too furious—with him, with the injustice of my ordeal, but also with myself for having failed to prepare what I would say when I finally saw him again.

"Liar!" was all I managed.

May pulled me to my feet and onto a stoop. Then he went up and down the street, gathering my disemboweled sundries into what remained of the bag.

"What the hell are you talking about?" he said, giving up on a sorry roll of toilet paper that had traveled the length of the gutter and now sat doomed in the intersection just outside Tufaah.

"There were *no* paintings on thirty-three," I said.

"Is that all? Jesus, Snoopy."

"It was just a garden."

"Yes—the rooftop where she paints. Did you look around for her easels?"

"There was nothing."

"That's too bad."

"You made it sound like they were everywhere. Paintings wall to wall."

"Now, hold on. I didn't promise you'd see paintings. I promised you a way up—isn't that the truth?"

It was clearly the truth. But slippery, and he knew it.

"You didn't tell me I wouldn't be able to get inside."

"Inside her *place*? I didn't know that's what you were trying to do."

"Yes, you did. You made it sound like I would. You made it sound like—there was a gallery, or something. Like the elevator would open straight into her apartment."

"That's just not true, Snoopy."

"You didn't say: it's just a massive rooftop."

"You didn't tell me you were looking to break into her *home*."

Here it was: the thing I hadn't thought of. The sliver of misinformation that would have been apparent to Ena. All my doubts about my worthiness were entirely warranted. I hadn't done enough—hadn't been clever or curious enough. And here I was, crying and unable to help it, and embarrassed that May was witness to my hapless, sodden rage. It served me right for being so disdainful of *his* tears the other day.

He gave me a nervous little squeeze. "Stop crying. Someone is going to call the police."

"Do you have the other key?"

"What other key?"

"The one for her *place*."

"No. And I wouldn't tell you if I did."

I blew my nose.

May went on looking at me. "Snoopy, I don't know what you're after in there—and, frankly, I don't want to know. I understand being young and bored and wanting to get into things. But there's places that are safe to break into. And then there's places that aren't. Those are big dogs. That's *their* place. You don't want to bust in on them when they're guarding it. You get what I'm saying?"

"Has she always had those dogs?"

He thought about it. "I guess so."

"How long were you super?"

"About five years, give or take."

"And that was what—ten years ago?" I said. "They've been around for fifteen years? Are they the *same* dogs?"

He smiled. "I don't know what it's like where you're from, Snoopy, but here people tend not to switch out their dogs when they get old."

"But shouldn't they be *dead* by now?"

This was clearly a suspicious and unexpected turn. "What are you actually asking?"

I shrugged. I could feel him watching me.

"Give me that key back."

"No," I said.

"You're going to do something stupid, give it back."

"It's mine," I said. "I earned it."

He smoothed down his trousers and stood up. "Snoopy, Bezi Duras is a very strange lady. You're lucky she didn't catch you up there. And I sure wish you'd leave it alone."

❧

MAY WAS AFRAID of the dogs, of what they might do to me. I couldn't explain that I wasn't because I knew they weren't dogs at all. What I feared instead was my own unworthiness. That I had failed to be adequately observant, adequately reverential. That I'd cut some unknown but vital corner, and that whatever forces were looking out for Bezi Duras—presumably kin to the ones that had eavesdropped on my mother and threatened my downfall in the various scenarios she had laid out for me over the years—were unimpressed by my efforts. Perhaps they had already decided that it was not for me to know anything more about Bezi Duras.

I returned to the rooftop the following week, determined to resolve the matter once and for all. If the time was right, the way would open to me. If it did not, I would give up until I drifted into the desired knowledge by some more deserving means. This might never happen—and I was all right with that.

Of course, the elevator key did not work on the penthouse door. I stood amid the rosebushes on Bezi Duras's front steps with my ear against the pale wood. Not a sound. Surely the dogs, if they were dogs at all, would have heard me by now. They should be going crazy in there. But nothing. Silence.

In all directions, the long-shadowed grid of the city stretched out. To the south, the buildings, stacked shoulder to shoulder like coffins, the pale roofs with their vandalized water towers, and between them the blazing figure of Dancing Girl. To the west, the endless park, black with trees, and beyond it the hazy smear of the bay.

The penthouse windows were huge but barred by blinds that rose up from the floor and ended just a foot or so from the top of the frame. The interior was visible, but only from an upward angle. I could see that Bezi Duras's walls were painted a blinding white, and that her fixtures were those same black chandeliers my mother was forever repairing on the lower floors. But apart from the occasional top of a mirror or the stray arc of a lamp, I couldn't see anything else. The dogs might very well be in there. They might very well be men. But from out here it was impossible to tell. It was almost comforting. As though by its very design, the architecture around me confirmed the secret it was hiding.

But then—where had I seen Bezi Duras undressing? There had to be an open window around somewhere.

And there was, on the far side of the building. Bezi's penthouse sat with its back against the shaft between the east and west wings of the Morningside. There, a wall neatly circumscribed the three-hundred-foot drop that plunged between the wings and into the courtyard below. That was how I had managed to see her. I leaned out over the chasm and tried to get a look at the windows, but the angle was impossible. Try any harder, and that would be it for me. What a sight I would make, whizzing past Mrs. Sayez's window. Imagine *that* fun card. WHAT WOULD MAKE YOUR NEW HOME EVEN BETTER? *Well, a parachute.*

Through a window on the eastern side of the building, I could see the top four or so inches of a long, leaning mirror. If I was going to try to gain some altitude, I should do it here. Luckily, there was a planter with a tallish tree pushed right up against the wall, and here I made my stand, throttling one bough as I climbed another, willing myself higher even though the whole flimsy trunk had begun to sway. The few feet of extra height got me nowhere near enough to see any portion of the room. Neither did the halfhearted jump with which I closed out my attempt before I came thumping back down again.

I stood up and took stock of the casualties. My hands were

scraped up. I had managed to sink an incriminating footprint into the flower bed. Thick, gooey fruits loosened by my trip through the branches lay smashed on the ground all around me.

They looked like figs.

And didn't they just smell of fig jam.

Without thinking, I raised a bit of the splatter to my mouth on the tip of my finger. Yes, it did taste familiar. That old-new sunlight taste.

I hadn't taken a moment to absorb the gardens at all. These were not, as I had blindly thought, just ornamental trees. They were fragrant, vastly different from row to row, bursting with fruit: lemons, oranges, plums. It wasn't a garden at all—it was an orchard.

Maybe you would have seen it sooner. But I didn't until right then.

The world tore open, and I looked and saw what was underneath it.

Bezi Duras was not a painter at all. She was a Vila.

One two three.

Of course. How obvious the signs were. The tower. The dogs, their magical transformation into men. Her secrecy, the purpose of which was to conceal this precious garden. The immensity of it caught me off guard. I sat down so I wouldn't fall.

A Vila.

Here it was, the "more" Ena had intended to share when the time was right.

I felt a great surge of pity-laden affection for May. Poor blind May, who had gone through all the trouble of stealing the key with the sole purpose of coming up here to look at paintings— all the while unwittingly trespassing into a Vila's garden. What a risk he had taken without ever realizing it.

The figs. I had four or five of them in the crook of my arm

already—some rescued from the ground, some pulled down in the minutes of confusion before I'd realized where I actually was. And there was nothing to do now but take them with me. I couldn't exactly put them back.

I don't know how long I'd been wandering there like that when the elevator chimed, and something inside the shaft whirred to life. Its rumble could mean only one thing: Bezi Duras was back.

In all the years Bezi had been living here, had she ever turned the key downstairs only to find that the elevator had gone back up all by itself? Of course not. She was the only person with the key. The elevator should be exactly where she left it. And if I hadn't loitered, hadn't spent so long hemming and hawing up here and trying to lizard my way up unclimbable walls, I would have gone back down when I was supposed to, and her suspicions would never have been aroused. But that possibility was gone now.

I fled to the far end of the rooftop, dived behind a lemon tree, and waited. An eternity later, I heard the familiar, faraway rumble of the elevator doors opening. Bezi Duras's shoes on the concrete, somewhere far up ahead, crossing to her front door. "Hullo?" she said distantly. "Is somebody up here?"

Better to stand up and announce myself than go on crouching behind my tree. Even if I somehow managed to steal away unseen, Bezi would find herself waiting for the elevator to come back up the next time she summoned it. And then she would know for certain that she had been right to be suspicious—somebody *had* been up here, after all.

Better to own up to it now.

But something small and cowardly sat pleading in my gut. It would not allow me to raise my head. "Get up," I kept telling it. "Show yourself." But it just twisted into itself, away from me. I went on crouching there until I heard the penthouse door slam behind Bezi. Then I slunk along the wall and into the elevator and went back down to the mortal world.

Downstairs, I laid the figs out on the dining room table. What would I say when my mother asked about where they came from? Ascribing my haul to a surprisingly fortuitous rations draw was out of the question. These tasted so much sweeter, looked so much fresher, than anything we had ever received in a government delivery.

There was nothing to do but sit down and eat them. One two three. Four. Five. After they were gone, I took myself to bed and lay there, letting the warm benediction of the Morningside dilute my nausea. Here I was, safe, content, unexpectedly full of figs, lying in a small fairy-book bed in the beating heart of this venerable old tower, a speck of dust five thousand miles from a home I'd never known. All around me lay the city, with its steeples and junkyards, its beaches of waterlogged debris, its water towers and mussel-laden piers, and the roaming tide. And everyone in it—the neighbors; the sneering Mrs. Gaspard; Mrs. Sayez, with her sweet, dull kindness; the entirety of the Dispatch, that faceless murmuration outspread among the different neighborhoods; the Dancing Girls on their billboards; and May; and even and especially my mother—they all inhabited the same world, in which Bezi Duras was just a painter.

And I? I inhabited this one. The real one. The world beneath the world.

I missed Ena terribly then. Her death, which so far had floated through my existence as a fact—undeniable, but cold—finally felt real.

I couldn't tell you what musings were scribbled on most of the fun cards I filled out during my time at the Morningside. The notable exception was the one I filled out that night:

WHAT IS YOUR LEVEL OF SATISFACTION WITH YOUR NEW HOME? *Greatest it's ever been.* WHAT DO YOU LIKE MOST ABOUT YOUR NEW HOME? *I am the only one who knows the whole truth of what it really is.* WHAT WOULD MAKE YOUR NEW HOME EVEN BETTER? *Telling my mother about it.*

THE BUILDING DID NOT BEGIN BEHAVING STRANGELY right away. At first, it was just the usual little disruptions: minor leaks, electrical surges.

A couple of lightbulbs shattered the following week as I was passing under them, at least twice in the company of my mother, who finally said, "They're really after you."

She meant it as a joke. We smiled about it together, but two days later, when she fell off a ladder and sprained her wrist, I began to feel unsettled enough to mention it to her.

"I think the building's being funny," I said.

"Funny how?"

"*Funny*'s the wrong word. More like—unfriendly."

"Don't be ridiculous, Sil."

She remembered this exchange several days later, though, when she walked into 32C to check the radiators and found a perfectly banked fire reddening the hearth.

"Did you do this?" she asked, after dragging me upstairs to see it.

"No."

"Then who did?"

"I have no idea."

"Sil, I want you to tell me the truth."

"But I am! Why would I do something like this?"

"I don't know. What you said the other day—is this a little prank to get me to see how 'unfriendly' the building is being?"

"Of course not!"

Then came the disastrous incident with the pipes, several of which began spurting sulfurously at the joints in the same twenty-four-hour period, all along different lines, so that we had to shut off the water to the whole building at once. Because my mother's arm was in a cast, repairs went more slowly than usual. Residents grew impatient, then furious. The phone in my mother's office rang insistently, all day long. I imagined I could hear it even on the upstairs floors. The chaos of the situation was amplified by the buzz of rage that now seemed to infiltrate not just the walls and hallways but the people roaming them, until we were all humming with it together. Residents walked right into the units where we were working to ask my mother when the shutoff would end. I would answer for her— "We're going as fast as we can"—and then brace myself for rebuke. Our torment did not end when we finally got all the pipes patched up two weeks later, but instead went on and on as city inspector after city inspector paraded through the basement and boiler room, directing us to various other issues that had to be repaired before they would allow the water to be turned back on.

And even when that happened, it still wasn't over. The true clincher came the following week, when the elevator jammed. Mrs. Golub, its sole occupant, already at the end of her rope because of all the repairs, pressed the emergency button. It was what she had been instructed to do on the many previous occasions she had found herself in the same situation. Only this time, the lights cut out and the elevator lurched groundward.

She could hear the shaft whistling by outside. Her life, she knew, was over. She was praying when her fall was suddenly interrupted. No crash in her fate, but six broken ribs from the force with which she struck the cab when she went flying.

She told us all this while lying strapped to a gurney outside the Morningside two hours later, while paramedics gave her oxygen and a fire crew worked to put out the blaze that had erupted when her unattended kettle boiled down to nothing and burst into flames, claiming her kitchen cabinets and curtains before somebody caught a whiff and pulled the alarm. Luckily, the firefighters were nearby, on the right side of the tide. They came fast enough to stop the blaze before it breached Mrs. Golub's living room. They were even able to rescue the wretched little dog, who looked suitably shook up and a little sooty, scowling out from amid its owner's blankets.

"Well, I'd say you're all very, very lucky," the fire chief said, then turned to go over the paperwork with my mother, who was standing by, cradling her bad arm, and strangling Mrs. Golub in the not-so-distant recesses of her mind.

The rest of us unhappy denizens of the now thrice-cursed building were dispersed in various tableaux of misery along the sidewalk. I scanned the crowd for Bezi Duras. She wasn't there. It was three o'clock, so it was plausible that she was running late in her return from her errands and might turn the corner any second now. But that didn't happen, and by three-thirty it was clear to me that she had stayed up in the penthouse with the dogs, because they were men, they were men *right at this moment,* and it was sounder to risk her life by remaining where she was than to bring them downstairs and expose them to the world.

"Jesus, Snoopy." May had appeared at my elbow. "What the hell happened?"

"Oh, you know," I said, checking to make sure my mother still had her back to me while she berated the fire chief. "Mrs. Golub."

"Well, well. She finally did it." May was craning his neck to stare up at where the spray from the hoses was glazing the side of the building. "How bad?"

"They keep telling us it could've been worse." I frowned at him. "What are you doing here?"

"I heard the sirens."

"Really?"

"I got to thinking, 'I hope that's not the ambulance coming to take Snoopy to the hospital in pieces because she ignored my advice.'"

There was something so accusatory about his tone that I went cold. I studied his face. His glasses had left false dimples where they dug into his nose, and his beard trailed off unevenly under his chin. Even now, standing in the shadow of our burning building, he looked almost wistful. Here was a true Islander, I thought: he had spent his life keeping an eye out for signs. He knew one when he heard one. And I? I was new to all of it, and apparently needed signs pointed out to me. All the petty little horrors the building had unleashed on us suddenly seemed so clear. Everything had been just fine until I broke into the Vila's garden. Pipes hadn't been bursting, and elevators hadn't been hurtling down the shaft until I stole and ate Bezi Duras's figs. May didn't know that she was a Vila, but he had certainly realized that I was up to something that wasn't right. And perhaps enough signs abounded now for him to see that I had achieved it, despite his insistence that I should not.

Whatever denial I was still managing to nurse about all this was obliterated later that evening, when I reached for the jam jar under my bed. To my horror, the last remnant of the fruit of my ancestors had mutated and was now overgrown with a nest of white fuzz. The intruding organism had grown up out of the jar bottom—putrid, odd, and alive. Here was the warning of all warnings, the final call to sense the Morningside could possibly give me, proof that May had been right. In the darkness beneath my bed, my misdeeds had been spurring this transformation. I had not drifted toward insight. I had done nothing of the sort. I had raided fruits from a garden I had no right to access. And for my mistake, this substance, which had bound me to the orchards of my great-grandmother, and to the spirit of my dead aunt, had been transformed into something monstrous.

I decided to take May's advice. I hung the elevator key around my neck on a length of yarn and hid it under my shirt, and went back to helping my mother with all the duties I had neglected in order to pursue my selfish desires. After all, maybe that was part of the problem. I had left countless chores undone. Countless apartments unchecked, unswept. Maybe if I went back to the tasks she had entrusted me with, I could reverse this celestial rebuke.

ONE DAY DURING this uneasy time, my mother sat me down at the dining table.

"I need you to write a letter for me," she said. "In English."

This was to be done longhand, on fancy paper she had somehow procured.

"Wait, wait," she said, seeing how eagerly I popped the cap off my pen. "Hear the whole thing before you start."

"All right."

"Don't get ahead of yourself!"

"All right."

"All right." She crossed her arms and closed her eyes. "So: 'Dear Mrs. Safiya al-Abdi.'"

I felt wounded by her rebuke, so I said, "What if she's not married?"

"Good point. 'Dear Ms. al-Abdi,' then. 'I came to this country last year. From Paraiso. I now live with my daughter at the Morningside. Every day, as I go about my work, I pass your little café, Tufaah, at the end of the block, and I think about you. What a wonderful place it must have been when it was open. How hard it must have been to leave it behind. I used to cook a little myself, Back Home, and I think fondly of my own little place, and how much I long to go back to it, though I know life will make that impossible. And I find myself wondering: Do you feel the same way? Do you plan to return? If not, please know that there is a person on your street who would very much be willing to take Tufaah off your hands.'"

By the time I reached the final sentence, though, my mother had changed her mind. "'Take it off your hands' sounds a little too casual," she said. "It sounds like I think it's a burden to her."

"You could say, 'Please know that there is a person on your street who longs to give Tufaah a new life.'"

"Yes," my mother said. "That's it—write. And then say: 'Very sincerely—'"

"Should we make it more assertive? Should we come right out and tell her to please write back if she wants to discuss it?"

My mother chewed her thumbnail. "'I hope you will consider discussing this offer with me, and get back to me at the following address.' And then write our address." But by the time I got to it, our address had become fraught, too. "What if she thinks we're a couple of rich old janglers from the Morningside?"

"She won't—we say that we came to the city only last year."

But this was too much trust to place in Ms. al-Abdi. She might breeze through the letter. She might not bother with inferences. The whole thing had to be rewritten, this time clarifying that my mother was only a humble building superintendent. As I read it back to her in English, I realized that I had managed to talk her into a greater commitment than she had intended. She had set out merely to test the waters with this mysterious Ms. al-Abdi—but by the time I was sealing the envelope, I had convinced her to make an actual offer. Given my current standing with the forces, I was the last person who should be convincing anyone to ask and ask for something. What if Ms. al-Abdi jumped at the opportunity?

I tried to reverse course. "Do we have the money?" I said. "To buy it from her?"

"Not yet."

"Maybe we should wait until we do."

"I want to put the idea into her head before somebody else does, Sil."

And then my mother, who never planned, who never put anything on paper, kissed the envelope and sent me downstairs, one two three, to drop it in the mailbox.

IT WAS A season of conflicting signs. Invasive vines crawling brilliantly up the walls of the old university. Coyotes whelping in the park. One day, someone called in to the Dispatch to say she thought she'd seen a goat in the overgrowth by the old Armory.

"But that's not possible, is it?" she said.

"A little bit of history, dear listeners," the Dispatcher told us. "Once upon a time, the parks department wondered what would happen if goats were brought in as an alternative to ordinary landscape maintenance. So they introduced a few of them to the eastern edge of Sorey Park—just a handful. They did their work for a time. A couple were probably snatched by coyotes. A couple by thieves. The others vanished into the park as the years went on. Every few years, even now, one crops up—I believe that's probably what you saw, caller. The descendant of that original herd."

This prompted more calls, from people confessing to having stolen one of the original goats or to knowing someone who had. In the end, the goats' reappearance was tallied among the auspicious signs.

One morning, we woke up to find the tide had gone so far out that the river had receded to its original channel. The highway, slick with algae, lay bare for the first time in decades. It was all anyone wanted to talk about on the Dispatch: how it felt to go down there and walk the greenway again and see the graffiti and the old Munsey Playground, with its merry-go-round strangled by brown seaweed.

"Don't get too excited, friends," the Dispatcher said. "I have a feeling low tide won't last."

It didn't. And when it came back in, another possible sign swam up from the bay with it. This new visitor first manifested as a giant, slow-moving ripple. A caller leaning over a balcony spotted it; but by the time he got his phone out, it had submerged, leaving behind only the ghost of itself.

"What do you think it is?" the Dispatcher wanted to know.

"I'm not sure," the caller said. "But it's massive."

It wasn't seen again until a week later, when a couple of kids playing on the old pylons of the Jennison Bridge heard a loud slap of something striking the water. They looked up just in time to register a disappearance, but when they called in to the Dispatch, they couldn't agree on what it actually was.

This went on until the visitor surprised a photographer who was taking a portrait of the chief Repopulation commissioner for the weekly paper. The commissioner had his back against the boardwalk railings and the setting sun behind him, so the images were blurry, but the photographer did manage to get a shot of the animal surfacing and emitting a huge, dappled spout. He summoned a friend, who sent a drone over the water, and within a couple of hours all of us at home were watching footage of what the Dispatcher dubbed the Island City whale patrolling the murk of the river.

Nobody had seen a whale since my mother was a little girl, so by morning the boardwalk was choked with people. The excitement was tinged by hesitancy. Nobody knew what to make of any of it. On the one hand, the whale's very existence was cause for celebration. On the other, the fact that it had gone up the mouth of a river and seemed unable to find its way out was inauspicious.

We stood there for hours, my mother and I, but the closest we got to seeing it was a flock of seagulls that seemed to move up and down the old, flooded highway, following something unseen.

My mother had taken the morning off. As noon started to close in on us, though, I could feel her turning her body away from mine to look at her phone. "The boiler might be down, Sil. We have to go."

I tried to hide my disappointment. "I thought whales had to breathe every now and again."

"I'm sure the damn thing will come up the second we're gone," she said, looking resentfully out into the water. "I'm sorry, Sil."

As the week wound on, everyone but us seemed to see the whale. Footage of it was only ever a minute long, the result of an apparently unspoken understanding that people should not advertise that they were in its presence until after the encounter had ended. It spent fifteen minutes putting on a show for a handful of teenagers crossing the Sorretti Bridge at dusk. The Dispatcher took a call from a psychic who claimed to be communing with it, as well as an artist who had caricatured it for the celebrity wall at Bertucci's, where it now sat in cetacean splendor, wearing a bib and awaiting a plate of spaghetti.

Callers could agree on little save that its time in the river should be limited, for its safety and our own. The authorities concurred. It was determined that an earnest effort must be made to drive the whale back into the bay. The problem was, nobody could quite figure out what route it had taken to squeeze into the channel, and so the farthest the coast guard got was corralling it down toward the Esplanade, where it would turn, dodge the guide boats in a few moves surprisingly fast for an animal of its size, and disappear upriver again.

A great deal of airtime was devoted to examining the whale's reluctance to leave. What did this mean for the city, the temperature and salinity of the water, the mental stability of the whale itself? Was it a sign of better days? Or yet another catastrophe in a long parade of them? A whale-extraction czar was appointed by city hall, and roundly mocked for everything from his title to his hairdo, until he finally called in to the Dispatch to explain his plan to get the whale back to open water by widening the gap in the Island City dam. This process took another week, during which time the whale, looking thinner by the day, kept appearing in drone footage on all our screens. The news began covering the heroes who were engineering its release: wreck divers working in insurance salvage down-island who were volunteering their time, rallying with their lamps and flippers and devilish grins to the lower dam, filling the murky water with sparks and drunken lights. My mother and I went down to the Esplanade to see them work, and this was where she met her first wreck diver: a tiny, whip-thin man named Fis Sarina. He was sitting on the retaining wall in his electric-green flippers, taking a breather, helping himself to something out of a flask, when my mother left my side and held out the coffee that had been cooling in her hand.

"What are you doing?" I asked her.

"He looks so tired," she said, in Ours. "Ask him if it's going to be all right. Ask him if it's going to succeed."

I did, and he nodded. "We'll know soon enough. The whale will either die in here, or it'll get through. One way or another, it won't be long. I'll miss being a hero."

My mother turned to me, and I translated: "She says she's pretty sure that what you're doing won't stop being considered heroic."

"You tell her I've been doing this work for fifteen years, and this is the first time it's being considered at all." While I relayed this message, he looked her up and down in a way that made me embarrassed for both of them. "Tell Mama she should try wreck diving. She's got the build."

We laughed about it together, my mother, Fis Sarina, and I. This still comes back to me. We laughed.

In another two days, they had the dam opened up. A whole fleet of trawlers and barges massed at the top of the island to drive the whale down, and this was when my mother and I saw it for the first and only time: a little ridge of fin and tail that broke the water once before gliding out of sight and away.

In the morning, I emerged from my room to find my mother clicking through a site I didn't recognize. The notepad beside her was a chaos of numbers. "Do you know that salvage divers can make three thousand a week?" she told me. "A *week*."

"Wow," I said.

"You have to take a course, I think, and get certified. But it doesn't seem to take very long. And it looks like there's so much work. Right?"

I leaned in sleepily to scan the page she was showing me. I could have told her she was wrong—that she had misread the salary and the want ads. But, unfortunately, I didn't.

All I said was: "What about your job here?"

"I'd do it nights. Maybe ask you to pick up a little here and there during the day? Just till you start school."

"Sure," I said. "Of course."

She gave me a squeeze and went on rubbing my arm while she thumbed down the page. "That man said I have the build for it, and look—what does it say here?"

I leaned over her shoulder for a better look. On the screen, a class of smiling graduates in diving gear were all leaping backward off a pier in comically exaggerated postures. I translated the caption: "'The best salvage divers are people of slight build with a high tolerance for enclosed spaces. We're looking for optimistic adventurers, people who can problem-solve and think on their feet. Is that you?'"

"That's *exactly* me," my mother said.

So my mother drifted into salvage diving. At the start of her certification course, her instructor—a toothpick of a guy called Sal—told them: "This work is really dangerous. But then most things are." Neither her descriptions of her preliminary fitness test nor the courses that followed were particularly frightening. She told me, "I sprinted on an inclined treadmill until I thought my lungs would pop, and then I had to jump off and scramble into this little crawl space all sticky and out of breath and find my way out in the dark."

I've often wondered whether my mother kept the details clinical in order to temper my fear or whether she simply found the experience itself to be clinical—interesting at most. Either is possible. It's certain that she was not afraid. And that lack of fear would probably have prevented her from thinking that the scenario might be frightening for other people. Mostly she just spun stories about the guys in her training group. Some were experienced divers. Others were as green as she was. Nearly all were crass eccentrics enthused by marine life—or what was left of it—and frustrated with the professions in which they had wasted their best years. They made her laugh despite her exhaustion, and for once they admired her athleticism and fearlessness. I found myself wondering whether they, too, had daughters who lay awake, imagining what it might be like to navigate a narrowing tunnel in the dark.

For the final two weeks of training, my mother began sneaking into the Morningside pool after hours. I would sit on the edge and watch her, a still darkness in the pale neon glare of the water. Viewed from that angle, what she was doing looked almost serene. She often came up smiling to show me there was nothing to be afraid of.

Most salvage divers at that time worked in either insurance or recovery. Half-flooded buildings in the tidal zone were always trading hands, depending on how optimistic sellers and buyers felt about news that the waters might recede. There was talk, too, that when the Repopulation Program reached critical mass, the administration might consider simply reinforcing basements and foundations and building a kind of floating city—making the water a feature of luxury down-island living rather than the hazard everyone who lacked vision was making it out to be. However, this meant a constant and unending verification of the stability of the buildings. Each sale mandated a new foundation check, so salvage divers often found themselves inspecting the same building twice, sometimes three times, a year.

Where insurance diving was a corporate matter, recovery diving was privately arranged and privately funded. Plenty of people had lost houses to the tide. Often, it was the descendants who were most interested in what could still be dredged up from their parents' ruins. They tended to be the kinds of people who had safes or panic rooms. Owing to the sensitive nature of what my mother might be retrieving, they required a live camera feed of the recovery, so they were in her ear all the time as she drifted through the silty murk of the drowned buildings. Their reminiscences tended to be strange: they might catch a glimpse, in the pale green bloom of her headlamp, of some beloved but irretrievable furnishing—an old dresser, or the writing desk of some long-dead, disaffected patriarch—and implore her to stop and examine it where it lay, upturned on what had become the sea floor. If her shift boss permitted it—meaning, if he accepted the bribe to let her linger over an item that wasn't listed on her job form—my mother would sift through the wreckage, open drawers that had somehow miraculously remained closed.

These were my mother's favorite dives. She would come home in the late evening, smelling faintly of stagnant water, so cold that I could feel the chill drifting from her skin and hair. I'd have tea ready for her, and she would spend the rest of our night reliving her journey through that slow green world. How she'd dived an old brewery and found the seafloor a mosaic of smashed bottles. How she'd gone into an old house, with its sodden, drifting draperies, to collect heirloom silverware, and had found all the plates and forks and cups in the dining room, inexplicably aloft in the water like coins of light. Once, a group of not very forthcoming clients hired her to dive into a space that turned out to be a bank. Over the course of eight hours, she unlocked the old safe and extracted the gold bars inside it, each one heavy as a cannonball, unaware of the scandal this particular incident would cause—because the city, it turned out, had been fighting a lawsuit for a long time with the building's original owners, claiming that the bank and everything in it, having sunk beneath municipal waters, now belonged to the city under maritime law.

She wanted me to feel her thrill. It was there in the pitch of her voice, her dexterity with the language of her new work. But all I felt was dread. I knew nothing about equalization, or buoyancy, or the poisons entering her blood in those noxious depths. Oh, she was careful down there. I was sure of it. But she kept going in. Kept putting on that mask and hoisting those oxygen tanks onto her back. For me, and for Tufaah, but a little bit for herself, too. Maybe that frightened me most of all.

I kept touching our protections: one two three. I kept myself busy, scuttling around the Morningside, hurrying through all my mother's duties. But there were so many things I couldn't actually do: Crawl spaces that were too small for me. Wiring issues I couldn't begin to solve. These fastened themselves to the end of each diving day. Fix boiler. Fix elevator. One morning, I woke up to an empty apartment. Thinking my mother had set off early for a job, I went about my day until I found her asleep at her basement desk, sitting still and upright, as if she had never been entirely alive. We laughed about it, but after that I moved my protections around, hoping I could cast a wider net more in keeping with the new risks that ruled my mother's life. The jam jar stayed where it was, but the scissors went into an air shaft in her office. The perfume bottle found a new home in the pool's skimmer basket. I would visit them periodically, not just in mind but in person, one two three, to make sure that they were still in place, still offering whatever small power was holding us together, because my practical help was doing my mother so little good. She was fading. And because of it, I felt like I was fading, too. And worse still, perhaps, *we* were fading—flickering more and more faintly toward each other from our respective worlds.

BOOK III

Mila

Just as my loneliness was becoming unbear-able, Mila and her mother moved into the Morningside.

One day, without warning, a light that didn't belong appeared under the door of 32C. Who knows how long it was there before it caught my distracted eye. My mother didn't remember leaving it on. When she went to check, the door caught against the chain. It hung there, open about three inches, just enough to give us a glimpse of a woman we had never seen before standing baffled in the empty apartment beyond.

"Hello," my astounded mother said. "Who are you, please?"

The woman took us in with wide, blank eyes and said, "No—thank you, no. Goodbye."

My mother wasn't quite fast enough to catch the door as it came crashing shut. "Hello?" She pounded once, forcefully. It was answered this time by a slight, thin-faced girl. Her hair was pulled back, and she had the huge green eyes of a night creature.

"Stop shouting, please," this new entity said. "It's the middle of the night."

My mother found her breath. "Who are you? How you get in?"

"We live here," the girl said. "Mr. Popovich can explain."

And she closed the door firmly.

My mother was beside herself. The nerve of Popovich, giving her no warning. The recklessness of Popovich, just handing a key to strangers. Sensing that Mila might be the kind of person to complain about our late-night intrusion, my mother made a point of beating her to it. "Some piece of work you've got up there in 32C," she said when she got Popovich on the phone.

I could hear him laughing dryly. "Take good care of them—they are my very special guests."

It was as my mother had suspected. "You know what I should have said?" she asked me. "I should have told him: 'You think that ingratiating yourself to people from Back Home will legitimize whatever thin claim you have to our heritage, and you know what, Popovich? It's pathetic.'"

"So call him back," I snapped. "Tell him."

I didn't care about Popovich, or Back Home, or anything else. All that mattered to me was that a girl close to my age had moved in and was living friendless on the thirty-second floor. I couldn't believe my luck. So what if she had been rude to my mother? Wouldn't I have felt similarly aggrieved if some angry foreigner had come pounding on my door at eleven at night?

I didn't see Mila again until the moving truck came. She stood in the street, directing a procession of huge, mummified furnishings down the truck ramp and along the sidewalk, completely unfazed by the expletives of the stalled drivers who couldn't get around her. The movers skirted her in wider and wider berths, deferential, unnerved, I guess, by her manner, and the way she barked at them when they did something objectionable. "What a little viper," my mother said, catching sight of the scene. But she hadn't been standing there as long as I had, so she hadn't caught the moment during the lunch break when Mila had hopped up on the truck ramp and tucked her knees against her chest, becoming a girl my age again. *That* was the version of her I was desperate to befriend.

A week after our initial encounter, my mother and I were summoned to 32C to take care of a fireplace that appeared to be backing smoke into the newcomers' apartment. We came in to find the fire burning merrily and the air completely clear. Mila's mother was sitting on the sofa, rubbing her hands together nervously, and Mila was standing guard by the mantel.

My mother set her toolbox down. "What is problem?"

"The place is full of smoke," Mila said.

Rather than insist that it wasn't, my mother put the fire out, opened the windows, and looked up the flue. Mila stood by with her hands behind her back. She watched my mother scrape off some of the soot that had darkened the firebox and then ascend her step stool and stand with her hips against the mouth of the chimney. "Smoke smell is from the dust," she said. "It is normal."

"I understand dust can be dangerous and start fires," Mila said.

"Not this little," my mother said, "or in such a fireplace as this."

"Could you remove it all the same, please? Thank you."

"Remove?"

"Yes, could you remove the dust, please? Thank you."

There was a face my mother made when she was flabbergasted by someone's lack of common sense. To the person in question, the face always came off as grimly sincere, even respectful. In truth, it meant she was laughing inwardly with all the disdain she could muster. This was the very face she made while she scraped the inside of the chimney. I could tell that an

earful about people my age was in my future. After an indeter-
minate length of time, she climbed back down and kindled a
new fire. "There."

Mila stood with her nose raised in the air, like a little blood-
hound. After a while, she said, "I still smell smoke." She turned
to her mother. "Don't you smell it?"

Her mother lowered her water glass onto the table, and then
nudged it away from the edge. "A little."

My mother stuck her head back up the chimney. The fire
snatched at her pant legs. "This is how the fire smell," she said
at last.

Mila sighed. "If you can't fix it, you can't fix it, I guess."

"Is fixed."

"All right." Mila shrugged. "But I'm telling you. My father
will notice when he gets here, and you'll just have to come
back."

"I will be here," my mother said. "He can call me."

In the hallway, she turned to me with a furious eye. "Be very
careful around these people, Sil."

"Why?"

"Because I don't want you wasting time with mannerless
little shits from Back Home." She stopped walking and turned
toward me so that I would know this next part meant business.
"I don't have to tell you not to let them know you speak Ours,
do I?"

She didn't, but I fought her all the same.

"What? Why not?"

"You know why."

It was the closest I'd come to stomping my foot in years. "I
don't."

"Because you don't know anything about them. Where are

they from? Whose side were they on during the war? How did they get here?"

"You have nothing but questions," I snapped. "Maybe we could get some answers if we actually talked to them."

She rounded on me. "I won't tell you again, Sil."

I felt the sting of it all the same. How was I supposed to befriend Mila if our only point of connection was off-limits? And what kind of friendship began with a lie?

My mother, however, was the least of my problems. By far the greatest impediment to befriending Mila was Mila herself. She managed to get herself into school right away. And when she was home, she was busy in a way that made her seem much older than her years. Neither the hopscotch grid I drew in the courtyard nor the stack of board games I laid out on the lobby table was enough to lure her away from the prodigious task of readying the place for her father's arrival. When she asked for directions to the library one afternoon, I led her there, taking the opportunity to stop by the playroom so I could show her the mural of the debauched dinner party, determined to impress her with how nonchalant I could be about the presence of something so grotesque in a room intended for little children.

But she only squinted at it from the doorway. "It's a little derivative of *The Last Supper*, don't you think?"

"Have you noticed they're eating meat?"

"That's funny, isn't it?"

"Well, it's awful."

"I mean: they're animals. They're meat themselves."

If she couldn't be impressed with something like this, I decided, she would have to be made to understand that I was the person who knew all the building's intricacies and intimacies.

I started posting up outside the mailroom so she would see me, headlamp on, ear pressed to the wall, on those rare occasions when she came downstairs with her mother's letters.

It took her five whole days to concern herself with my vigil. "Are you looking for toxic mold?"

"No, no," I said. "I'm just waiting for the ghost."

"Oh." She paused behind me, also waiting. "Who's the ghost?"

"This boy who got crushed in the elevator."

She frowned. "Recently?"

"About twenty years ago."

"Has the elevator been repaired since then?"

I had no idea. "Of course," I said.

"Well, I hope you see him."

"Do you want me to come get you when he shows up?"

"No, thanks. I grew up in Aguila and never saw a ghost. I doubt this one will amount to much."

I was starting to grow desperate. She'd been living upstairs for three whole weeks, and I was still no closer to knowing anything about her. Not her age, not her interests. Certainly not that she was the kind of person who liked to sneak off and sit by herself— something I learned when I visited my talismans in their hiding places. I had just confirmed the presence of the perfume bottle in the pool's skimmer basket when I looked up to see Mila, perched on one of the wooden benches on the far side of the room. The moment she realized I'd seen her, she shifted her position. Her stillness, it turned out, had been very deliberate.

"What are you doing here?" I asked her, going cold with surprise.

"Sitting in quiet contemplation."

"It's rude not to let a person know that you're in the room when they come in."

"Is it?"

"They might do something private."

"Is that what you're doing? Something private?"

"No," I lied.

"So what's that you've got there?"

"Nothing, just something for the skimmer."

She got up and came around the long end of the pool, while I hurried to replace the basket with fingers that felt leaden and huge. Mila bent down and opened the basket back up and lifted the bottle. I'd never noticed how vulnerable it looked, how old, the pink glass flaking away in all the places my fingers had touched it.

"I really don't think this belongs in there," she said. "So I guess I'll take it."

"Don't!" I said. "It's part of the filtration system."

"I don't believe you."

"Yes it is—look. I do this for a living, and you don't."

"Tell me what this really is, and I'll put it back."

"It's for protection."

"Protection? From what?"

"This is a really old building. There are things you don't know about and can't know about."

She stood there, the vicious little thing, with her mouth twisted up at the corners, and for a moment it looked like she was going to accept this answer. But then she turned on her heel, bottle in hand, and started for the door.

"Please don't!"

"Protection from what? What's going to happen if I don't put this back?"

"Something terrible." It was true, I wanted to tell her. Everything was so carefully balanced. "It's a—a careful system. There are things in this building that need balancing against."

"Like the ghost?"

"No, it's more serious than that." She waited. My poor, desperate brain, reaching for its triad of comfort, got as far as two and fumbled. "We have a Vila."

She frowned. "What's that?"

What had I done? It had taken me many long, laborious hours to learn what I knew about Bezi Duras. Even longer to commit myself to learning no more. I had managed it in secret for months, evading my mother, negotiating with May, stealing keys and robbing mailboxes, all in the hope of making myself worthy of definitive proof. And instead of heeding the obvious signs to move on, I had reversed course, casting everything I knew at the feet of a stranger. My only hope now was that she would not disdain it as she did everything.

"It's a kind of spirit," I said.

"It lives in the building?"

I nodded.

"Where?"

Some semblance of will was starting to come back to me. "I can't just *tell* you."

"Why not?"

"That's not how this works. You have to earn it."

For the first time, Mila looked moved toward emotion. Of course, it was the irritation that you might have expected of her rather than the awe I wanted her to feel. But it was emotion nonetheless. "Well, then. Never mind." She dropped the perfume bottle back into the skimmer and left me there.

I felt torn about how this had gone. On the one hand, I had protected my efforts around Bezi Duras. On the other, I had pushed Mila away, perhaps for good. But I needn't have worried. She found me a few days later, a glint of curiosity animating her face. "So I did some digging around about that spirit you mentioned. The Vila. What makes you think we have one in the building?"

I went back to mopping the stairs. "There's a lot of evidence."

Mila thought about this. "Like what?"

"This isn't something we're supposed to talk about."

"Why not?"

"We're just not supposed to."

"So tell me what you know, and I'll stop talking about it."

"I know that she has magical powers."

"Like what?"

"Turning people into animals."

"That's impossible."

The bit of Ena in me came right out to bare her teeth. "If you're going to doubt me, I just won't talk about it anymore." I turned away and followed my mop down the hall.

"Why does she turn people into animals?" Mila called out after me.

"Because she can."

"Who are the people?"

"That's one of the things I haven't yet found out. They're dogs by night. But during the day, they're men."

"You're talking about the old woman upstairs. The one with the dogs—what's her name?"

I had never thought of Bezi as old. Pale-haired, perhaps. Stately. But never old. In the mirror at the end of the hall, I caught a glimpse of Mila, still standing behind me with her arms crossed.

"You've seen it happen?" she said. "You've seen them turn into dogs?"

I stood there, trying to figure out what to say. I could put a stop to this here and now. I could say, *No, it's just something my dead aunt told me,* and steer Mila away from the whole thing.

But this was the first time I'd gotten her attention. And I couldn't bring myself to give it up. So I said, "I've seen plenty," picked up my bucket, slung the mop over my shoulder, and left her to mull it over. Sure enough, she tracked me down a few days later to find out what exactly counted as plenty—by which time, I had organized my thoughts about what I would and wouldn't reveal. So I told her: Bezi Duras was a painter who lived on the thirty-third floor. A torturous quest had given me access to her garden, but I hadn't seen the inside of her home yet, and that was where the transformations took place. The task before me—and before anyone who wanted to sign on for my endeavor—was to solve this final piece of the puzzle.

"Where does she take the dogs at night?" Mila asked.

"Up the street."

"And then?"

I shrugged.

"You haven't followed her?"

I was forced now to reveal tender rules that had never before required saying aloud: I could not speak to Bezi Duras, nor ask her questions, nor follow her. Whatever knowledge I happened to gain would simply come my way if the time was right.

"Why?" Mila asked impatiently.

"That's just how it works. I don't make the rules. Do you understand?"

She did—she said so. But the next time she laid eyes on Bezi Duras, she called out from the courtyard while I watered the flowers. "Hey! Ms. Duras! Where do you go all night?"

Ice floes heaved in my heart. All my efforts, my delicate little secrecies—upended by a single, reckless, prospect-destroying question.

The Vila turned our way. She looked amused. She came back

from the gate and gave Mila the once-over. "What's that accent?" she asked, in one of her own.

"I don't have an accent."

"You certainly do."

Mila stood there shaking her head. Bezi Duras leaned forward and asked again—this time in a language that sounded very much like Ours.

"I'm sorry," Mila said, with her chin stuck out. "I don't understand you."

"That's too bad," Bezi Duras said.

We watched her leave. I was at a loss: How to reprimand Mila for her carelessness without driving her away?

"That was very godless of you," I said.

"What do you mean?"

"Only that—well. You're not supposed to ask her anything. You're supposed to find out."

"How do you find out if you don't ask?"

"I told you already. There are rules. You're supposed to find out *on your own*."

She thought this over. "Why?"

"It's just how it works."

"Your rules are ridiculous, Sil."

"I didn't make them," I said. "But I know they have to be respected."

Mila hopped up on the wall and walked the imaginary balance beam. I had the sense, looking at her, that she had never fallen in her life. "All right," Mila said. "Let's find out on our own, then. Let's follow her."

Never mind the impossible task of explaining to Mila about the checks and balances of not asking for too much, or the fact that I had already felt the consequences of trespassing too far into Bezi Duras's life. Even if I could somehow convince myself, following the Vila on one of her walks would require freedom I didn't have. For one thing, my mother could tolerate my being out of her sight for hours at a time—but only because some preternatural electricity told her that I was generally where I was supposed to be, somewhere nearby, in the building. No matter where she was—underwater in some submerged bank lobby or toppling off the back of a barge out in the bay—if a hair on her head rose on the premonition that I had wandered out into the city, she would know. And knowing, she would turn the place upside down trying to find me—then turn me upside down when I came back. One two three.

"We can't follow her."

"Well," Mila said. *"I'm* going to."

This threat plunged me into despair. I'd revealed just about everything I knew about Bezi Duras—and now this interloper, this newcomer to all my hard-won intelligence, with no stake in the mystery's answers, had come along. And she was going to reap all my efforts and advance toward the answers herself, and leave me behind.

At least I had the elevator key. I hadn't told her about that. She could follow Bezi Duras to the ends of the earth, but she could not follow her up to the penthouse. Unless she asked and somehow gained permission. In which case, it would turn out I had gone about everything the wrong way after all. Back and forth I went in my torment, until Mila found me after school one late afternoon.

"Guess what I got?" she said, gesturing to her backpack.

She wouldn't show me until we had concealed ourselves in the basement bicycle room. There, she opened the tablet she'd gotten from school and swept through its programs until she arrived at a real-time calendar of the city's tides. I watched her swipe through the days, and the water levels in the little squares up- and down-island rose and fell, going from red to green and back again.

"Now we can figure out where she goes," she said. Then she laughed at herself a little irritably. "Or, rather, where she *doesn't* go!"

From the Morningside's position on Battle Hill, we traced all possible trajectories for Bezi's route on the next evening that Mila could slip out: three streets east and one street south; two streets west and five blocks north. We let the timer tick down and watched the waters crawl up and recede. It was decided that Bezi Duras's likeliest route was west for at least two avenue blocks, and then winding north along the old park. Beyond that, she would have to either keep walking north or head eastward—but there were only a handful of places she could end up without having to either turn back or take a boat.

"Maybe that's what she does," I said. "Maybe she gets on a ferry."

Mila thought about this. "We should go out ahead of her and wait. If she passes the junction of 150th and Hill, we'll know we're on the right track."

"I don't know," I said. "We shouldn't do it. We haven't earned it yet."

She rolled her eyes. "What does that *mean*, we haven't earned it? We're earning it now, aren't we? Do you know how much trouble I'll be in if my teacher finds out I brought a tablet home?"

I hated to guess, but I suspected the answer was *Not a whole lot of trouble you couldn't bully your way out of.* And it was exactly that kind of bullying that brought me to the corner of 150th and Hill a mere two days later, waiting for the approach of Bezi Duras's footsteps in the dark while my trusting mother was stripping off her gear on some decrepit down-island pier. It was a perfect night: balmy, fragrant. The moon sat between the darkened buildings, as though it were actually in the city with us.

Beside me, Mila could not keep still. Every few minutes, she would stride out from our hiding place and peer around the corner, then come running back. "Nobody's coming!" And then again: "Goddamn it, *nobody's* coming."

We crouched there for hours and saw nothing save for a patrol and a couple of teenaged boys who fought fiercely and rather clumsily about the infrastructure required to pirate a radio station before sharing what looked like a first kiss for both of them. By ten, Mila was raging—not so much about the wasted hours as the fact that she'd been wrong about where to position our stakeout.

"We'll do better next time," she said the following afternoon, having forgiven herself at some point during her wakeful hours.

It suddenly became all right for the tablet to go missing for one more day.

Having reconsulted the map, we decided that Mila had not been wrong after all—or, at least, that she had not been *that* wrong, and that Bezi Duras was just as likely to have taken the only possible alternate route. We didn't get a chance to check this theory until the end of the week, by which point we were met with a far less favorable evening. The weather had cooled, and a seawater stink was off-gassing from the west. A funnel of cranes wheeled shrieking in the distance.

"Ew," Mila said, holding her nose. "What *is* that?"

"Mussel rot," I told her, proud of my ability to supply this information. The mussels had been beached by the receding tide, and a half million of them were opening their shells, dying, stinking the place up. "It happens every couple of months."

"You know," Mila said, hurrying alongside me, "where I come from, the air smells like jasmine all the time."

"Didn't you grow up in Aguila?"

"That's right."

"I read there's a beach in Aguila, where the garbage boats come, that's made entirely of old clothes. Cliffs and cliffs of them, just sitting there in the heat. Doesn't that stink?"

"Come on, Sil." She grinned at me from beneath her pinched nose. "I didn't grow up in *that* part of Aguila."

Eventually, the buildings parted, and we found ourselves standing practically in the open, under the mirthful gaze of a Dancing Girl I'd never seen before. Her dress was the same yellow as the one on Battle Hill, but tasseled. I felt an odd twinge of territoriality about her choice of dance partner—not the lamp with whom she waltzed outside our window but a paltry broom instead.

Here, in this vacant spread of the upper city, the train left its ivy-laden tunnel and shot northward across the edge of the park and out into the north bay. Junction girders that had once held the old trains aloft had created a kind of aboveground cavern, metal arches spanning away and away. The tide was here, too. It had come up Green Street and settled between the pylons, singing quietly against everything, even the tips of our shoes.

"Well," I said. "We'd better settle in."

We found a low wall to hide behind. Reassuringly few dead pigeons lay at our feet.

Around ten-thirty, Mila shook me awake. Below us in the street came first the shadows and then the forms of Bezi Duras and her companions. They were dogs, all right, but the moonlight had changed them somehow—lengthened them, perhaps, or made them less canine in their movements. They clicked and scraped all the way down the street and under the railway bridge, then turned left and disappeared from sight.

"Come on," Mila said, disastrously. "Let's go."

"Wait," I said, grabbing her jacket. "We have to *wait*."

"If we wait, we won't see where they're going."

When she finally wriggled free from me, she crept along the wall. But there was no need for stealth. Bezi Duras and the dogs had disappeared.

"We lost them!"

"I'm sorry. I didn't want them hearing us."

She wandered around, ankle-deep in the water, kicking it occasionally in frustration, while I struggled to placate her. "At least we know to come here now!"

A few nights later, we tried again. It was hotter than it had been all summer, and the heat had turned first into a sort of hollow stink, then into a grayish fog that coalesced around everything. You couldn't see more than two feet in front of you—terrible conditions for following anybody.

"I've been thinking about it," Mila said. "And I know where they disappeared to last time."

"Where?"

"You'll see."

This time, it was Mila who insisted that we wait for Bezi and the dogs to pass us by. Once she was satisfied that they had vanished, she circled the railway pylons, inspecting each one carefully. They were littered with mazes of graffiti that read REBELS OUT, and a particularly mystifying THEY ARE LIES scrawled in a medicinal tint of purple.

"Sil," Mila called softly from the other side of the span. "Come on."

She had found a staircase, unreasonably steep and over-grown with crisp, stinging grass, that led straight up onto the railway track. Climbing this was no easy feat. Weeds had long since overwhelmed the track, and the shining rails thinned northward until they disappeared among bolts of trampled grape and wild rose.

"This is a mistake," I said. "She can't be very far ahead. What if she sees us?"

But there was no talking Mila out of an opportunity to con-firm that she'd been right. She led the way, high-stepping over the brambles like some tiny antelope, while I fell farther and farther behind, imagining all the ways she could come to grief and have to be rescued. Would I be able to grab her hand and pull her up by one arm if she went over the side? Maybe. But could this scenario play out without signaling our presence to Bezi Duras? I doubted it.

Eventually, the track rose into the middle of the fog, and the ground below vanished.

"We should turn back," I said.

"You can, if you're scared."

"I'm not scared. I just don't want us to get caught out here after dark."

"Right. Because you're scared."

She turned away from me and went ahead, and in just a few short steps was gone from view. "Mila," I said, terrified to raise my voice.

The fog before me was silent. I would wait for her, I de-cided, for three minutes—but after they had passed, she still hadn't answered me or reappeared. All the same, I thought, that should not undermine my decision to turn back. She had attached herself to my investigation of Bezi Duras like a bossy mollusk, irreverent and careless, utterly bullheaded in a way that endangered us both and had probably made it so that the answers I sought would never reveal themselves. If I wanted to turn back, I should. So I did.

I had gone perhaps ten or twelve tentative steps when something sounded out of the congealed air behind me. It was a yowl—low and brutish. Certainly a dog. It was followed by an unintelligible bolt of reproach from a low female voice garbled by distance.

Mila's own voice, not very far away, whispered: "See?" As though she knew I was still there. "That's them. Come on, Sil."

We went blindly on. Eventually, the slow-rising parabola of the track leveled off. The fog rose a little, so that we could see its edges against a length of dark water below. Now it began to feel inevitable that Bezi Duras would grow tired of shushing her dogs, turn around, and head back toward us—at which point we would surprise her on this narrow strip of ruined track, and one or several of us would end up in the bay.

To make things worse, it was now well and truly night. I'd been reluctant to admit it to myself because my overtired eyes were casting electric amoebas into the denseness of the fog, but the gray before us was certainly dimming. The wind, when it did rise, was now edged with cold. The bay below had gone from green to black.

The track began to slope downward, gently at first but then steeply enough that we had to wedge our feet in against the ties to keep from slipping. This got harder when bushes began to appear out of nowhere, intruding onto the track. Mila was tall enough to throw a leg over the first one but was obliged to clamber through the second. It was while she was holding the thicket back for me that I realized it was not a bush at all but the crown of a tree. There were more downslope as the track arced toward the ground.

A muted oval of orange light sat unmoving in the fog ahead. Finally, the track widened and came into a station. High overhead the solitary orange light hung above a sign that read BRIGHTWOOD. A ticket desk leaned, empty and dilapidated, from the wall. The platform, with its torn-out benches, was striped with shadows. Mila tried the turnstile, but it didn't budge. Beyond it, a staircase cut right and down into pale gray below.

"I bet they went down here," she said.

I had too many misgivings to let her just run with this conclusion. "I'm not sure," I said. "That turnstile looks like it hasn't moved in years. Maybe they kept going."

To my surprise, Mila gave this some thought. She looked back toward the overgrown rails. "Well, how far to the next station?"

"I have no idea."

"It must be a five-minute ride at least," Mila said, seemingly unbothered by the fact that she had never taken this train and knew nothing about the line. "So how far is that on foot? Maybe twenty minutes? Right?"

"What if it's forty?"

"All right. Let's say it's forty. Would it be reasonable for them to keep walking for forty, or even twenty, minutes when they could just take the stairs right here?"

"That depends on where they're going. We don't even know where *here* is!"

But that didn't matter. She boosted herself over the turnstile and disappeared down the stairs. I followed, feeling my way along the slick handrail.

The fog was stagnant below, thick as a dream. No sign of Bezi or the dogs in any direction. Only tendrils of pale orange air dissolving against the dark forms of what looked like trees.

"We've lost them," Mila said. "This is your fault—going along like a goddamn snail."

"Maybe we can find their tracks."

But there was no earth to find tracks in underfoot. Just slabs of what had once been sidewalk, burst open by sprays of grass and shrubs, with an occasional black root elbowing its way out from between the cracks. The spidering course of the broken street brought us to a low fence of rotted wood, which after several yards gave way to an empty gate frame. Beyond sat a house, a ghost of one of those townhomes on the Dancing Girl billboards. The windows that weren't boarded up had been staved in.

"We *mustn't*," I said.

"Oh, come on," Mila said. "This is *clearly* the place."

She sped across the flagstones and peered inside. Looking like some small, thin-legged tribute standing there, a child sacrifice pressed against the face of the yawning gargoyle she'd been sent to appease.

She screamed and jumped back, and my knees went. By the time my heart had slowed down a little, she was laughing.

"That's not funny," I said.

"I'm sorry, I couldn't help it."

"She'll hear you!"

"I'm sorry."

An apology from Mila, that rarest of things, felt like a direct blast of sunlight. I found myself striding up the walk, and for once it was my shoulder against the door, me pushing to get into the house.

Very little fog within, but it was the darkness playing tricks now. A banister with no staircase. The noose of a vanished chandelier. What was left of the floor led through the front room and into what would have been the kitchen, where a

handful of remaining drawers hung open. In the corner lay a
tattered heap that I felt certain would be a dead man, but instead turned out to be just an abandoned sleeping bag, waterlogged, bristling with pale mushrooms.

When we got back outside, the streetlamps looked dimmer.
"What's that?" I said.

In the fog ahead, a light was intermittently flashing. Rhythm-
less and distant. Neither close nor bright enough to sharpen
the details around us, but impossible to ignore.

"Looks like lightning," Mila said.

"Is there a storm?"

"I don't hear any thunder."

It occurred to me then that I had no idea what time it was.
Working backward from this moment, I tried to divide the evening by minutes—had it taken twenty to get here from the
train station? Thirty? How long had we been following Bezi
Duras? And before that—how long had we waited for her to
appear? Three hours, or four, or six—it was impossible to know.
Bezi Duras would soon be turning back, setting up the possibility for an encounter on this unknown terrain. My mother would
soon be coming home to find me gone. If there was still any
hope of leaving this place before either of those two things
happened, it was waning fast.

"We have to leave."

"Just a minute," Mila said.

But it took far longer than that to reach the next house, open
the door, and look around. Once we were there, it was impossible to stop Mila from continuing on—even though, by then,
it was reasonably clear what we could expect to see in all the
houses that followed. In each we found more or less the same
scene, save for one. Inside, a huge nest of twigs and papers and
rags lay sodden just below a gaping hole in the roof. A rook

crane, tall as a man, stood alongside it. I had never seen one up close. Its eyes were like stones, still and molten in their sockets. It had to turn its entire head to watch us as we crossed the room to better position ourselves before it.

"Let's go," I said.

"But we haven't seen anything yet."

What I couldn't tell her was that I feared we *would* see something. The darkness, the fog, the relentless wreckage of the place had destabilized my senses. I knew exactly how it would happen: I would see something, and Mila would not. I would carry the memory around with me forever, and Mila would not. I would go mad, and Mila would not.

"We can't keep skulking around here. They could be halfway home by now."

"*Fine,* Sil," Mila said. "Fine."

And then the door on the far side of the room opened, and a shadow came in. I felt more than saw it, but so did Mila. Her arm stiffened against mine. She was breathing very slowly, very quietly, and this made me more afraid than I thought possible. The unseen newcomer left the door open and moved softly along the far wall, morphing and rippling across the torn wallpaper. In the moment it crossed the light drifting through the uncurtained window, I saw that it was tall, and stood on two legs, and then it disappeared into the darkness again. Moments later, a long arm left the shadows and helped itself to something from the nest—one, two, three, four. Then the robber shadow flared up again in the doorway, and was out in the street.

The shock of it was still singing through me when I finally found the courage to look over at Mila. Surely the blood must have left her hands and feet. But no. She was smiling. "Did you see him take the eggs?"

"Who?" I said.

"That boy. Come on—before we lose him."

And, unbelievably, she rushed out into the street. I staggered along behind them, leaden with fear and disbelief. There was Mila, out here in the oily moonlight like a girl in a trance. Unafraid, because she had no sense of a world beneath the world. Everything to her was as it was on its face. This new figure we were now following was just something to be understood. Something to be asked to account for itself. It owed her answers—and so, apparently, did the second figure who joined it out of the looming darkness when we reached the next cross street. Mila wasn't even bothering to stay quiet anymore, running a little to keep up with the two of them, and I was trailing farther and farther behind, windlassed by the reality I couldn't make her understand. We were not supposed to be here, following two—no, now *three*—strange boys down one alley, and then another, and then another, in this forsaken part of the city. We were supposed to take all this for the warning it was, and grab each other's hands and go home.

Ahead of us, the boys were humming with laughter as they hurried along. They turned in at the last house at the end of the block and disappeared inside. Mila, breathless and smiling, reached the gate, and stood there waiting for me.

"We need to *go*," I called. But whatever was working itself into the air around us had already made its way into Mila's eyes. I wasn't even sure she could hear me.

The boys had left the front door partly open and were sitting down to a meal. Their table was pushed toward the middle of the room, away from the stove. By the light of a couple of camping lanterns, we could see their faces, and the kitchen beyond, where an old, almost bald woman in a dark coat was dropping the crane eggs into a pot on the stove. She took something out of the oven, brought it in, set it on the table, looked up, and saw our bewildered faces looming in the doorway.

"Excuse me," she cried. "Who are you?"

"I'm sorry, we're in the wrong place!" I said desperately, shoving my whole body back against Mila, who was leaning into me to get a better look inside.

"No, we're not," Mila said cheerfully. "Hullo!"

The woman was peering more closely at us. To my horror, her face brightened. "You're Muriel's girls. From the hospital, right?"

Mila didn't miss a beat. "That's right."

"How's your mother?"

"She's fine."

"Don't just stand there letting in the air, girls, come in. Shut the door. Have you eaten?"

"No!" Mila said delightedly.

"Well, come on, it won't be long."

With a final shove, Mila popped me out of the doorway. I leaned into the corner while she made her way to the table and sat down. The boys were all huddled on a bench against the wall, trilling away together in what I now realized was some tinny language I couldn't understand. The table was huge, and not an inch of it was free of netting or wire or wooden boxes, among which was interspersed the occasional bowl of cracked seedpods or steaming greens.

"Hullo," Mila said, taking it all in. "It's a party!"

I could scarcely bring myself to look at the faces around the table, but I felt sure they must be as leveled by her cruelty as I was. Mila, meanwhile, was making herself at home. She found an empty plate and drew it in front of her, then fished a fork out from under a pile of string lights.

"Please start," the woman said from the stove. "Boys, pass

our guests some food." She noticed me, still hovering in my corner, and frowned. "Sit down." I followed her finger to an empty chair beside Mila.

One of the boys was looking at me with his head cocked to the side. "Who are you?" he managed. His voice was small. Outside, he had seemed long and lean, adolescent in his expansive movements. But he couldn't have been more than seven or eight years old. Big-eyed, bird-boned, so pale his veins shone in little rivulets around his eyes.

"We're Muriel's girls," Mila said.

The woman brought the boiled crane eggs over in a basket and pulled up a chair at the head of the table.

"And how is Muriel?" she asked.

"Oh," Mila said. "You know."

"Hard week at the hospital?"

"Even worse than last week."

"I can only imagine." The woman looked straight at me. "She's lucky she has you."

If she noticed the terror melting my smile, she didn't show it. Instead, she sent a bowl along the table, past boy after boy, one, two, three, until it got to me. I spooned the contents onto my plate, pleasantly surprised to recognize cabbage. Odd, I thought: just moments ago, I could have sworn the bowl was full of something dark and slimy. I tried to pay better attention as the next offering headed toward me, but it was so dark— could I really be sure that the platter of boiled potatoes now warming my hands hadn't been hiding somewhere on this table, in this morass of tangled rope and tin cups? I'd sat down determined not to eat a bite. But I hadn't eaten all day. Would it really be so terrible to take a mouthful, just to be polite? One two three, I thought, and there was Ena, asking me if I was out of my mind. Did I know anything about these strange, chittering boys and their obviously confused guardian? Did I think any good could come of indulging the crazy lie Mila was spinning for them? It would serve us right to get poisoned here.

Mila clearly wasn't victim to any of these thoughts. She surveyed the feast before her and pushed a fork into a mountain of crispy onions. I watched its arc back toward her mouth. And there I was, knocking it out of her hand. The fork sang off the tiles, and the boys stopped their whispering and stared.

"Sil!" Mila said, with exaggerated affect. "Please excuse her. She has a lot of deficiencies."

"I'm sorry," I said stupidly. "I just—our hosts aren't eating yet."

This wasn't true. The boys' mouths were full.

The old woman tried to move us past the moment. "I'll get you a new one." I made some halfhearted gesture to beat her to the punch, but she had already swooped down on the fork. She crouched in front of me with her dress pooling around her body, and as she stood back up, she laid her hand against her chest. She smoothed that fabric down down down, and I caught beneath it the glimpse of a long, grinning scar. And now it all came to me.

Three boys. Of course. Bezi Duras and this woman crouching before me were one and the same. And her dogs? Their skins were lying somewhere in a back room of this dank and horrible little house. They had put on trousers and shoes, shaken the howls out of their voices, and gathered around the table. They were not human by day—they were human by night, and they were not just three men pulled from some random corner of her life. They were not men at all. They were boys. Thin, fragile sons. Ravenous and lost. And right there, sitting at that table, it made all the difference in the world. Had they been expecting us? This meal, was it *for* us? And this bowl that was being pressed into my hands, and from which I was helping myself to a much-too-liberal scoop of something fragrant and wonderful-smelling—this bowl I was now passing to Mila, my friend Mila, sitting there to my right with a look of smug expectation—was it enchanted with something that would visit the same curse upon us? Would it turn us into animals? Me into a toad, and Mila very obviously into a cat or weasel, or some other sly, contemptuous thing? All this time, I had thought that Bezi Duras was a static entity, locked in ritual, coming and going, someone whose power had been worn down by the distance from home, condensed into a diminished version of herself, nothing but essence. But the city had turned her instead into something more sinister. She was coming here to feed, and to nourish her sons on these strange offerings, raising her boys on barbed wire and nettles. There was nothing she wouldn't do for them. Nothing they wouldn't do for her. And here we were, intruding into their midst.

A new fork had materialized in my hand. Mila took it.

"What are you doing out so late?" the woman was asking.

Mila said: "We're looking for someone. A woman who maybe came by here not too long ago? With three dogs?"

I inched my foot over to her and gave the edge of her shoe a firm, slow press. She let me down immediately by looking under the table.

"Three dogs?" the old woman was musing. "I don't think so."

"You'd know it if you saw them."

I heard my lost, wretched voice say, "Mila."

Next came the rook crane eggs. They were huge, big as river stones, and speckled with a rust-colored splatter. The boys passed and passed the basket, grumbling, pouting, staring longingly at it once it ended up in Mila's hands. She looked at the four eggs and the five other faces around the table and said, in a voice larded with politeness: "Oh, I mustn't."

The woman said: "Please. Go ahead."

Mila helped herself, then thrust the basket into my hands. She steadied the egg and tapped the crown of it with her spoon. The boys were practically out of their seats. Then she paused. "What if there's a chick in mine?"

The woman's jaw stretched into a smile. "Then you're lucky."

That was when I finally found the courage to stand up. "I think I hear our mother calling." I got hold of Mila's elbow and squeezed, and this somehow got her to her feet. "Thank you so much for having us."

"But the eggs," the woman said, only I was already halfway to the door, reaching for the handle and praying it wouldn't disintegrate in my hand.

Outside, Mila turned on me. "What the hell, Sil? I want my egg!"

"Your egg—are you crazy? You'd probably crack it open to find your own face inside, staring back at you! Don't you see what's happening here?"

"What are you talking about?"

"It's *them*," I hissed.

"Who?"

"Bezi and the dogs. That—that woman. The boys."

"What are you saying?"

"She brings them here so they can spend the night as their *actual selves*. They're her sons."

"Who?"

"The dogs—that's *them*."

"Oh, come on," Mila said, and I realized I'd only imagined

the trace of discomfort in her voice. Didn't she have any sense? Wasn't she from Back Home?

"We need to *go*," I said. "While we still can."

Dizzy with fear, I was imagining the interminable walk back, the tracks probably all but vanished in the overgrowth, twisting away to misguide us. I felt weary just thinking about it. The absence of recognition in Mila's face, her blank stare, firmed up exactly how alone I really was. If I didn't get us back, we'd probably be stuck here forever. We might wander these still, abandoned streets for hours that were in fact years, while back in the real world behind and before us, our mothers put up flyers and embraced over our empty graves. My mother would take a long time to get beyond her fury to a place of mourning—being stuck here forever was, perhaps, a bit of a mercy for me—but she would get there eventually. And then she would be totally and utterly alone in this world. No Ena. No me. Just my mother, swimming in the dark.

"I'm going," I said, and started up the murky street.

Mila gave a little roar of frustration. "Ugh! Wait! Just a minute." I turned back to see her running down the walk and back into the house. What was I going to tell her mother? Your daughter refused to listen to sense, she went back into the Vila's lair—after being allowed to leave, no less—and I never saw her again?

Some interminable minutes later, Mila came bounding out, and I found my breath again.

"All right," she said. "Let's go."

"Why did you go back?"

She smiled at me smugly. "I forgot to hug our hostess goodbye."

Brave, reckless, extraordinary thing. "Mila—why?"

"We have to see if you're right, don't we?"

"What do you mean? How?"

"I dropped something in her jacket pocket. If you're right, we'll find it upstairs tomorrow."

But I didn't care about being proven right. My belief had ripened into certainty, and it didn't matter anymore whether Mila believed me.

WE MADE OUR way back to the train station and started home in silence. With every step, I counted one two three. Something new and as terrible as what we had gone through was now looming: the prospect of sneaking back into my own home. I didn't know how late it was or how long it would take us to get back, but my belief that we might still have a chance of returning before our absence was noted had dissipated entirely. My mother was certainly home by now. She had certainly put her head around my bedroom door to make sure I was asleep. She had seen no illusory lump under my blanket. No paper-stuffed human facsimile had been planted there to delude her. She had certainly begun calling my name, and hearing no reply, she had begun walking the halls. Here, a few variables entered the picture. It was growing light in the distance. Did that mean she had given up her search and called the police? Was her terror vast enough to override her fear of them? Did she believe they had the authority to begin searching the apartments she could not—those belonging, of course, to any suspect bachelor who might have snatched me, unobserved, from the corridor?

WHEN I FINALLY eased the apartment door shut in the pink haze of five in the morning, my mother stood up from where she was sitting at the foot of my bed. I could see her from the entryway—the sound of my arrival roused her from what had probably been a sort of fevered half-sleep. As her fear disintegrated into anger, she seemed to double in size.

"I guess you're going to tell me some lie" was the first thing she said.

"No, Mama."

"Where the hell were you?"

"With Mila. In town."

"In *town*?" A smile of delighted disbelief overtook her face. Apparently, the notion was hilarious. "What do you mean *in town*?" She did not wait for a reply. "Do you mean out there, in this rotted fucking city, wandering the streets where God knows who could do God knows what to you, and you'd never be found?" This time, a vowel made it out of my mouth before she started in again. "I thought you were smarter than this. I thought you were smart enough for certain things not to need saying. Like: Don't wander off into the night with fucking Mila without letting anyone know where you're going, without so much as a word or a note left behind, so that when I get back here, I have to pick up the phone and call the police and be told that you probably ran away, and you'll come home when you're hungry." *In fact, I am hungry,* I considered saying—but immediately envisaged, with lightning-crack clarity, how fast she'd get to me from where she was standing. Besides, there was no interrupting her. "And then to have the policeman laugh at me when I say, *My daughter wouldn't do a thing like that.* Laugh. When I tell him my daughter is missing. You know what else I didn't think needed saying?" She held something up. It was a packet of Mrs. Sayez's fun cards. "Don't put your fucking *critiques* on paper and then offer them up to the government that took you in."

"I didn't mail them," I managed to say.

"But you filled them out."

"They're anonymous."

"Anonymous? Your fingerprints are all over them. Your fingerprints, which *they* have, up in that fucking clinic where they held us when we first arrived." I could see her struggling with how to emphasize what she was saying. Would it be an epithet or a gesture? The dramatic won out: she flung the cards down with as much force as she could muster, and they went hissing all over the floor.

"And you lied to me," she said. "You're a liar."

Somehow, I drew myself up. "I was out with Mila. It's the truth."

"No." She came toward me. "No—months ago, I asked you what these cards said. And what did you tell me? Light and easy questions about our happiness here. Well, I've been learning. At the dock, I've been learning to read. And I know enough now to know that you *lied* to me."

There was a tremor in her voice that indicated her upset was rooted in more than just anger. To combat it, I said: "Well, you lied to *me*."

"*I* lied?"

"Yes," I said, dizzy with misplaced courage. "You said you hated the farm. You said we had no other relatives. All these things that Ena told me about—"

"You and fucking *Ena*!" She was yelling now. "What else did Ena tell you?"

I struggled to think of an answer. There was a repository somewhere, in the furthest recesses of my sleepless, light-blinded brain, but all I seemed to be able to draw from it now was chaff. Grandma stringing her violin with her own hair. My mother's wild fox companion. "She told me the truth," I managed. "She told me you're a—a *foundling*. Just left there on her doorstep like a"—I reached for the worst thing I could imagine—"a baked ham."

These words did not have the intended effect on my mother. Her mouth twisted with scorn. "The truth?" she said. "You idiot. The truth." She started to leave, but paused in the doorway. "In all her truth-telling, did Ena ever bother to tell you why *she* left? It wasn't the war, you know. She left *years* before any of that happened. Because she couldn't be what she was at home. Because that very same Baba playing the fiddle in all those happy pictures beat her black-and-blue when she caught her kissing another girl. Did she happen to mention that? Oh yes. *That's* the truth. Did Ena tell you that when word got around town that she'd had an affair with a married woman, the same boys she'd grown up with and had been friends with all her life started leaving dead cats on our doorstep? Started trying to run her off the road, if they passed her on her bicycle at night? It got so bad she couldn't leave the house. So she took every penny she'd ever saved, and some of my money, too, by the way, and she left without a word to anybody. And when she came back years later? With Beanie? In those pictures you saw on the fridge? Well, we had to pretend that none of it ever happened, and that Beanie was a spiritual adviser who was helping her change her ways. So. Make a little folksy story for yourself out of *that,* if you can." She had one final thing to say: "You go anyplace with that girl again, I'll skin you alive."

To say that life turned cold would be an understatement. My mother rose at three-thirty every morning and was out the door by four. Upon her return, she would eat whatever I'd warmed up and fall asleep, often right on the sofa. I, meanwhile, stayed in and dozed through a procession of virtual courses and snuck around carrying out my mother's Morningside chores without deviation, generally doing my best to remain unskinned by her and unnoticed by Bezi Duras. Every so often, it occurred to me that I might curry some sympathy with my mother if I explained what had happened. Contrary to my previous beliefs, we were not living in a tower with some diminished old-world spirit. We were here on the sufferance of a witch who was very real. Maybe, in her old-woman form, she had failed to recognize me. Maybe it would hit her like a thunderbolt the next time our eyes met in the courtyard. Or maybe her sons, in their canine form, would recognize my scent. And then what?

If my mother knew the peril I had endured to gain this knowledge, her stance toward me might soften. On the other hand, whenever I thought about telling her about it—imagined myself even beginning the conversation, let alone trying to explain to her the certainty of that world beneath the world—my stomach convulsed. She would not believe me. It would only infuriate her and remind her of a transgression I hoped she was at least part of the way toward forgetting. So I stayed silent. Stayed out of everyone's way. And for good measure I visited my protections in their hiding places, one two three, as often as I dared. They all felt so futile, so puny. The only real way to avoid whatever might be coming was to get out of there completely, leave the Morningside. But that would require convincing my mother. Which brought me, once more, to the impossibility of telling her.

"Snoopy," May called through the gate one afternoon. "You look terrible."

"I've been doing my courses."

"What courses? The Insomniac's Guide to Slow Mental Collapse?" He rattled the gate gently. "Snoopy, come on. I kid. At least you've got a new friend—who is she?"

"Mila."

"What's her story?"

I shrugged. "She lives on the thirty-second floor."

"Bet she doesn't let you forget *that*."

I'd bumped into her only once recently, a few days after my mother's terminal directive. "Will we go up to the penthouse on Saturday?" she asked in her usual graceless way.

"I don't think so," I mumbled.

"Sunday?"

I had been walking around under a sort of radioactive halo of shame that warmed up anytime I was forced to interact with anybody. But Mila seemed undiminished.

"I can't go anywhere, anytime. My mother caught me sneaking in. She was furious."

"Oh." Mila said this as though the prospect of parental fury had never occurred to her.

"Wasn't your mother angry?"

"No. She was asleep."

"Well. Mine wasn't. I'm punished until further notice. So."

"All right," Mila said. "Let me know when it passes."

Despite this fundamental misunderstanding, she did me the courtesy of leaving me alone. But this, too, was poison. Fear twisted at me. What if Mila, fed up with waiting for my punishment to "pass," decided to undertake the journey to the railway and over to the abandoned island again by herself? For comfort, I allowed myself a few stolen moments in 16D, from where I could verify that Bezi Duras was indeed still heading out every night—and, more important, that my fears about Mila had not yet manifested. Relief on both fronts: reliable sightings of Bezi and the dogs, but never one of Mila. Apparently, even she wasn't reckless enough to brave Island City on her own.

IN EARLY SEPTEMBER, the cadaverous Mrs. Gaspard crept up on me as I was cleaning the basement laundry machines. "I don't see your aunt much these days," she said.

"No."

"Where's your mother?"

"In the security shed."

She stuck her head into the little basement office. "I must say the place has never been neater."

"She'll appreciate hearing that."

Mrs. Gaspard looked at her watch. "Has she been told about the annual Board meeting on the seventeenth?" I said I didn't know. "We meet in the library at seven o'clock. A very casual affair, but vital, so we'll need her there to do the serving and so on. And she'll have to pick up our catering from Saint Martha's."

"What the hell is Saint Martha's?" my mother asked me that
night. She had just come off a three-day job in the outer bay
and looked frailer than I'd seen her in a long time. "Where the
hell is that?"

It turned out to be a ferry ride away, down-island, past the
western edge of the Marsh. I'd never seen so many rook cranes
before, dozens of them wheeling and silhouetted against the
yellow sky while pickers walked the ridgelines of trash below.
We disembarked, and walked east from the terminal to the
cross street Mrs. Gaspard had written down for me. But when
we got there, the stretch seemed to hold only old warehouses,
mostly boarded up. "I don't like this," my mother said. We went
along, looking for a shingle, a sign, anything to indicate that we
were in the right place.

"I must have misunderstood," I said, mere seconds before a
man in a baker's coat emerged from behind a steel door up the
block. He was wearing a cap that read SAINT MARTHA'S. My
mother sprinted to catch the door with her foot, and we stood
there until the man vanished around the corner.

A vast, warm, coal-fire smell wafted from the stairwell below.
"Do you know what that is?" my mother asked.

Shamefully, I did. "It's meat."

Saint Martha's was a dimly lit, high-ceilinged basement
warehouse teeming with silent shoppers who drifted among its
aisles, meeting no one's gaze. You didn't have to wait for your
eyes to adjust to the poor lighting to understand that food was
in play—the smells that hit you as you came down the stairs
made that plain enough. Meat, yes, but also warm yeast, bright
citrus, and a bouquet of things so foreign to me and so wonder-

ful that I could scarcely stand upright. Painted signs suspended above the aisles pointed toward unimaginable delights— BAKERY, PRODUCE, DAIRY. In the far corner, under a sign that read PICKUP, sat a small counter behind which a pile of huge paper bags climbed steadily all the way to the ceiling. Manning this point of interest was a tall, uninterested brunette in a burlap apron, who, after several minutes, finally gave in to the pressure of my stare and took the trouble to lower her tablet.

"I'm sorry," I said. "We're here to pick something up."

"What building?"

"Sorry?"

"What building are you picking up for?"

"The Morningside."

She isolated four bags from the pile behind her and pushed them across the counter in my direction. "You can pay up front."

On our way up front, however, my mother detoured into the displays. I followed, and nearly lost her amid the pyramids of bright fruit.

"Look at this," my mother said. I came around the corner to see her holding a glossy purple orb out to me.

"It's a plum," I said.

"Yes, but have you ever seen one that looks so—plummy? It's like a *picture* of a plum." She lifted it to her nostrils, then held it up to mine. "Smell it."

"I don't smell anything."

"Exactly." She shot the whole display a murderous look. "Might as well be plastic."

We sniffed more inodorous fruit, then paused to watch a small thundershower soak the quivering greens in their crates. "Why?" my mother said. When she disappeared around the corner in the direction of CHEESE, I didn't follow. She seemed unable to muster anything but contempt for the place, and I knew that I should feel the same—after all, somewhere in here, somebody was roasting flesh, and I had been assiduously trying to avoid looking with any interest into the distant BUTCHER vitrine, behind which huge tubs of red matter were laid out. But I was too awestruck, too light-headed from the smells that seemed to be emanating from everything but the fruit. I found myself in an aisle boasting canned goods—but these were not the gruel to which I was accustomed. Asparagus and beets. Olives and artichokes. At the top of the aisle, a blond man with exquisitely manicured fingernails offered me a piece of orange melon wrapped in some manner of pale cheese. He tried to hide his shock when I pulled it off his knife with my teeth. Embarrassed, I fled into the bakery, where flushed women in hairnets were shoving huge platters of crenellated pastry into the case. CHEESE, the display cards read. JAM. ALMONDS. Suggestion notes accompanied everything: Try this chestnut spread with your rye. This quince paste with your pumpernickel. Here was a bread baked underground—the "ancient way." You must be sure to try it with a dollop of horseradish and salmon.

Taking a left, I found myself in the jam aisle, face-to-face with my mother at last.

"Do you know what this is?" In her hand sat a round, fat jar, exactly like the one that was at this very moment rotting with the miasma of all my trespasses back home. A bright panic lanced my chest. *Jam,* I wanted to say. *From grandmother's orchard.* Everything about the jar looked eerily similar. The same purple lid, the same glass burl sitting just above the label. It even had the same heft when my mother handed it to me.

"What is it?"

"Fig jam from home. I grew up on this stuff." She turned it

over to look at the price. "Right," she said, and put it back. Up front at the cashier, however, she produced it again and set it wordlessly down on the belt.

"Won't Mrs. Gaspard see it on the receipt?" I asked nervously.

"I don't care," my mother said. "We'll say it was a misunderstanding."

I bristled at this. *We* wouldn't have to say anything—I and I alone would be the one explaining myself to Mrs. Gaspard, and making a valiant play of ignorance. My mother clearly had no sense of the extent of that woman's hatred for me.

On the sidewalk outside Saint Martha's, amid the shuttered warehouses, in the thick afternoon air, my mother popped the lid off the impostor jar and held a wooden spoonful of its contents out to me.

"Don't chew, just sort of let it sit there." She was watching my face, making it impossible to hide my emotions. This jam from the store tasted exactly the same as the stuff Ena had shared with me all those months ago. Exactly the same. The whole situation felt inherently dangerous—as though I were meant to confess now that I'd tasted it before or admit that it was just like Baba's. "You don't like it?" my mother said.

"It's wonderful."

"Isn't it good? Have some more."

"No—you."

I watched her face for signs of something sinister, but there was only her smile, and that look of remembering. "Yes," she said. "That's it, all right."

Afterward, we took separate ferries: my mother down-island, to the docks, and I back to the Morningside with our wares carefully nestled against my side, disguised in plain burlap bags so that nobody would recognize where I'd been and, in my mother's words, "mistake me for the kind of person worth robbing." I had to keep reminding myself to pay attention so I wouldn't miss my stop, but I felt as though I'd floated away. All of Ena's talk about Baba's orchards, the last of the ancestral jam at the bottom of the jar. The guilt I had felt for its ruination—when, in fact, it seemed possible now that it might not have come from those orchards at all. If there even *were* orchards—if there ever had been in the first place.

THE BAGS FROM Saint Martha's turned out to contain several platters, each densely packed with assorted, delicious-smelling offerings arranged around a bunch of grapes or a deck of crackers. There was cheese on all of them, and on some there were indecipherable rounds of something called coppa, too. The realization that it was meat, when it finally came, blindsided me. What was I supposed to do now? Lay it out or just put it back in the bag and throw it away after the meeting? Neither option was especially appealing. What would Mrs. Gaspard say when she came down here and realized that I was attempting to serve her and the other Board members meat? Would she even remember that my only role in this had been to go and pick up the order? That I hadn't placed it myself? Never had I felt so blindly grateful for my mother's absence, for the fact that she did not have to be the one making a decision in this case, or taking the blow of retribution.

I had the huge mahogany table in the library wiped down by six o'clock, and had wretchedly resigned myself to displaying all of the platters, come what may, by the time Mrs. Gaspard drifted in.

"What are *you* doing here?" she said with alarm.

"Just laying out the food," I said. "I hope—" I fought with

how to phrase this. "I hope—I do hope everything is to your satisfaction."

She cast a glance over the offending platters. "Where's the pumpernickel bread?"

"Um."

I went through the bags, one by one, loudly and in full view of her, so she could see that they were all empty. "Thieves," she eventually said. "They'll be hearing from me." She seemed suddenly to remember that I was there. "Where's your mother?"

"She's very ill," I recited. And then, though I'd promised to be as vague as possible: "She didn't think she should be around all this food."

Mrs. Gaspard blanched. "And you? Are *you* ill?"

"No."

"Even so. Better stay back there behind the bar." She peered down at a platter. The cheese was beginning to sweat under the yellow library lights. "Did you lay this out?"

"Yes."

"With your bare hands?"

By seven-twenty, the last of the janglers were in their seats. I wielded the wine bottle at any empty glass that happened to drift in my direction, but otherwise stayed where I'd been ordered to and busied myself wiping out the cabinets. How strange to see them all in one place, these people I'd encountered in the halls and knew only by the household malfunctions for which they summoned my mother. The Curtises, with their endless noise complaints and leaking refrigerator. Red-faced Mr. Payne of 23F, who lived on the water line most commonly afflicted with pressure problems. The fragile Miss Calorann, who insisted that something or someone was trapped behind the wall of her kitchen, and wouldn't believe us when we told her it was just the pipes clanking on those rare occasions when the overnight temperature dipped. Mrs. Golub, of course, with her foul-smelling little survivor dead-eyeing everyone above the rim of her purse. Until this moment, they had existed separately in my mind, each a denizen of their own floor, of their own gloomy, solitary woes, circling back to the same questions, the same complaints. And yet, here they were, forking lengths of slippery ham off the platters as though it were the most ordinary thing in the world. As though eating it didn't carry a fine, and it hadn't been secreted here from a nameless warehouse across town. As though there were nothing to be ashamed of, and nobody looking.

I'd often wondered who among them had been the culprit behind the chicken bone that my mother had been so distressed to tong out of the gutter all those months ago during the raccoon's midnight raids. Well, here was my answer. It could have been any of them.

Mrs. Gaspard was already on her third glass of wine when Mrs. Sayez swept in, late and out of breath. She made apologies and waved away the wine I offered her, but did help herself to the last piece of salami, much to the poorly concealed dismay of Mr. Payne, who had been eyeing it for some time across his empty plate.

"Any other business?" Mrs. Gaspard wanted to know.

"Yes." Mrs. Sayez fanned herself. "The Repopulation fundraiser."

"What, already?"

No petulant exhalation was going to derail Mrs. Sayez. "As you know, the Repopulation Program has made great strides this year. We have welcomed a record seven hundred families from all over the world. More than half of them are already employed across different municipal sectors—hospitality, service, salvage, and engineering. We have broken ground on two

Repopulation housing developments on South Falls Island. Our polls show that support for our efforts has never been greater. So this fundraiser is a great opportunity for members and donors to not just honor the glory days of our beloved city but to celebrate the progress we've made in getting it back to itself."

"That's wonderful, Clare," Mrs. Gaspard said, in a voice that suggested it was anything but. "Even so, we're all wary of how entrenched this building has become in your fundraising obligations. We're not Repopulation headquarters. You're the only Repopulation representative living here. And yet, every year, we spend valuable resources arranging something that lies outside our purview."

"I like the parties," Mr. Payne said. "Get dressed up, meet nice people. What's the harm?"

"Get dressed up and meet nice people on your own time, and on your own dime." Mrs. Gaspard flattened her meeting notes with one hand.

Mrs. Sayez sat forward. "I understand your concerns about the extent of the building's commitment. Really, I do. I think you'll be glad to hear that Ms. Duras has volunteered to organize this year's festivities."

Mutters of excitement coursed around the table. I climbed off my step stool and edged closer.

"Volunteered?" Mrs. Gaspard again. "That's not like her."

"She hasn't thrown a party in *years*," Mr. Payne said.

"Well, that's what I mean." Mrs. Gaspard looked down the table. "When was the last time she had anybody up there? And now she suddenly wants to host? Why?"

Mrs. Sayez rallied to the front. "I believe, as a refuge seeker herself, she wants to offer her support to the Repopulation efforts."

"Can't she offer it in the form of money?" But the hum of enthusiasm around the table was growing louder, and Mrs. Gaspard could feel her position slipping. "What date again?"

"October nineteenth."

"And how many people are we expected to tolerate?"

"I have the details right here."

A paper was uncrinkled, loudly passed along the table, and contemplated in silence. "I suppose it could be worse."

When I turned around again, Mrs. Gaspard was still studying the note. The others sat watching her breathlessly. She turned the page over and snorted. "'It goes without saying that the Board members and trustees are all welcome.' Goes without saying. I should say it needs saying. How often have we approved these things without so much as a thank-you card—let alone an invitation from Bezi Duras?"

"We get to go?" someone said excitedly. "All of us?"

"Well, if you want to spend an evening hollering over the wind and peering at some nonsense on a canvas," Mrs. Gaspard said, "it seems you'll have your chance."

"Her parties really are something," Mr. Payne chimed in. "I went with my sister, when she was invited with the ballet guild. That must have been fifteen years ago. Bezi had done all these little original studies of the ballerinas. And there were ribbon dancers!"

"I doubt there'll be any ribbon dancers at this one," Mrs. Gaspard said. "Unless some of those Repopulation kids turn out to be handy at it."

This drew less of a cackle than she seemed to expect. Mrs. Sayez gave her a tight smile. "A few of our Repopulation families will be attending as guests—but they won't be expected to provide entertainment, of course. However!" There was a long, terrifying pause. I looked up to find Mrs. Sayez grinning brightly at me. "Sil—I'm sure your mother will be helping the caterers and so on, but how would *you* like to go to a party?"

"**WHAT'S THIS?**" my mother asked.

Even from across the room, I could tell she was pointing to the October 19 square on our calendar, which had been circled in pale green for the better part of a week. I'd picked the driest marker I could find for this dubious honor, hoping she might fail to see it, but unable to bring myself to sabotage her by leaving it off the calendar completely. Now I made a big deal of coming over to the fridge and squinting.

"That's the party!"

"What party?"

"The Repopulation fundraiser."

"So why am I only hearing about it now?"

"Mrs. Sayez said she talked to you," I lied.

My mother took an exasperated journey through the October pages of her planner. I couldn't position myself to look over her shoulder, but based on the sounds she was making it did not look promising.

"Sil, I'm sorry," she finally said. "I can't."

"Oh," I said, trying to sound more disappointed than afraid.

"It's the last night of a big excavation. You'll have to do it."

"Of course."

She hovered close, looking at me. "Do you want me to take the evening off?"

"No, no. Don't. I'll do it."

Her hands came to my head, and she squeezed my temples. "So much work, Sil. I hope you know how thankful I am."

"Mama," I said. "Don't start."

I walked around with this secret in my heart for the entire following day. Here it was: the opportunity I'd been waiting for. The chance to walk right into the Vila's home and linger and take it all in. This time, there was no denying that I hadn't asked to be admitted. But I no longer had any desire to go upstairs or see any more of whatever eerie forces Mila and I had encountered on the abandoned island.

And now there was the question of Mila, who would surely jump at the chance to do just that.

I'd had some success in avoiding her, but the week I learned about the party, she became increasingly determined to find me. We'd glimpse each other on opposite ends of a hallway, and she would start hurrying my way while I would remove myself into the elevator or the service stairwell as quickly as I could. One evening, she pounded on my door for five minutes, then went silent—only to begin pounding again the instant my stockinged feet hit the living room floor. "Sil! Are you in there?"

When she did finally catch me, on the stairs between the library and the lobby, she stretched her whole frame between the banisters to block my escape.

"Sil!" She was humming with undiluted energy. "Guess what?" Before I had the chance to answer, she had pulled a card from her pocket and sailed it down the stairs to me. I caught it. Gold lettering on a dark background. A formal invitation to Bezi Duras's party for Mila and her mother.

"October nineteenth!" Mila said excitedly. "I've been trying and trying to tell you." Her expression sank a little. "But I didn't know if—will you be out of punishment by then?"

My hand, clutching the invitation, looked bloodless and guilty—the hand of a traitor. Here I'd been doing my best to make sure that Mila didn't catch wind of the party. And all the while, she'd been trying to clue me in.

"Oh," I mumbled. "I think I might be helping the caterers."

"How perfect!" she said. "You'll have something to wear!"

THAT SOMETHING TURNED out to be a stiff black jumpsuit, which arrived in a paper bag the morning of the party, accompanied by a note instructing me to check in at five o'clock. By then, the penthouse elevator was already being guarded by a black-suited bulwark of a man, who rummaged around in my bag before pointing me upstairs. No secret key this time. No pretense. My mother and I had carefully planned my explanation of her absence: "She sends her apologies—she has a bad sprain." I would say it matter-of-factly to anyone who asked, in a way that suggested that perhaps I didn't know much about my mother's sprain, or sprains in general.

The doors opened to a blazing sunset and preparations already underway. Twinkle lights were being strung around the orchard. One side of the balustrade had been walled off by a long white curtain behind which people on ladders were shouting instructions. A platform was being set up amid the rosebushes at the bottom of the steps that led to Bezi Duras's front door. Ornate panels screened the southern part of the garden, and from behind them I could hear the clink of kitchenware and see steam and smoke rising.

As I stood there, one of the waiters touched my shoulder. "Are you here to help?"

I nodded.

"Then help," he said, tossing me a tablecloth.

I tailed him around the rooftop, slinging linens, setting votives between empty chafing dishes on the long tables that lined the balustrade. A mandate to help unpack the serveware brought me around the decorative screens, behind which a makeshift kitchen was humming with tension. An army of cooks, clad in white, rushed silently around, hauling trays out of ovens, tonging vegetable sculptures onto rows of tiny plates. By the time the musicians showed up, maybe an hour later, I knew the truth. This was going to be an outdoor party. All of it. The kitchen, the entertainment. Even the bathrooms were out here, discreetly tucked away in a little metal cabin behind a giant topiary of the Posterity Initiative umbrella.

What an unbelievable stroke of luck.

But my relief was short-lived. What would Mila say when she came upstairs and found out?

Before long, the elevator doors were parting to release streams of extravagant strangers. In they came, suits and silks and feathered skirts broken up by flashes of pale leg and collarbone. Jangling hands swooped in to snatch crackers and little finger sandwiches from the trays I held out in front of me as I hurried to and from the kitchen. Every now and again, a thin heel, kicking free from the train of a dress, would lance across my path. Bezi Duras was among us, seemingly everywhere at once—shaking hands, admiring silhouettes, urging people to help themselves to more. I couldn't go three feet in any direction without bumping into some part of her and then hurrying away with my head down. Did she already know it had been us in that abandoned house, one two three? Or would she have to meet my eye to realize it?

Perhaps the enchanted didn't carry knowledge over from one part of their life to the other. I needed to make Mila understand that this was the best we could hope for. There was no sign of her yet, for which I was grateful, because there was no time to think about what I would say to her.

But there *was* a yellow dress. A distant flash of it startled me from between the columns of dark finery. It was draped in cheerful cascades around a slender Black woman who sat at the corner of the bar. I found an ice bucket that needed refilling, and scurried closer. From behind, the woman had been stoically elegant, all nape and shoulders and sculptural updo. But she was younger than she was trying to appear, pert-nosed and apple-cheeked. She sat alone, peering suspiciously down into her napkin. One of my little crackers lay there, half-eaten, and she was trying to illuminate it with a decorative votive.

"That's caviar," I said. "Apparently."

"So I hear," the woman said. She frowned at me. "What are you, twelve? Are you supposed to be on that side of a bar?" I held up my bucket, and she nodded. "You're one of the Repop kids."

"Sorry?"

"Repop. Like my new friend Sherni over there?"

She pointed back through the crowd. Her new friend Sherni was a girl maybe half my age, at the far end of the balcony. She was dressed in a shapeless gray frock and snugged between an uneasy-looking pair who must have been her parents. The cloud of her brown curls had been vised into a ponytail with considerable force. Whenever she reached back to jiggle her scalp, one of her mothers would bat her hand away. All the while, the three of them held the same tight smile directed at nobody, the same look of apprehension as food tray after food tray passed them by.

"I don't know Sherni," I said. "I live downstairs. My mom's the super."

"So, you're Repop."

The word sounded right to me, but I didn't have time to acknowledge it because Mrs. Sayez materialized out of nowhere in a path-clearing tulle gown.

"Jane!" Her arm went around the young woman, who met the embrace sideways, holding her drink out of the way. "Thank you for coming."

A volley of perfunctory banalities followed: Of course, Jane wouldn't miss it for the world. How was Mrs. Sayez? How were her kids? Fine, fine, upriver—and how was Jane? All right, a little worried about fires in the West, for her mother's sake, but that couldn't be helped. It certainly couldn't—though we were all doing our best, weren't we? Here more than anywhere. And what a beautiful dress Jane was wearing! So festive.

"Like Dancing Girl," I said. They both looked at me. I had the bucket full by then, and a distant, jacketed arm was waving me over. But now that Mrs. Sayez had seen me, there was no getting away. "Silvia! Have you met Jane?"

"Yes," I said. And then, because I was feeling embarrassed about having been possibly misunderstood, I ventured again. "You look like Dancing Girl in that dress. You know—on the billboard?" I struck a pose with an invisible lamp.

"Ah yes!" Jane smiled. "The deliverance dance."

Mrs. Sayez looked around. "Where's your mother?"

"Somewhere," I said, pretending to scan the crowd.

"Well, you must get her over here to meet Jane. Jane, this is Silvia—she's one of our program's great success stories. She came from Paraiso last year, and now she lives right here at the Morningside." Jane held out a hand. I wiped mine and shook it. "Jane works for the *Island City Sentinel*—she's here to write about the fundraiser. Tell her how you like the program!"

"I love the program," I said, stupidly.

Jane nodded. "I'm glad to hear that," she said. "*I love the fundraiser." She looked down at the contents of her napkin. "I haven't had caviar before."

"Bezi wanted to treat us all to something special," Mrs. Sayez said. "Isn't it marvelous?"

"I didn't know it was legal."

"Well—this kind is. This time of year, anyway. I think."

The party went on. Sauce spatter. Tubs of dirty dishes. I had just delivered a champagne saber to the headwaiter when Mila found me. She was scowling. "It's outdoors!" she shouted, startling a nearby violinist, who quickly caught up with the tempo again.

"I know," I said, feigning misery. "I know."

She stood looking around. "Maybe things will move inside later?"

"When?"

"God, Sil—every party has a *later*."

"I doubt it." I pointed toward the screens. "Everything's out here. The kitchen, the bathrooms—everything."

No version of Mila was less pleasant than the recently thwarted one. She stood there, chewing the inside of her cheek. "Shit," she said.

I went on watching her. This wasn't so bad. There was resignation in her rage.

But then her eye caught something in the crowd, and with a quick "I can fix this," she sped away from me and straight over to a flock of swaying suits, among whom, I now realized, stood Bezi Duras.

"Excuse me," Mila said. "I need to use the bathroom."

Imagine the horror. Me standing there in my apron with a tray of garlicky snails on my shoulder, unable to look away while Bezi Duras stopped short. The long fingers of her left hand emerged from a balloon sleeve to rest on Mila's arm. The other hand pointed toward the little metal cabin behind the topiary.

"You don't want me to go in there," I heard Mila say. "Your other guests won't appreciate it."

"You're funny," Bezi Duras said.

"Can I go in your house?"

Bezi bent down, down, down until she was crouching face-to-face with Mila. "I tell you what. You can go in my house—if you ask me in Ours." She smiled oddly. "And just for formality's sake, I'd like to hear you address me as the 'thou' I'm owed. None of this 'you, your, you're' shit."

Mila tilted her head. "I don't know what *you're* talking about," she said.

I had never admired anyone more, nor respected anyone less. There she was: Mila, with her night-creature eyes and her deranged boldness, trampling all my carefully laid guardrails, yanking on Bezi Duras's sleeve in the middle of a party. And what had she used this perilous moment of connection to reveal? An urgent and fictitious need for the lavatory.

Bezi Duras got up and turned away. Mila came smugly back.

"I wish I knew what's wrong with you," I said. Her lips moved, but I couldn't hear her. "What?"

She leaned in close, and forced something cool and jagged into my hand. "Here you go."

"What is this?"

"Her key." She shrugged. "I picked her pocket."

She pulled the snail tray out of my hands, flung it onto the nearest table, and took my arm. For the next thirty seconds, her braid was all I saw as I tailed her through murmuring knots of strangers. Behind the bathroom, through the rosebushes, up the steps, and around the corner to Bezi Duras's front door.

Mila's cheeks were flushed. "Do it quick," she said. "Before someone sees us."

The key was still in my fist, but I hadn't had time to untangle what it was she wanted us to do. "You mean—break in?"

She rolled her eyes. "It's not breaking in if you *have* a key."

"But we weren't *given* it. You stole it."

"So what? I'll put it back." She looked over her shoulder. "Hurry up."

I stood there with the unearned key in my numb fingers, with the violin-tinged croon of the party behind me, and thought of the dim kitchen on the abandoned island, and the hollow-eyed boys. "I can't," I said. "I won't. We don't want to do this."

A sheen of fury brightened Mila's temples. "I should've known you'd say that." Then the key was out of my hand and in hers.

"Don't!" I said, but she was already turning it. There was some resistance apparently, because she looked over her shoulder again and then moved into me so that she could put more of her weight behind the effort. There was still time to stop her. It wouldn't have been terribly hard—she was hunched over, and so invested in the effort of twisting the key against its lock that her whole hand had gone completely white. Then her face did, too. She stepped back.

All that remained in her hand was a twisted brass nub. "It broke."

"How?" I cried wretchedly.

"I don't know—I don't know. I must've . . . it must be the wrong key." She bent to the door and tried to dig the tip of her nail into the keyhole, but it was no use.

"I told you," I hissed. "Didn't I *tell* you?"

"Oh, *shut up*, Sil. You with your earnings and your balances. You sound insane, you know that?"

She lashed the remaining half of the key onto the ground. I heard it sing where it struck—once, twice—and then fall silent. I dived into the bushes after it, dimly aware that Mila had already left my side. Back to the party, no doubt, perhaps even to tell Bezi Duras what we had done.

I was still on my knees, feeling around, when the hum of the party began to subside. They had seen me. They were stopping, one by one, in confusion and discomfort at the sight of this girl who did not belong—not in this building, not on this rooftop, and certainly not in the dirt on all fours. But when I looked up, nobody was facing my way at all. The entire party had turned to bunch around Bezi Duras. She was standing in the middle of the avenue of trees, striking her champagne flute for silence.

"Excuse me," she said, in a voice that seemed too soft for oratory. "Thank you all for coming. Thank you especially to all the caterers and waitstaff and cooks who have worked so hard to make tonight's gathering a success."

"It's wonderful, Bezi!" a woman shouted.

"Thank you—isn't it? How about this shrimp? I've never met such a well-traveled crustacean." She waited for the laughter to subside. "My gratitude to the members of the Repopulation Program, and the very special guests they brought here. We have the Fayed family from Atam. The Burgos family from Aguila. We thank you for tolerating our use of you for this spectacle. If any of you are sufficiently disgusted, please know I would be glad to finance your relocation to quite frankly anywhere else in the country." Bezi let the applause and the ripple of laughter—frenzied, a little too loud—die down. "Many of you have been asking why I volunteered to host tonight. I suppose that should make me rather embarrassed. When one is faced with the same question over and over, one must reckon with the kinds of things one has allowed to proliferate about oneself. And I suppose your questions shouldn't come as a surprise—I *have* been reluctant, over the years, to involve myself in the Repopulation Program's efforts."

Mrs. Sayez whooped. She was drunk. "Thanks for coming to your senses, Bezi."

"Thank *you*, Clare. The truth is: once I saw who was going to be in attendance—the Patersons, the Wallfields, not to mention journalists from outlets I both admire and mistrust— I found it impossible to say no. Especially because it seemed the best imaginable opportunity to debut my own latest project, which is intimately tied to the program's efforts." More applause, thinner this time. A line of waiters stepped up and in unison pulled down the long drape that had extended all the way around the balustrade, revealing a wire line along which huge photographs had been strung. Everyone pressed forward to get closer, affording me the opportunity to slip into the crowd. Once there, however, I found it a great deal more difficult to maneuver out—which is how I wound up face-to-face with a four-by-three print of a house that looked extremely familiar. Fog surrounded it, and a yellow lamp shone in the distance. I had a sudden, gutting feeling of violation—as though I once again knew something I shouldn't. There, through the window, was the little kitchen with its junkyard table. No sign of the woman or her boys—but then, of course, there wouldn't be.

Somewhere ahead, Bezi had begun speaking again: "Over the past two years, I have grown interested in tracking the progress of the so-called settlement structures on South Falls Island. So I started traveling there to photograph it. On foot, more or less every night. It's not far—though I do have to change my route more and more as the tide comes farther in on the North End. As you can see, if you get closer—do get closer, Joyce—most of the progress on South Falls Island has been sylvan in nature. It's all woods and brambles. There are some townhouses and schools and hospitals—most of them abandoned thirty years ago. The ones still standing are ruins, and occupied by outer island people whose families they've belonged to for decades. The images you see here are just a tiny fraction of what I've photographed. And they raise a question: Where exactly are the houseworks and blocks of apartments that are being advertised by the Repopulation Program?"

A hush had fastened over the rooftop. Uneasy stillness from everyone except Jane. She had hoisted her phone above the shining middle parts and carefully wound twists, and was thumbing the shutter as fast as she could. When a white hand appeared over her shoulder and attempted to take it from her, she wrenched her shoulder back into the offender with such force that a glass shattered several bodies away.

"Fuck off, man," she said. "Don't touch me again."

I looked around for Mila, but the suits and gowns were too dense. Somewhere up ahead, Mrs. Sayez's voice was beginning a tremulous reproach. "Bezi," I heard her say. "This isn't— right. You're not telling the whole story."

"I'm not interested in telling a story, Clare. I'm interested in asking questions that give the truth an opportunity to surface. Questions like: What does the Repopulation Program intend to do with the communities that still exist in these promised places? And what exactly is the Repopulation Program doing with all the government subsidies that are meant to go toward its projects? They're certainly not going to the people the program has promised to help. Or to the revitalization of ruined parts of the city it has promised to repopulate.

Which leads me to ask *further:* What is the nature of the hope we are selling to the people we lure here with the promise of an improved life? They work in the belief that they will be given a place to live. But where, exactly, is that place?" Bezi had begun to move along the balustrade. "Is it here, on the southernmost tip of South Falls Island—where the water is so poisonous that the area has become completely uninhabitable? Or here, at the Brightwood Station, where the jungle has grown in and the mold is two inches thick? Or here?"

Jane hopped up on a chair and called out, "Ms. Duras, did you bring us together this evening to condemn the efforts of the Repopulation Program in their entirety?"

"I'm not condemning anything," Bezi Duras said. "I'm simply taking this opportunity to ask reasonable and necessary questions, since so many people who *should* have those answers are assembled here."

"It's an ambush." A man's voice.

"Bezi," Mrs. Sayez said despairingly. "Couldn't you have come to me with these questions? This is distressing to see, and yes, it seems we have to investigate what's going on at South Falls Island, but—just because a portion of our plan seems to have hit a little snag doesn't mean we should cast aspersions on the whole thing. There's nothing wrong with wanting people to come back."

"But, Clare, we're promising something that doesn't exist. A city on the verge of a turnaround, when in fact it's just the dying gasp of a time that's all but over. We bring them here *not* to build the city back up—but to hold the edges while it finishes falling."

"But we live here, too."

"Yes. But it's one thing for *you* to live here, Clare. You've lived here all your life, and you have the means to make continuing to live here bearable for yourself. So do I. But you've lured these people here under false pretenses, and you're keeping them around with promises you can't fulfill. And the whole thing is so nakedly obvious that a solitary person, moving on foot a few times a week, can find evidence of it without much effort."

Slowly, whispers began to break up the silence that followed. One throng of partygoers drifted closer to the photographs. Another shuffled for the exit. I had the feeling that I should make my escape before the party thinned out enough to expose me. I cut into a cluster of dresses to my left and let myself be carried along toward the elevator, an innocuous presence, perhaps somebody's badly dressed child.

AROUND MIDNIGHT, IT seems, Bezi Duras showed the last of her guests to the elevator. The waitstaff were packing up the tables and winding up the twinkle lights. The orchestra had long since gone home. Bezi took her shoes off and walked with them in hand up the stairs toward the door. That was when she felt around in her pocket and discovered that her key was missing. The remaining staff scrambled to sweep the rooftop for it, to no avail. Then somebody offered to pick the lock—which led to the discovery that it was already jammed.

My mother painted this picture for me the following morning while she hurried into fresh clothes on her way to the penthouse to meet the locksmith.

"What does it all mean?" I asked her.

"Sounds like somebody took her key and tried to break into her place."

Somebody. "That's terrible," I said, stretching my vowels a little too much.

"She's raging," my mother said. "She had to spend the night with Mrs. Sayez."

I could just picture it: Mrs. Sayez looping her arm through Bezi's, urging her downstairs, offering her tea, trying to make amends. And Bezi's sons? How had they spent the night? Had they crowded around the door, howling for their mother, until the rising sun turned them back into dogs? This was exactly what we needed: an enraged Vila, whom we had separated from her children. I felt sick.

My mother tugged a brush through her hair. "How was the party?"

"Fine."

"Did you get enough to eat?"

"Mmm," I said.

"I'm sorry I wasn't here." She crouched down and started lacing up her boots. "Did anything interesting happen?"

I looked at her. Of course. She didn't know. My mother hadn't been there, or spoken to anyone, or tuned in to the Dispatch yet, so she didn't know about Bezi Duras's project, the murky photographs, what they revealed, and what those revelations might mean. She didn't know that in this world—hers, and May's, and everybody else's, apparently even Mila's—the painter Bezi Duras had been going to South Falls Island to prove that something on which our lives depended did not exist. There were no parks, no houses, no gardens for tending, no new schools. I had seen it with my own eyes. I had been there without even realizing it, blundering with Mila through a haunted fog, because I had been after the world beneath the world—the one in which the most important thing about Bezi Duras was that she was a Vila.

But my mother did not live in that world. I had never managed to gather enough evidence to invite her into it. And now, it was too late. This bigger, more pertinent reality had displaced everything. I couldn't untangle all its implications, but I still knew what it meant for us. No house. A tenure at the Morningside that would stretch on and on, perhaps forever. The possibility of not getting into a real school. And Tufaah? Forget Tufaah. I thought of my mother's letter, sitting unopened in some drawer—or, worse, Safiya al-Abdi's reply winging its way back to us with a note of thanks or, God forbid, an acceptance of terms. My mother's poor heart, which had made the mistake of daring to hope.

She was still looking at me. "Sil?"

I smiled and gave a little shrug. "Bezi showed us some pictures."

I would have to tell her. Perhaps not right away—but certainly before Mrs. Sayez had the opportunity to come downstairs and honey it all up for her.

Tonight, I told myself. But then the locksmith didn't appear until four-thirty that afternoon, by which time my mother, as a precaution, had called in to hand off her diving assignment to somebody else. The locksmith chatted her up while he worked, lingering, trying to make her laugh. It was almost eight by the time she got back downstairs. She hadn't slept the night before, so she was too tired to talk, too tired to do anything but eat her rations and fall asleep so deeply that she missed the call from the salvage company the following morning. And then, because she didn't want her foreman to think she was slipping, she accepted the insurance dive at the Martinique Hotel—yes, that one. The one you've heard about.

THAT AFTERNOON, WHILE MY MOTHER'S SALVAGE team was drilling in the flooded tunnels of the Martinique, a piece of siding the size of an infield sheared off the front of the building. It fell, creating a wave that ran the whole length of the flooded sub-basement, and the force of it knocked out two load-bearing pylons, which also fell, trapping the divers in the freezing dark below. Two of them—Roth Marrin and Vic Aslo—swam out. My mother and three others did not.

"We got brothers down there," Roth Marrin said when the evening news crew swung the camera into his battered face. He was wrapped in a thermal blanket, wild-eyed and sobbing, and he was confused. He had forgotten to say "sister." We got a sister down there.

They had known her for five months. Whoever had shot footage of the collapse had begun filming after it was already underway, after the first boom of debris hitting the water made them look up. What I saw of it started about twelve seconds later—twelve seconds, give or take, after my mother had died or become doomed. I didn't know yet which it was. Rescue efforts were commencing, they said, and would continue through the night. Through the night.

I suppose it would be reasonable to guess that I immediately sent a fun card heavenward—WHAT WOULD MAKE YOUR NEW HOME EVEN BETTER? *The return of my mother, please.* But it did not seem safe in that moment to ask the vengeful universe for anything more. I had been asking and asking and asking, despite having been given so much already—and the cumulative effect of all that asking was that the only thing I really cared about and depended on had been taken away.

On television, black helicopters were beginning to circle the staved-in remains of the Martinique Hotel. An expert called in to the Dispatch to weigh in on the dangers of the salvage-diving industry, how difficult it was to insure workers, since incidents like this could happen anytime.

Incidents, he said.

Out into the hallway again, down the elevator, around the lobby, seeing no one. Into the pool room. I turned the lights on and stood there, looking down into the glimmering water. What a mistake it had been to not move the perfume bottle holding down this part of my protective triad when I'd first thought of it. Would there be any point in moving it now? Or was it actually doing its part to somehow preserve my mother? To keep my hands from doing something calamitous, I knelt down beside the skimmer basket and put my face on the cool, rough tiles. I could hear the water in the filter sloshing gently. I mustn't open the basket. If I did, I would certainly move the bottle. And then whatever small good my protection might still be working on my mother's behalf would be completely obliterated. One two three.

I headed instead into my mother's office and touched the shelves she had organized. I turned up the radio. Some intolerable down-islander was flogging goods he had found in his mother's attic—at this hour, in this crisis.

"There you have it, folks," the Dispatcher said, when the caller paused for breath. "Vintage Bundt cake pans as far as the eye can see. And while we wait for our next caller, does anyone have an update on the Martinique situation?"

A voice from the North End belonging to a Carlos called in. He had the names of the three men who had been trapped. He was getting reports that there'd been a fourth, but he didn't know who they were.

I picked up the phone on my aunt's desk. I knew the number by heart. While the line rang, a small army of callers rambled about the unfortunate predictability of the situation and the need for more oversight. Someone living just across the street from the Martinique had been watching pieces of its façade crack and fall away for months. Finally, the ringing paused and there was a click.

"Drowned City Dispatch, what are you calling about?"

"The Martinique collapse," I said. "I'm calling about the fourth diver."

"Hold, please." A moment later, the voice on the radio and the voice in my ear merged into one. "Well, friends, it seems we have an update on the fourth diver—who am I speaking with?"

"Silvia," I said. "Sil."

There was a pause on the other end of the line. "Go ahead, Sil. What can you tell us?"

"The fourth diver is actually my mother," I said. "I thought you should know because—well. Because it's her."

"What's her name?"

I told him, and he repeated it several times for whoever was just tuning in. "What else do you want us to know about your mother?"

My mind went blank. "She's little," I said. "Like a fairy person."

"We'll be keeping our lights on for you, Silvia."

"Thank you," I said, and hung up.

I stood there in the office among my mother's things, hot with embarrassment. Of all the things I could have said.

When I got to the courtyard, I found a folded sheet of paper taped to the ground just inside the gate. SNOOPY, I'M SO SORRY. COME TO 55 WEST PARK PLACE, MY DOOR IS OPEN. LAM.

For a moment, this didn't seem like a terrible idea. West Park Place wasn't far. It would be quiet, I decided. A neat little apartment, modestly but carefully furnished. May would be the kind of person who collected books and kept an antique teakettle and had all mismatched tableware, lucky survivors of years of haphazard dishwashing. Exactly the kind of setting where I might actually be able to fall asleep. But I wasn't sure I had the strength to climb into my own bed, let alone pack a bag and go roaming around the city alone. On the other hand, if May came back. If he grew worried and swung by the Morningside one more time before turning in—I could see myself following him. It would not be such a labor, to follow a person I trusted. It would not require much mind or body.

But he didn't come back, and after a while I went back upstairs. The news was still on, still playing the same twenty-second clip of dust plumes rising from the Martinique. Daytime in that footage, with a kind of glazed brightness that deadened the camera lens and made the whole thing seem fake.

AROUND TWO IN the morning, there was a knock at the door. It was Mila. She brought me upstairs, where her mother made

us tea. From their south-facing living room window, we
watched the electric sweep of the search helicopter weaving
between the buildings down-island. When I remember this
moment, I remember the thrum of the blades, though I know
I couldn't possibly have heard them. I guess that much light
looks so loud, you're surprised to find that it doesn't produce
any sound. "Eat," Mila's mother said. "Eat something." When I
finally bit into the sandwich she had given me, I felt sorry for
Mila. My mother was no cook, but at least she knew to salt her
butter. Knew how to crisp the edges of even the blandest
canned spread. That something was deficient about this meal
was not totally lost on Mila's mother. She kept glancing at me
and then at her daughter, and then, despite her best efforts,
back at the darkened hallway behind her that led into the bedrooms. After twenty minutes of this, Mila struck the table with
her palm. "Oh, Mother." She turned to me. "Sil, my father is
going to join us."

She disappeared down the hallway and returned moments
later with a man I'd never seen before. He had a large square
face and was dressed comfortably in soft slacks and a button-
down. He looked, in my mother's parlance, like a gentleman—
which I had always taken to mean a person of good manners
and easy graces.

"Good evening, Sil," he said. "I'm glad to meet you at last.
I'm sorry to hear about the trouble with your mother."

I thanked him, and he sat down beside me while Mila put
together a final sandwich for him, and then we went on sitting
in silence, as though I didn't have a thousand questions about
him. Mila had been awaiting his arrival like a cat on a
windowsill—why hadn't she mentioned that it was imminent?
Why hadn't he been at the table or in the kitchen to greet me?
If Mila hadn't blown her fuse, would they have brought him

out at all—or had the plan been to keep him somewhere back there in one of the bedrooms until I finished my dinner and withdrew downstairs?

"Have you been in Island City long, sir?"

"About five days." He had a slow, tired smile. "Mila tells me you're the very best of friends." Mila nodded and, to my surprise, petted me on the head. "You must stay with us until your mother comes home, of course."

I hadn't planned for this eventuality, but clearly they had. A brand-new toothbrush awaited me in the bathroom. A sleeping bag had been laid out for me beside Mila's bed. I dreaded our moment of inevitable solitude, Mila up on the bed and I on the floor, and nothing but the half-dark and the way Mila was going to gut me with whatever question, or observation, or misfired endearment she had been chewing over during our meal. But, to my surprise, she fell asleep right away, leaving me to my thoughts, which wandered for a long time, until I finally gave up, eased out of the sleeping bag, and returned to the living room.

Mila's father was still at the dining table. He patted the chair beside him, and we sat together and watched the wandering lights in the distance.

"There's only one helicopter now," I said, feeling that if I voiced it, I might invite contradiction. Keeping it quiet in my heart was certain to make the worst possible outcome true.

"That's right," Mila's father said. "But sometimes that's because they have more information and have narrowed the search. They know they only need one." His huge face came swiveling toward me. A hand rested on my head. "It does not mean they're giving up."

I felt as though he'd taken my whole heart right out of my chest, given it a squeeze, and handed it back.

"Are you hungry?"

"I'm all right," I lied.

"You don't like spread sandwiches."

"I do!" But he wasn't buying my protestation. I looked down at my feet. "I like them better than nothing."

He clapped my shoulder. "Well, let's see if we can do better than 'better than nothing.'"

From a high kitchen cupboard, he removed a jar whose label I couldn't make out, and spooned a dark, glossy spread across two slices of bread: one for each of us. We ate these miraculous sandwiches, full of sweet, nutty cream, dipped in milk.

"What is this?"

"The best thing in the world," he said. "Milk and hazelnut cream."

"Wow."

"Isn't it good?"

"I've never had anything so good."

But then, a widening doubt. There I was, on the thirty-second floor of the Morningside, wondering if it might be possible to negotiate another milk-and-hazelnut sandwich, while my mother—my mother who, despite everything, had never let me go hungry, who wanted nothing more than to heap food onto my plate in a little place of our very own—was somewhere below, in that electric maze down-island. They were turning in for the night down there, or taking a break while the tide rolled in, or planning their next move. Or admitting to one another, perhaps, how hopeless the search was. How hopeless it had always been. And I could see it all. The entirety of that collapsed building was visible to me from where I sat—which meant that my mother was, too. I was looking right at her. She was right there, in my line of sight. Merely obscured by distance and rubble and water. She was right there, right *there*.

And if she wasn't dead, she was thinking of me. And I? I was thinking of milk-and-hazelnut sandwiches, and how comfortable it was up here, and how lucky Mila was to have been raised by this kind man.

He noticed my tears right away. "Oh, honey," he said, and patted my hand. "Whatever you're thinking right now, stop. It does your mother no good at all. You must stop."

He got a jigsaw puzzle out of the credenza and spread the pieces all over the table. We sat across from each other, trying to corral them by color into quadrants that resembled the picture on the box: a woman in white raising her hands sunward while a confusion of wild roses unfurled down her body.

"This is really beautiful," I said.

"It's a picture of a story from Mila's homeland," her father said. "This is the pagan goddess Remiša, calling her daughter, the Sun, higher into the heavens for the birth of summer."

He edged a huge, rose-clogged puzzle piece in my direction and I dropped it in the pile designated for my eventual battle with the lower-right corner of the board. "Where are you from, Sil?"

"Paraiso."

He didn't bother to hide his surprise. "Really?" He wanted to know where in Paraiso we had lived, and this I managed to parry back because I could still remember the little balcony overlooking the eastern edge of the city, the ancient market with its overabundance of spring onions sharpening the air as the yellow afternoon turned into a furnace.

"Piazza dei Folletti."

"Did you like going to the *festa* in the springtime?"

"We never went."

"You must keep up your mother tongue," he said. "It's rare to find someone to practice with."

"It's not my mother tongue," I said.

"What is?"

"We were in Vesvere for a while."

"Are you from Vesvere, then?"

Was I? Was I from Vesvere? Of course not. He was asking because he knew, or at least sensed, the answer. He wasn't going to let me get away with vague, curt, twist-away responses. And he knew more than the people who'd asked before, who were asking so they could fill out a blank space on a form or place my accent so they could put it, and me, out of their minds.

"We came from Sarobor," I finally said. "Right before the war."

How did I expect him to react? I can't remember now. I guess I had spent so long in the grip of my mother's cautionary prescriptions that I hadn't gotten as far as imagining what would happen when I finally told someone the truth. Because it had always been something I must not do, it had likewise always felt unavoidable—a mistake I couldn't help but make. An inevitability, burning somewhere down the road of my life. But I had imagined neither the moment of revelation nor its consequences.

Mila's father didn't seem to mind. He simply smiled a little and said, "Sarobor was a beautiful place, once," which edged me closer to tears again. "I went there, many years ago. It wasn't too far from Uvala, you know. Where Mila was born."

"My mother and I came through Uvala."

"Do you remember it? No, you would've been in a swaddle. Well, I'm not surprised. You and your mother were among thousands. Tens of thousands. You couldn't get to places like Paraiso and Vesvere without going through Uvala. A hard thing, you know, for a town that small. Not easy for us to feed and clothe so many drifters."

"She always said it was the most dangerous part of the journey."

"Of course it was. Very dangerous. People on the move, with no home of their own, are always very dangerous. A lot of criminals, a lot of young people feeling desperate. No papers, no accountability, no way to tell the good from the bad. Those were hard times."

I wiped my eyes and nodded, though I wasn't sure we were talking about the same dangers.

"Your mother is going to be all right," he said, in Ours—or in a dialect that brushed up against Ours, faintly accented but still close enough for me to understand.

"I don't speak Ours outside the house."

"Well, we're inside the house."

"I guess we are."

"But I know what you mean. I don't like Mila speaking it, either. That's why I've taught her hardly any."

"Why?"

He thought about it. "Because Ours is a big language. Like a river with a lot of little channels. And anything about these little channels can let people guess where you're from. The way you stretch your vowels lets me know you're from Sarobor. The way I stretch mine tells you I'm from Uvala. And based on those little channels alone, some people—not everybody, but some people—might start making assumptions about one another."

"What kind of assumptions?"

"Well—what it means that you're from Sarobor, for instance. What side you were on during the war. Why you left and came here. That kind of thing."

"That's dangerous."

"It's always dangerous to give people a way to tell themselves

stories about you before they get to know you. Always." He patted my shoulder. "So mind your mother. She's not wrong."

But she had been, I thought. She *had* been wrong. She had
made it seem as though breaking open that secret, uttering a
few sentences in Ours to someone other than her, would be
like stepping off a cliff—terrifying and terminal. But instead, a
perfectly normal conversation had ensued. It had brought me
into the confidences and wisdom of a gentle and caring person.
And as a result, if my mother perished out there in the deluge
of the lower city, I would not be alone.

She had to be told. I would explain, if she came home, that
she had been wrong to be so doubtful, so reserved. There were
people around who knew our language and loved Back Home.
Her secretiveness had confined us to solitude, to a loneliness
that had ruled us both for years and then turned out to be
unnecessary—but there was time now to change that. Of
course, my mother would meet this news with suspicion and
anger. But she would eventually soften up to the truth. I would
pull her with me into its warmth.

And what if she didn't come back? What if all that noise and
strobing movement down-island was for nothing? What if she
was dead already, gone from me since the moment of collapse?
One two three. The search would drag on for a few more days,
and then the timbre of conversations about it would slowly
begin to change. The Dispatcher would start talking about my
mother in the past tense. This removal from the present would
become ornamented with a few details about her life. Perhaps
her veterinary ambitions. Perhaps her place of birth. Perhaps
by then somebody—some caller who had tuned in when I gave
my mother's name—would remember that there might be a
daughter somewhere worth checking up on. It would probably
be Mrs. Sayez. She would put me in her spare room, and fuss

over me. And when whatever authorities were responsible for orphaned children came to take me off her hands, she would tell everyone how she had tried to save me. Well, maybe I wouldn't give her the opportunity. Maybe I'd pack up a couple of things from Ena's place and sneak into the boiler room and live hidden in the walls of the Morningside, subsisting on pigeons, rattling the pipes, leaving behind cryptic fun cards for the residents to find. WHAT IS YOUR LEVEL OF SATISFACTION WITH YOUR NEW HOME? *Low.* WHAT DO YOU LIKE MOST ABOUT YOUR NEW HOME? *Slowly driving Miss Calorann mad.* WHAT WOULD MAKE YOUR NEW HOME EVEN BETTER? *More dead pigeons.* I could become one of those feral cases we sometimes heard about, a sort of string-haired half-being that appeared to new residents, who, having arrived in a restored city many years in the future, would catch a glimpse of me behind some long-closed door and become isolated by their belief in my existence.

May probably wouldn't let that happen. He'd get tired of waiting outside the gate, find a way into the building, and bring me down to 55 West Park Place. And then what?

Maybe—and this seemed the most preferable, and therefore unlikeliest, of all scenarios—maybe Mila's parents would take me in. A providential turn of events: Mila and I, born in neighboring cities but spun away from each other by the derangement of war, eventually reunited as sisters by heartbreak in a distant land that was becoming our own. What a story for the Dispatch.

WHEN MILA CAME HOME FROM SCHOOL THE FOL-
lowing afternoon and found that her father and I had finished
the puzzle without her, she was bemused.

"What happened here?" she said, studying the woman in the
finished piece.

"We got carried away!" her father said.

"He's trying very hard to take your mind off things," Mila
told me later, when we were alone in her room. "Don't mind
it—he can get annoying."

"He's been really kind."

"But puzzles won't do the trick." She clapped my shoulder.
"Come on."

I didn't really understand what we were doing at first. Not
when she led me downstairs into the back alley courtyard, nor
when she held her hand out for the penthouse elevator key.
And even while we stood there in the tight little swaying car,
my mind wouldn't quite draw sense out of what was happening. A haze of exhaustion had overwhelmed me. I felt as though
I'd been breathing smoke, and my brain couldn't get free of the
lull. Soon enough, I would pass out—and when I woke up, all
would be clear again: what had happened to my mother, and

what would happen to me, and all things, good and bad, that would follow these eventualities. One two three.

I believe I did say, "Let's not!"—only once, when Mila was already picking the lock of Bezi Duras's place, and only because I found myself sharply aware for the first time that we were, in fact, just kids.

"But I've been practicing," Mila said. "For you."

"Why?" I felt suddenly, irrationally angry. "You don't really believe any of this stuff. You don't care if it's true."

"But we *have* to see if you're right."

I watched her struggle with the lock. "I don't even know how we would go about that."

Mila winked. "Ah, but remember? I put something in her pocket back on the island."

"What is it?"

"I can't wait to show you."

The evening light behaved differently in the penthouse on thirty-three. It seemed to move upward, from floor to ceiling, traveling from mote to shining mote. Bezi Duras's place was like no other apartment in the Morningside. No hallways. No bedrooms hidden from view. Just one pure white outspread rectangle with a gleaming kitchen near the front and an erratic proliferation of decorative walls that came nowhere near the ceiling and seemed to exist only to hang paintings upon. And there *were* paintings. May had said there would be, and there were. On every wall. Stacked like lumber in every corner. Hidden behind chairs and under sofas. Paintings from Bezi's early days and her later ones—thickly textured and raucous in their color, fragmented celebrations of something that felt both distant and alive. Your eye, scanning the room, would sweep across an abstraction of wild colors and translate to your mind an image it hadn't actually seen: a trumpet, a bicycle, a naked girl shaking a tambourine. Farther in, the forms became more legible. Thin, gold-flecked women smiling tautly down from woodland thrones, cliffside thrones, thrones in cathedrals and on beaches. There was a small array of charcoal rook crane studies. Mr. Payne's ballerinas. And the photographs, of course, from the night of the ill-fated party. The smell of all that varnish and dried oil would choke the sight from your eyes were it not for that impossibly high ceiling, from which the black chandeliers hung like huge, sleeping spiders.

Mila didn't seem terribly impressed with any of it. "Where do you think she keeps her coats?"

She found a hallway rack and started riffling through the hangers, rummaging in pockets and bags.

"What are you looking for?" I said.

"You'll see."

For a while, it seemed that I would not. But then her hand closed on something that made her whole face change. She loosed an excited little cry and held the thing out to me. I blinked at it stupidly, the tethers between my vision and my brain slack and numb.

"Mouthwash?" I said, confused. She stood there looking triumphant. "I don't understand."

"Don't you recognize it?"

I looked again. "No."

For the first time, her face fell. She brought the bottle closer for inspection. "No, Sil—look. This is the thing from the pool."

"What thing from the pool?"

Everything in me went still. The perfume bottle. It hadn't been in the skimmer basket at all. I had been reaching out and reaching out into empty space, one two nothing, all this time. While we were on the island. While my mother was diving. And last night, as I lay facedown by the pool, willing myself to resist moving the talisman to somewhere it might do more good, it had been gone. Not even up here but in the pocket of some forsaken coat on South Falls Island. No wonder the building had collapsed. No wonder my mother was dead.

"I told you to put it back," I said.

"Oh, Sil."

"When did you take it?"

Mila shrugged.

"When?"

"Does it matter?"

She turned her back to me and wandered farther into the room. As though the idea that I might bash her skull in for what she had done hadn't occurred to her at all.

"Sil," she called. "Come look at this!"

Leaning up against the west wall, surrounded on all sides by smaller works, stood the biggest canvas I'd ever seen. Wide as a city gate. The strokes of which it was composed were quick and ragged, but the scene was easy enough to make out: a young woman, thin-lipped and anciently inhuman, was crossing a bridge from some little riverside town. Around her stood three empty spaces where the paint seemed to have been scoured away. Three empty spaces—for three enchanted sons. This, I suddenly knew, was where they lived. This was how she had brought them here from Back Home, all those years ago.

But they were not in their human form now. They were rousing themselves from where they lay sprawled out on the tarp below the painted girl's feet, sitting up one by one—as surprised, I think, to see us as we were to see them.

What did I know about dogs in general? They had strong skulls and weak stomachs. What did I know about these dogs in particular? They were not dogs at all. They were boys—and like all of us, they had been punished. And they lived in a schism of mind and body, knowing one life, living another, save for those few precious and undetermined hours when both halves combined and they could live only as themselves. They were not themselves now. They were flat yellow eyes and wide, white teeth. And they were standing up.

What would have happened had Bezi not come back at that exact moment, I really can't say. We probably would've ended up as one of those tragic statistics you read about in the paper that teach you what kind of being is safe and what kind is not. But there she was, in the doorway behind us. And there we were, Mila and I, caught between her and the dogs.

"Explain yourselves," said Bezi Duras. She dropped her bags on the counter, and the dogs coursed past us and went to sit at her feet.

"We wanted to see your paintings," Mila said.

"I see." She leaned back against the counter. "You—you were at my party. What's your name?"

"Mila."

"Mila what?"

"Mila from downstairs."

"You were the one who tried to break in here that night—weren't you? The one who broke the lock?"

"No."

"No? You must admit that's hard to believe, given that you're in here right now."

"We just wanted to see your paintings."

"That's all you have to say?"

"Your work is quite interesting."

"What a generous observation." They stared at each other. "Tell me again, in Ours, how interesting my work is."

"I don't know what you mean."

"You're like a stone, aren't you? Not a soft thing in you, all the way down."

I stood invisibly by. Bezi Duras did not look at me. She was peripherally aware, I'm sure, of another body in the room. A taller body, somewhere behind Mila. But Mila, really, was all she saw. Mila was memorable. She had picked her out of the hazy impressions of all our run-ins—because Mila had announced herself. She had charged in and made their acquaintance hostile from the beginning. And in that hostility, she had found acknowledgment. And, if I really admitted it to myself, a certain amount of admiration. It sickened me. Admiration, after she had done what she had done, all for the sake of seeing what would happen. All this time, I'd thought that if I stayed on the outskirts, if I adhered to the rules that Ena had set out, the answers I sought would find me when the time was right. When some cosmic calendar aligned. But now I wasn't sure of this at all. Now it seemed far more likely that the role I was meant to play was intermediary. I was here not to receive the knowledge but to bring Mila and Bezi Duras together. Because Mila was the one Bezi Duras recognized. The one Bezi Duras admired. And for all this, I had lost my mother to the darkness of death.

I knew it, and I could not breathe.

So what did I say, standing at last in that pale cloister into which I'd been striving to be invited all this time? "I know we didn't earn the right to be here."

Bezi Duras finally looked at me. "That's certainly true."

"But you see," I said. "My mother."

"I heard. I'm sorry. But that doesn't excuse or explain what you've done."

Something had condensed in the air. I saw Bezi and I thought of the Vila, high up on Modra Gora, impossibly alone and wishing only to remain so, asking tribute of those who wouldn't let her be.

And, in Ours, I said: "Please."

She studied me. "Please—what?" she said, in Ours, too.

"Please don't take my mother."

"I don't understand."

"Take someone else."

Over the years, and throughout my teens especially, I convinced myself that she said a lot of different things in reply. Sometimes, her response comes back to me as incredulity. When I want to remember that she had no idea what I was talking about, she says, "What?" and laughs. When I want to remember her absolving me of what I was actually asking her to do, she says, "No."

But—and this is the truth—what she actually said was: "Whom?"

BOOK IV

My Mother

WHAT ELSE HAPPENED THE WEEK I ASKED THE VILA to take someone else in my mother's stead? Rodney Earl Boone died, unsurprisingly, from a heroin overdose, and within hours offers for his gold-plated guitar pick were flying back and forth across the Dispatch. The last female Tabik turtle at the Island City Zoo died, too, leaving a male—Claude—as the species' only survivor. The administration passed a law that prohibited the teaching of what they called "extraneous histories." And on Friday, a rescue diver found my mother. The initial wave from the collapse had dragged her almost a hundred yards from where she'd been working, back and back through the roaring current, into an air pocket, and for three days and nights she had treaded water between what would turn out to be the two elevator banks of the Martinique Hotel.

There wasn't much footage of her rescue, save for a five-second clip of a black chopper racing for the upper city. The newscaster said my mother was aboard, but the truth is it could've been stock footage of any black chopper on any flight over the city. On most broadcasts, this sequence was usually followed by a few close-ups of the hospital where my mother was being treated for hypothermia, exhaustion, and some sort of arrhythmia. The only photo of her actual self surfaced two days later, when a camera crew snuck into her hospital room and caught a glimpse of her lying back against the pillows. They drove a beam of light into her swollen and unrecognizable face, and she sat up and said, "Please help my daughter—she's dead."

You may have seen this footage—it's been featured on one or two of those lists of the era's most iconic moments. In that context, my mother was often misidentified as a woman who had lost her child in an entirely different incident, another building collapse that wouldn't happen until the following year. The first time I saw it, however, I was sitting between Mila and her father on the plush sofa upstairs. I heard my mother say those words—"Please help my daughter—she's dead"—and felt my whole being drain of warmth. Mila's father hit the mute button and turned to me immediately. "People get confused in hospital," he said. "She doesn't know what she's saying."

Of course, I thought. Of course she doesn't—why would she think *I* was dead? Surely my mother knew that it was *she* who'd been carried away. Plunged into darkness, beyond all knowledge. Surely she knew that, all this time, it was *I* who'd been certain of *her* death.

She wasn't sent home for another week. Fellow divers invaded the Morningside, readying our place for her arrival. They stocked the fridge and laundered the sheets, and when the time came, a small procession of them followed the care vehicle in which she was lying all the way to the Morningside. She was already asleep by the time Mila's mother got the call that I could come downstairs. She looked so small, lying there among the plumped-up duvet and extra pillows, with the huge bedside bouquet arching over her like some watchful bower. I wasn't sure if she had always been that small, or whether the darkness had torn bites out of her while she'd been gone. The divers milled around for a while, murmuring in the kitchen, offering me tea from my own cupboard, but the last of them was gone by ten o'clock, leaving me in dread solitude with my mother. She hadn't said a word yet, or really woken up except to smile at me once, hazily, as though she recognized my face but was too far away to make out my features.

I had thought I would feel relief. But all I felt was anger. I didn't want to share silence with this small, changed person and bear witness to her helplessness. I wanted her to sit up and get well again so that I could tell her, freely and without guilt, how wrong she'd been about absolutely everything.

I glanced up from my book later that night to see that my mother was awake and looking at me.

"Are you hungry, Mama?" It seemed important to ask her before she got the chance to ask me.

"No, my heart," she said. "You?"

"Are you hurt?"

"I'm just very tired."

"Can I get you something? Some water? Some soup?"

"Have *you* had anything, Sil? You look so pale."

"Don't worry about me," I said bitterly. "You get yourself better."

I made myself scarce. Slept on the sofa, where I could hear her if she needed me, but far enough away to prevent spontaneous questioning or confessions. I feared what I might say if I started talking: "You're here on grace—you've been swapped for somebody, and I don't know who." The wellspring of my resentment was infinite, and uncertain. The feeling left me only once or twice during those first few days. Whenever it did, it was replaced by a feeling of shame so profound that my eyes clouded up, and I had to remove myself to the kitchen so she wouldn't hear me sniffling. It was not her fault that the building had collapsed. It was not her fault that whatever happened to her had diminished her so much. After all, we had both been equally certain that she was doomed, and that I would be orphaned. But she had been the one treading water in a black hole down-island, and I had been the one weeping into milk-and-hazelnut sandwiches and making hellish bargains with the enchantress upstairs. And however acute my terror or my memory, I must never share it with my mother, because she would feel responsible. She would feel guilty that she had caused me so much pain. I, in turn, hadn't caused her any pain—but I still felt guilty. How could I explain that in order to get through the past ten days, I'd had to abstract the whole ordeal so that I wouldn't think about it too much? How would I explain that I had allowed Mila to break me into Bezi Duras's apartment, where I had begged for my mother's life? These things were unutterable. I could barely admit them to myself. And certainly they would have to take a back seat to whatever it was she wanted to say: about the dark, and the cold, and the terror of her solitude down in the broken building.

But my mother never brought it up. Days passed. By and by, she started sitting, standing, shuffling to the kitchen to get her own tea. Started going out into the hallway, smiling at the residents who offered her words of welcome and vague concern, and even at the ones who made it clear that if she'd just been honest and humble enough to confine herself to the work they had provided her, she would not have been in the Martinique when the building gave way. All the while, she never said a thing about the collapse, or about how she had survived it. Never mentioned feeling a sense of relief, of fate turning her way, that might have coincided with the moment of my bargain with Bezi Duras. I waited for some hint of what had happened down there, for tears or nightmares. My mother kept most things to herself—but this incident, surely, could not be one of them.

I waited, but it never happened. Not for years, anyway—but we haven't even come back to this morning yet.

She seemed preoccupied with what I'd been doing during the three hellish days when her fate was unknown. "Were you alone the whole time? Wondering what had happened to me?" she asked me.

"No," I said. "I was upstairs at Mila's."

"Well, thank God for that. At least the girl's good for something."

"They took really good care of me."

"Mila and her mother?"

"Yes," I said. "And her father."

"He's here?"

I nodded. "Arrived just a few days before you left."

"What's his story?"

"He's a very gentle man."

My mother grew fixated on the idea of thanking them "properly" for taking care of me. "I have to go up there," she said, at least once a day. "And thank them face-to-face."

"You don't have to. You wouldn't want somebody taking time out of their recovery to thank you for something that was just the decent thing to do."

She stroked my face when I laid out these protestations, but it was hard not to feel like some part of her suspected that I was just saying things that sounded like the right thing to say. I, in turn, couldn't help but feel it, too. My skin crawled whenever an endearment came out of my mouth. Here I was, this false daughter. This untrustworthy darkness, waiting at the end of amnesty to let fly with everything that was really on my mind.

One day I came home to find my mother in her best clothes.

She had put on a blouse and a pair of slacks I hadn't seen her wear since Paraíso. She'd found time and ingredients to bake a lopsided little tea cake, which was sitting wrapped in a kitchen towel in the crook of her arm.

She looked me over. "Don't you have anything nicer than that to wear?"

"What for?"

"We're going upstairs to say thank you. Change into something nice—hurry."

A dress that had been too short for me even way back in January was the most decent thing I had hanging on my side of the closet. Covered with smashed-looking flowers, it was loathsome to put on, an accelerant for my rage. If she was well enough to order me around, perhaps she was well enough to hear what I had to say. I would certainly be in the mood to tell her after Mila passed judgment on this vernal garbage bag.

But then—perhaps going upstairs was the best way to bring the issue to a head. After all, Mila's father knew I spoke Ours. I had told him the truth about our past. He would surely raise it with my mother. She would be surprised—unpleasantly, of course. But a little blindsiding wouldn't hurt. She would see, firsthand, how wrong she had been.

When Mila's mother finally answered the door, she threw her arms around my mother without hesitation and without asking. "Oh," she said. "We were so worried."

She looked tearful enough to make me wonder if she might be drunk. Mila's response was more reserved. She accepted the cake my mother held out and unfolded the tea towel around it.

"Oh my," she said. "Look how it's risen."

"I wish to thank you for taking care of Sil while I was away," my mother said in English. She said the word "away" as though she'd been delayed at the ferry terminal.

"Oh please—don't mention it." Mila's mother was already setting out plates beside the cake—only four, I noticed with a sinking heart.

"Won't your father be joining us?" I asked.

"He's not feeling well."

"Oh, that's such a real shame!" my mother said. "He was so kind to Sil. I wish to thank him. He did not have to care for the stranger's child."

The ongoing exchange of looks between Mila and her mother seemed to soften a little. "Mila," the woman said. "Why don't you just peer your head in and see if your father isn't feeling better?"

Mila stood there, hesitating, holding her ground on some unacknowledged battlefield. "All right," she said eventually with a tense smile. "All right, I guess I will. I guess it would be a shame to sit this out. This cake, Sil's dress. Both so wonderful."

Mila's mother, I noticed, immediately laid out a fifth plate. We sat around the table and waited. Eventually, Mila led her father out of the back bedroom. My mother was already getting up before his huge, gentle hulk cleared the hallway. He closed the distance between them in two strides and shook her hand.

She was in the middle of saying "I wish to thank you—"

That was as far as she got. Mila's father was the kind of man who was disposed toward being effusive before a sentence directed at him had ended. "We're so delighted that you're safe and sound. And how we love Sil—she is Mila's very best friend, you know."

Mila gave me a soft little kick under the table and smiled.

"Yes," my mother was saying. "Yes, very good friends."

She looked around to get her bearings before sitting down, and this was the first time since he'd come in that I caught a glimpse of her face. She looked odd. Perhaps standing up too quickly had made her go pale. But then there were her knuckles. So drained of blood they were practically green, clutching the back of her chair to steady herself as she eased down into it. She sat, facing away from me, her whole body completely rigid.

"What an ordeal you've been through," Mila's father said. "Do you remember what happened?"

"You know, is not so easy to remember."

"Of course. I suppose these things come back later on."

"Yes."

"And are you feeling better?"

"Yes. Much." She gestured widely to encompass the vastness of the feeling before her, and in so doing knocked over the tea Mila's mother had placed, unnoticed, at her elbow. Amid a slew of apologies, she tried to mop up the liquid with her sleeve while Mila's mother rushed in with a napkin. "Oh no, oh no. You know, I only wished to drop off cake, not bother you. Really we are very busy." She stood up, and in my fury and embarrassment, I did, too. Here she was, pretending—and the only one unaware that this was what she was doing. I would put a stop to it.

"Mama," I said, in Ours. "It's all right—we can stay a little while. Can't we?"

It is actually beyond my powers to describe the look my mother cast my way. I had never seen it before. It should have reduced me to atoms where I stood, but I felt invincible. I had done it. I had revealed at least some part of my terrible betrayal to her, and here she was, caught out. Swaying a little, still holding on to that chair, until Mila's father broke the silence.

"Yes," he said in Ours. "Please do sit down and stay awhile. You're among friends!"

How like him to recognize the battle raging in my mother at that moment. How important to reassure her of his good intentions. The blaze went out of her eyes, and she sat back down. "You know, we couldn't be happier to know you this way," Mila's father went on. "Sil told us all about your journey here."

My mother's hand went into my hair, but I couldn't really feel the touch itself—just the tips of her nails, needles trembling against my scalp. "Oh, she doesn't remember. She was so small." She was speaking Ours now, too—but putting on some strange accent, as though her native language were as unfamiliar and ragged as her English. I pulled primly away from her hand.

"You're from Sarobor?" Mila's father asked.

"That's right."

"We're from Uvala."

"Ah. Beautiful Uvala."

"Sil said you came through, on your way here."

A sort of shuddering exhalation, perceptible only to me, left my mother's lips. "Yes. However, we have cousins in Vesvere, so we went straight on." This was a lie—but I was charitable enough to let it slide.

"This is a very good cake," Mila's mother said, switching to English. "I can't remember the last time I had cake at all. You must give me the recipe."

"Thank you. Most of it live up here"—my mother pointed to her temple—"but I will try to remember and write it out for you."

"I've never been able to cook from memory."

"You can hardly cook at all, Mother," Mila said.

Mila's mother laughed lightly. "It's true."

"My grandmother always say—you must have true desire to cook. Otherwise, why do it?"

"How extraordinary," Mila's father said, making his way in from the outskirts of this culinary detour. "Your daughter seems to have retained more of her native tongue than you have!"

I was surprised at how deeply this insult stung me. I wanted to tell him: *No, she's not really speaking, she's bungling it on purpose. She's a joker, my mother. A poet. She knows words so specific to Our language that they can't be translated into any other. No one knows how sharp she is, how funny. She won't let anyone see.* But to imagine saying this was to imagine the rebuke it would incur from my mother. And I already had the creeping sense that one was forthcoming. It seemed vital to delay it for as long as possible.

"She's really good at languages," I said. "She speaks almost six."

"Almost six?" Mila's father said.

I listed them, and he nodded along, obviously impressed.

The meal stretched interminably on. The cake was discussed at length, admired, its ingredients dissected. Mila's grandmother had made a similar one—with a different sort of crumb, and a different sort of fat, but then so few things from Back Home could be found or replicated here. They were just nostalgic substitutions. And then there were the rations—how was anybody supposed to bake anything? By the time we veered into this territory, I had begun to acknowledge the hollow opening up in the pit of my stomach. My mother was not relaxing. She was not growing more comfortable with each passing moment, or ruminating on how mistaken she had been to withhold Our part of herself from people in general, and these people in particular. She was inching her way through this encounter with a fixed smile and glazed eyes, so that she could escape with what she had calculated to be the least possible degree of further discomfort. And I was going to hear all about it the moment we were alone.

When we loaded into the elevator—my mother, her palpable fury, and I—she finally turned to look at me. "I don't understand," she said. "What possessed you to tell him we're from Sarobor?"

"He asked" was my dumb reply.

"He *asked*? How did he ask? Did he dangle you out the window by your feet? Hold a knife to your throat, push your head underwater?"

"No."

"Because I can't think of any other circumstances that would have led you to tell him."

"He *pressed* me."

"Pressed you."

It was true, up to a point. He had pressed me about languages while we sat there doing the jigsaw puzzle, for sure. But my abandonment of the rules by which we lived owed less to his relentlessness and more to my own frailty. I had been tired. I had felt alone. It hadn't taken much to break my resolve. My mother knew that. As always, she could simply *tell*—and now, somehow, the balance between us had shifted again. In mistakenly believing my mother too fragile for a confrontation, I had missed my opportunity to have one. Now I was back in the wrong—firmly and irretrievably, because she was furious, and disappointed, and blind to the fact that Mila's father, though liable to ask intrusive and relentless questions, meant no harm.

"They were taking care of me," I said. "I didn't want to be rude." But that didn't matter to my door-slamming, cold-shouldering, silent mass of a mother.

I WOKE THAT NIGHT TO NOISES FROM HER ROOM. A nightmare at last, I thought, hurrying across the hall to wake her. But I found her on her hands and knees inside the closet, rummaging through the old backpack where she kept our documents.

"What are you doing?" I asked.

"Go back to bed," she said, without looking at me.

She tormented me with her silence all the following day. I tried to read her face for signs of softening, but there were none. Just the old grimness from before the Martinique, the shuttering of something that had begun to open. It made me miserable enough to head to bed early—but I wasn't there long before she was shaking me awake.

"Come on," she said, thrusting a backpack into my hands.

Hazy with sleep, I followed her down the hall, into the elevator, and down to the sub-basement garage, where we sat for ten minutes trying to get Ena's ramshackle little car to turn over. The inside of it was close and airless, but behind all that muted stink of disuse blew an old note of Ena, of cigarettes and cinnamon gum. I must have been lulled by it, the incongruence of smelling her and knowing her to be gone—because the next thing I knew, my mother was shifting the stuttering little hatchback into gear, and we were inching jerkily toward the open garage gate and out into the street.

"Where are we going?" it finally occurred to me to ask.

"Put your seatbelt on."

My reward for doing as instructed was to receive a slim, book-sized tablet. "Open that," she said, "and guide us north."

"What is this?"

"A tide map. Hurry up—we're on Pike, heading east."

Pike heading east put us on one of two surefire ways out of the city—labeled on that particular map as PERPETUAL ROUTES and highlighted in bold red. "Turn left in two streets, I think," I said, and she did.

"Now what?"

"Where are we going?"

She tapped the top of the map. "The bridge."

"But where are we *going*?"

She didn't reply. I had never navigated these streets in a vehicle before, let alone interpreted a map at such speed. The moment I got my bearings, we had already skirled past wherever it was I had intended to guide us. "Slow down," I said— but my mother seemed to be able to do so for only a few minutes before picking up speed again. I looked from the brightness of the map to the darkness of the street, and my eyes filled with meandering electricity. The tide map kept shifting. We might find water anywhere.

"Where next?"

"I'm not saying another word unless you tell me where we're going."

Her futile effort to wrench the tablet out of my hands failed. "We're leaving."

"Leaving? Where?"

My mother did not turn from the road. "Anywhere."

"Anywhere? Are you craz— Stop!"

She took a sharp left to avoid the frothy water massing at the bottom of the hill before us. Now we were driving north toward the railway lines. I imagined myself jumping out of the car—and suddenly, I was doing it. The door offered no resistance when I pulled the handle. The cool air and the noise of the road rushed in.

"What are you doing?" my mother said, turning my way for the first time—but it was too late. The seatbelt clip shot up toward my face. I pulled my arm out of the strap and leaned sideways—reaching out, gently, for the road. For the briefest moment, I was airborne. Whatever plans I might have formed about how I intended to land evaporated on impact. I hadn't counted on how much it would hurt, or the effort it would take to roll. I dropped and lay there.

My mother, who had hit the brakes the moment she heard the belt click, now rolled to a halt about twenty feet ahead of me. My whole right side was on fire—but the fact that I was getting up firmed my belief that I must be in one piece. Before I had a chance to rally or even contemplate my next move, my mother was out of the car and on me. I tripped over the curb moving backward to get away from her, but she was holding on to my coat.

"Are you crazy?" she kept shouting. "Jumping out of the car—are you crazy?"

A light went on and a head emerged from a window across the street. What did this stranger see? A small, one-woman whirlwind buffeting a scarecrow of a girl who towered over her, and an empty car drifting slowly down the street. Apparently, this wasn't worth sticking around for. The head disappeared.

"The car!" I shouted, to save myself. "Mama—the car!"

The interlude necessary for her to catch up to the car and pull the hand brake gave me a moment's reprieve. I considered taking off down the street, but I couldn't really tell which way to run. My mother was calmer when she came back.

"What were you thinking?" she said. "Are you hurt?"

"What the hell do you care? Get away from me!"

That wounded her. She stood there, looking from me to the car. In the rush of triumph at having caused her distress, I made the mistake of reminding her why we were out here in the first place. "I'm not going *anywhere* with you." Which, of course, brought her forward in a fresh assault. She grabbed my lapels and flung me back into the trash cans behind me with incredible force for such a tiny woman.

We were both crying by that point, so it was hard for me to make out what she was saying. "What?" I said. "What?"

Her tearstained face emerged from the nest of her hands. "Why did you have to open your big, stupid mouth?" she cried. "What have I been telling you all these years? Keep your fucking mouth shut—and if somebody asks where you're from, you say *Paraiso!*"

"Why?" I roared. "*Why?*"

"*Because,* goddamn you. Because I've seen an inch or two more of the world than you have, and if I tell you to do something, you *do it*. You don't whine and mope and blow everything up the instant my back is turned."

"If you've seen more of the world than I have, it's news to me!" I cried. "I don't know a goddamn thing you've seen or done, or anybody you've ever known, or anything you've ever cared about. It's all just rules and insanity! Insane superstitions about the fucking—the weather, the wind!"

But my mother was on her own path, and there was no derailing her. "And then to tell him *where*—and in Ours! What's wrong with you? Don't you have a shred of sense, you stupid, stupid girl?"

This broke something in me. The next thing I knew, I was screaming, "He was nice to me!" alternately in English and Ours. My outburst brought a few more interested heads to the surrounding windows, one of which promised to call the cops if we didn't fuck off out of here and yell that drivel someplace else.

This put us in another phase of the fight. My mother grabbed my arm and started pulling me toward the car. Unsure of what to do next, resisting her to the point of lunacy, I sat down in the street. What a sight we must have been for our spectators in the darkened buildings—me rooted stubbornly on my ass, and my tiny mother turning me around by the arms so that she could control more of my body mass as she hauled me step by step to the waiting car, which had at some point begun to smoke. We were yelling indecipherable cruelties at each other in both languages now, and I suspect we would've gone on for a long time had a tall man in sweatpants not emerged from the building opposite and slammed the door loudly behind himself. He went on standing on the stoop until we fell silent. When I finally got up, he said: "You okay, miss?"

"Mind your own business," my mother shot back.

"I wasn't talking to you." He nodded at me. "You want me to call the cops?"

An unprecedented crossroads. Here was a person looking to me for guidance—and there was my mother, wiping off a handful of my hair on her pant leg. Perhaps most galling about it was my sudden clear understanding that, despite everything that had happened in the last forty-eight hours, she fully expected me to cooperate. She expected me to rally to her against this stranger, who was on my side, offering me help. And who, whether she realized it or not, was more likely to trust me than her, because the moment I opened my mouth, the words would come out crisp and clean and unaccented. Here I was, holding our fate in my hands, just as I had before I'd jumped out of the car. And my mother still didn't know it. And she still didn't know to be afraid.

"It's okay," I said. "Thank you. It's a family thing."

It took the stranger another moment to go back inside. By that time, tears were streaming down my face. My mother and I stood leaning against the car. "Why do you hate me so much?" I sobbed.

"I don't hate you." My mother sat on the curb. "I don't hate you. You made a mistake." I came over and stood by her. I had feared that she had come back from the darkness a totally different person, but here she was: Exactly the same. Intractable and terrified.

"What did I do?" I asked wearily. "What did I do, Mama?"

She shook her head. "Do you have any idea who that man is?"

"That man?" I looked back at the stoop for my would-be rescuer.

"No. Mila's father. I wasn't sure until he started speaking. But then—my God."

"Mama, what's wrong? Who is he?"

"Have you heard of Natra?" I shook my head. "Of course not. I never wanted you to." She was crying again. "Sil, he knows I recognized him. And after you admitted we're from Back Home. I know you don't understand, but we *cannot* stay."

"Who is he?"

"A wanted man."

"Wanted?"

"So they say."

The way she said it enraged me. "Why are you laughing?" I asked.

"To be a wanted man, you have to be wanted *by* somebody. Someone in power has to search for you. They have to care about what you did. And, my heart—nobody cares."

"What did he do?"

She shook her head, and it enraged me further. No, I didn't know about Natra—but she had brought it up, not I. And now here she was, with the past right up against her door, and unwilling to name it again.

"You're *exactly* the same."

"What?"

"Well, if *you* don't care, who the hell else will?"

"What do you mean, I don't care? Haven't you been listening?"

"How? You've just figured out this man is here, whoever he is, and all you want to do is run away. You're not going to tell me who he is. You're not going to confront him. You're not going to make *his* life difficult. You're just going to change *your* life and let him go on living his at the Morningside." I was surprised by my own clarity on this point. How strange not to feel muddled at all.

My mother remained sitting on the ground, looking up at me. "What do you expect me to do?"

"You have to tell someone," I said.

"Who?"

"Anyone," I said. "Anybody. The Dispatch!"

"The Dispatch." She laughed. "What for? You think someone will care enough to come haul him away before he's killed us in our beds because I recognized him?" She shook her head and stood up. "We have to leave."

"What about Mila? What about her mother? Are we just going to leave them with him?"

"They're his family. They probably have no idea what he's done. Or they know, but don't mind." She wiped her eyes and took one last, unavoidable swipe at me. "Didn't you say he was kind to you?"

"Please," I said. "We can't just run away. Tell someone. Anyone."

"Who is there to tell?" Around us, the buildings were silent. She moved back toward the car and held the door open. "Come on, Sil."

And then it hit me. "Wait," I said. "Wait. I know somebody. I have somebody."

Number 55 West Park Place was a narrow, three-story townhouse on a quiet block. May didn't open the door until the third or fourth time we knocked. By then, my mother was all second thoughts and already moving back down the stoop in the direction of the car.

"Snoopy!" May said. He opened the door wider and saw my mother in the walkway. "And Mama. What's going on?"

May's place was dimly lit and too warm. A living plant on the windowsill leaned its blushing flowers against the glass. I'd never seen so many books. They took up every inch of available wall space, some on shelves, some stacked in piles on the floor. The one surface free of books was a desk at the back of the living room, home to what looked like a huge keyboard, over which a microphone was crooked. I'd been wrong to think that May's place would be quiet. The machine on the table was whirring. A telephone was ringing. The Dispatch was on. And from somewhere above or below came the quiet roar of a passing train—a sound machine, I realized.

"We've come at a bad time!" I shouted over the noise.

"Not at all, not at all. Please, sit."

He turned down the Dispatch and the sound machine, but

the phone just went right on ringing while he overturned the kitchen, looking for something to offer us. By the time he came back with a can of warm cola, I was irrationally furious with him, and with whoever kept calling him so persistently.

"Are you going to answer that?" I asked.

"The machine will get it." He gestured toward the dining table, and we arranged ourselves around it awkwardly. He turned to my mother. "Snoopy says you need my help?"

My mother shifted in her seat. "We don't need anything," she said. "I do not know why we come here."

May smiled patiently. "I wish you'd figure it out," he said. "It's four o'clock in the morning."

"You have much to do?" This made him laugh a little, and an ease started to settle between them. I couldn't tell if my mother's sharpness was due to the general stress of the situation or the fact that she was still convinced he might have designs on me.

"We're running away," I blurted out.

"Why?"

"There's this man my mother recognized," I bulldozed on before my mother could stop me. "He's a sort of criminal."

"What kind of criminal?"

My mother shot me a dark look. "I don't really know," I said.

I thought if I could just drag her to the threshold of all this, the words would come more easily. But they didn't. I should have known, from my own experience, that you couldn't just suddenly dismantle all the effort that had gone into keeping silent. But I'd assumed that my mother would not be subject to the same weaknesses that could so easily stifle me.

May looked at us. "Let me get a pen," he said. He was gone for so long it began to feel deliberate.

"He's calling the police," my mother said.

"Don't worry, he's not."

But she sat with her backpack in one hand and the unopened cola in the other until he returned with a legal pad and a couple of pencils, and a fruit cup presumably dredged up from some forgotten corner of his pantry. He placed it in front of my mother and put a spoon on top. "Tell me about this man. The criminal."

Where, May wanted to know, did he live? In the city, my mother said. All right—did she know where? In our building, of course. Was he a new resident? She nodded. How did she know who he was? He was easy to recognize. She knew his face. It wasn't the kind of face you could ever forget. And we were here because—well. He knew she had recognized him. And it had become impossible to remain anywhere near him. May nodded. Was he dangerous? Yes, my mother said. Yes, very. He was there at Natra. May had probably never heard of him—and that, my mother said, was exactly what she had expected. She shouldn't be here, talking about him to somebody who didn't know, who didn't understand.

"I don't know," May said. "But I do want to understand. I do."

The phone startled us again. "Someone is very much wanting to reach you," my mother said.

"It's all right," May said. "They can leave a message."

"It is quite late—might be an emergency?"

"Don't worry about it."

"You should pick it up. You should pick it up, and we should go."

Her attempt to stand was met with a lot of protestation on May's part. His hand rested on her wrist, and he spoke slowly and quietly enough for her to eventually sit down. She cracked open the cola, but didn't drink it. It sat hissing on the table between them in the brief moment of silence before the phone started ringing again.

"You have heard of Natra?" my mother asked.

"I think so."

"You think so."

He looked embarrassed. "Something happened there."

"Oh yes." She sat for a moment, with her lips pressed tight. Then she turned to me. "I don't have the words," she said in Ours.

"So tell me," I said. "I'll translate."

"When the slides started and people moved inland, Natra was the second stop for our people fleeing north. There was an old textile factory at the edge of town where they set up a medical tent and a sleeping area for us. And at first they really made us welcome. Hot food. Mattresses. The kids all lined up to give us clothes and toys. You saw the pictures, I'm sure, that week or ten days it got coverage. Heartwarming stuff. I guess they thought there were few enough of us, and that we wouldn't stay long. But then the slides dragged on, and the wildfires started, and people just kept coming and coming. So cities farther along the refuge road started turning newcomers around. And there was nothing to go back to, so things got backed up in Natra. Bottlenecked. Once the factory ran out of beds, people slept on the floor. And when they ran out of floor, they slept outside in the heat. The relief groups started running low on food and water, but people just kept pouring in. Dirty and hungry and half-crazed with panic. When you're out like that, with no home to go back to, you're crying most of the time. Desperate. The men get angry. They get violent. And the locals started getting sick of us, so petty gangs would come in at night, starting fights, setting fires. When the police got overwhelmed, they brought in the troops to keep peace. And at *their* head was Rait

Belen, who had one job in Natra, and that was to clear the place out."

"Clear it how?" May asked.

"However he could."

"And?"

"Oh my God—are you please going to answer the phone?" my mother suddenly shouted. The incessant ringing had faded out for me, but not for her. She put her face in her hands. May got up, went to the back of the room, cracked the coat closet door, and edged his arm inside. The phone fell silent. The red light above his desk went on blinking insistently.

"Please answer," my mother said into her hands.

"I'm telling you, don't worry about it."

"Someone is in an emergency."

"They're not, I promise." He sat back down. "Please, go on. How did he clear it out?"

"Well—first he cut our rations. Then he introduced new rules: you couldn't sleep in the same place for more than two nights in a row. Soldiers would come through, and if they found you in the same spot, they threw you out. Getting cited for trespassing meant you lost rights to whatever you'd brought with you—your clothes, your bags, any equipment. You'd be standing there watching these tiny old women holding on to their backpacks while some jacked-up soldier head-to-toe in body armor tried to walk away with everything they had. I knew this kind of thing went on everywhere, all over the world, but I was surprised by how gleeful they looked, those soldiers. We were pretty afraid, and I started thinking we still weren't afraid enough.

"All this boiled over—there were a few brawls. After that, Rait Belen changed course. There were these jobs, he told us. Roadbuilding and tree clearing, that kind of thing. For the men only. Buses started arriving, and any man who wanted work was welcome to board, with the understanding that they would return in a week or two. But that didn't feel right to me. Why were these people, who didn't want us there, suddenly going to the trouble of finding jobs for *us* when they could hardly get any work themselves? So we started asking around. Why were these buses coming in the middle of the night? When were we going to hear from the people who'd gone away? There was always an answer, you know. The liaisons would tell us: 'Oh, the buses come at night because the drivers are volunteers. They have their own jobs during work hours, we're very lucky to be able to get them out here at all.' I wouldn't say that Sil's father had no reservations—he wasn't stupid. But he was hopeful. He'd been a teacher Back Home, and he wanted to get back to some kind of work. He didn't want to be helpless. He wanted us to be able to move on with some sense of safety. I could tell he was ready to take his chances. 'Don't be a fool,' I said. 'Something's wrong with this. Nobody wants to give us jobs—they just want us out of here. They want us out, there isn't enough of anything for anyone.' But he had a firm belief in the decency of people. And he was afraid of waiting too long and missing his chance. So when the next buses came, he went. Didn't make a big deal of our goodbye, just went off the way he'd headed off to school every morning."

Here was my heretofore unmentioned father. His existence bloomed from nothing to the few seconds of breath my mother and I stopped to catch in the middle of her story. All the other versions of him I had imagined over the years vanished at once. He was tall and timid. He had my lopsided smile, and I had his. And then my mother and I went on.

"After I hadn't heard from him in a week or so, I started asking other women if they were getting any letters or calls from their husbands and fathers. Most of them said yes. I believed them. Why would anyone lie about something like that? But when people are desperate and afraid, they get cruel. They do and say stupid things to reassure themselves. They'd tell me, 'Oh, what a shame you're not hearing from him—maybe he left you.' But he wouldn't have done that. Ever. He loved us both very much. And then of course it turned out that none of *their* husbands were writing or calling, either. All those men and boys went off to work, and nobody was brave enough to admit that we never heard from them again. At least not until much later.

"But a couple of the younger mothers and I said: 'This is going to get worse. So much worse.' And we got ourselves together, went out after dark, and just walked. Babies on our backs, all the way to Vesvere."

"I'm so sorry," May said.

"And then a few years later, there was an investigation. For show, of course. But it helped us put together what actually happened. That officials and liaisons had taken bribes from neighboring countries to stop people from advancing farther inland. Stall anyone coming from the coasts, and you could get a nice little sum to retire on. There was never any proof, of course—but you have to wonder how much Rait Belen cleared for every man who got on one of those buses and never turned up again. Enough, I'm sure, to buy his way here and set himself and his family up at the Morningside. And what will we do? We can't go back there now. He knows I recognized him."

"Are you sure it's him?" May asked.

"Of course I am. Ten years is a long time in this wretched world—but you don't forget a face like that."

MY MOTHER WAS tired, so May set her up in the bedroom. I stayed at the table. The red light above May's desk was still blinking. It made me nervous. I got up to let the blood back into my limbs, and I went along his bookshelf, mouthing the titles quietly to myself, feeling smug that I had been right. Of course there would be this many books. He dressed like a man who liked them. He had left his closet door open a crack, and I pressed it just a little wider, expecting to see that salmon-colored linen coat I knew so well. But there were no clothes in there at all—just a bunch of old-looking machines. They were humming.

When May finally emerged from the bedroom, I said: "All this stuff. It's like you're the Dispatcher or something."

He laughed. Because, of course, he *was*. And he'd mistakenly assumed I'd known it from the moment we'd walked in.

So there I sat through the remnants of a night that had only grown stranger and stranger, watching May run his pirate radio station from a tiny desk in the building that had once been his grandfather's antiques store. The Dispatcher. One two three. Between calls, he let me ask questions. Is it really you? Yes. Is this how you knew about the fire at the Morningside? Yes. Do you have any help? No. When do you sleep? Whenever I can. Why do this? I'll tell you sometime. Every now and again, I closed my eyes and put my head down and listened for the similarity between the voice he used in real life and the voice I'd been hearing on the radio for months. It just didn't sound the same. That was part of the spell he had woven, and not even knowing the truth could break it.

In the morning, he let a couple of hours of music play and was out on Battle Hill before I was even up, sitting on a low wall, pretending to do nothing when Mila's father came walking by. He brought back photos on his tablet. He and I sat comparing them to the few snapshots available online from Rait Belen's military days. The passing years had stacked comfortable weight on him, but the flat blue eyes looked the same.

"It's him," I whispered.

"Are we sure?" May said.

"Of course—just look at him."

He shook his head. "I still can't get my head around how he got here unnoticed. All the steps it took to get here, all the people who saw him, and she's the *only* one to recognize him? How is that possible?"

He didn't know my mother yet, so he didn't understand that the story itself was proof enough. She had gone my whole life without breathing a word of it. Nothing about my father, nothing about Rait Belen, nothing about buses or the textile factory or her journey before or after them. The great, rushing force of what she knew had followed her everywhere we went. It had followed me, too, even though I neither recognized it nor knew its name. And then, in a place she had finally felt relaxed enough to call home, it had caught up to her at her moment of greatest vulnerability, forcing her to relive it and call it what it was.

It couldn't all be for nothing.

While we tried to figure out what to do, the three of us settled into an uneasy routine, playing musical chairs with the bed and sofa and reeling from our respective terrors. Whenever I felt too cooped up, I went up to the roof, where May's enormous old antenna stood among the abandoned buildings, invisible to everyone except the rook cranes nesting next door. My mother did not go outside, except to stand in the little courtyard behind May's brownstone and look around at the boarded-up back-building windows and the rotted laundry lines twitching overhead. Whenever May ventured out for supplies, she added some item essential for our getaway to his list. Flashlights. Water. A tank of emergency fuel. He brought them home one by one, but they just piled up in the corner while we played cards and he wrangled callers long into the night.

My mother kept insisting, "We'll be on our way soon."

"No rush," May always said. "I don't mind the company."

Where exactly did she think we were going to go? We had no people anywhere. And as she kept reminding me, mostly in order to remind herself, Popovich would soon realize that we had disappeared. He would let himself into our place. And then the few things we had in the world would be at his mercy.

Beanie's maps. Ena's albums. I imagined Popovich standing there while movers wrestled my cot out the door; he would find the jam jar, open it, grimace at its contents. Then he'd toss it into the trash without a second thought, never realizing what it actually was, or what it had meant to us.

PLAGUED BY THESE THOUGHTS, I WENT BACK TO the Morningside one afternoon while my mother napped. May was moderating a heated debate about the reintroduction of the city's old motto and didn't see me slip out and into the street.

I was pleased to find that my old gate key still worked. There was nobody in the courtyard. No one in the lobby, either. I stood at the desk, with its empty chair, unable to decide what to go for first. The scissors? The jam jar? Which one would I stay up nights thinking about, if I was seen sneaking around and had to make a break for it?

The scissors were older. I'd carried them around with me since Paraiso. But the jam jar—it was all I had of Ena. And the apartment was so full of her things, so full of Beanie's. Maybe it was more important to get up there and grab everything and anything I could.

I got as far as the mezzanine when I heard that familiar, crisp step somewhere behind me. Too late, I ducked into the service stairwell. I was down a flight and a half when a door somewhere above me opened, and Mila's voice fell in all around me: "Sil? Sil!" But I didn't look up, not even when she started after me, her footsteps quick and light on the stairs. "Sil, I can see that it's you! Where have you been? *Wait!*" Some vein in my chest fluttered at the lack of control in her voice, the growing urgency. How strange to have her on the back foot for once. But there was nothing to do but keep descending, even when it sounded like she was leaping down after me three steps at a time. Into the basement, into the superintendent's office, where I shut the door and locked it behind me. The radio was still on in there, murmuring softly. Of course it was. No one had been down here during our absence. I cranked the dial to drown out the sound of my breathlessness, and the Dispatcher's voice—May's voice—filled the room around me so that I could barely hear what Mila was yelling while she banged on the door.

"I'm just saying," a thin-voiced caller insisted. "I'm not surprised they're being investigated."

"I don't disagree with you," May said. "But not for the reasons you think."

Mila kicked the door again. "I'm not leaving, Sil."

Suit yourself, I wanted to say. I sat down and put my face on my knees and imagined myself in the thick hum of May's makeshift office.

"Don't tell me," the caller said.

"No—look. I think it's important that all this stuff is coming out about the Repopulation Program. And it should be investigated. But more on my mind is the question of why. Why do things like this happen. Why does every step we take forward have to be followed up with some predictably human setback. It's like we don't know the fight's already over or something."

"That's a real shitty thing to say, Dispatcher."

"I guess it is." May paused. "If you tune in to this station, you know I don't like to tell stories myself much. I want to hear yours. I want to let you hear each other. I worry that most stories I know aren't mine to tell. But listen, The other day, a caller notified me about a man who had moved into our neighborhood. This man—well. He's wanted. A criminal."

"What, like a thief?"

Imagine May, taking a deep breath, shaking off the ghost of his younger self. May, on every radio in Island City, and yet totally alone. All those old fears and misgivings obliterated in a single moment of self-recovery.

"No," I heard him say. "A *real* criminal. War crimes. His name is Rait Belen. Look him up. He did things so terrible it sickens me to even mention his name. Anyway, the other day my friend recognized him just walking down the street. And I've been wondering ever since: What made him choose *this* city? Of all the places he could have gone in this world, he decided to hide out here."

Imagine my mother, sitting up at the mention of Rait Belen's name. Confused, frowning. Sticking her head around the bedroom door to look at May at his desk. I was surprised not to hear her in the background. Please, I thought, let her sleep through this.

"See?" the caller was saying. "Another Repopulation failure. How did he get in, you know?"

"I know *how* he got in," May said. "That part's no mystery. All he had to do was pay the right person to get him the right papers with a fake name, and then he was nothing but another white man looking for a better life for his family. The Repopulation Program didn't have anything to do with it. And sure, people here made assumptions about him. They thought, 'War.' They thought, 'Poor guy.' But they imagined themselves into his struggles, and they did not think, 'Killer.' My point is not the how. It's the why. I'm asking why such a person would choose to come *here*?"

It struck me that I could hear more clearly now that Mila had stopped pounding on the door.

May was still talking: "What made him so confident that he could come here and just live his life? Walk outside among ordinary people, go about his day, stand in line for rations with the rest of us? Did he really think nobody would recognize him? Or did he feel sure that even if somebody did—we wouldn't care?" May paused for such a long time I almost moved the dial to see if I'd lost the feed. Then he took a deep breath and continued: "If it's the latter, well. If it's the latter, alas poor city, what have we become?"

"You ought to report him," the caller said.

"I'm not sure how much good that would do."

"But people gotta know, don't they? Isn't he dangerous? What does he look like? Where does he live?"

I turned down the volume.

"You knew," I said through the door. "You knew exactly what he was."

Silence from beyond the door. I slid forward on my hands and knees and looked underneath, and then I got up and unlocked the door. There was no sign of Mila.

BY THE TIME I GOT BACK TO WEST PARK PLACE, MY mother and May had already gone through whatever fight his on-air revelation had provoked. They both looked exhausted.

"He told the whole city," my mother said.

"I know." I looked at May.

"I had to, Snoopy," he said. "You know that."

"I don't think it was your story to tell."

"Maybe not." He shrugged. "But this is my city."

And so it was.

We settled into a period of waiting, though what for I really don't know. My mother seemed to think it was retribution. She felt certain that Rait Belen or one of his cronies would show up at the door in the middle of the night and murder us all. May didn't seem entirely immune to this possibility. He started going out for rations less often, always a little nervous that he might not come back. My mother was constantly reassuring him that we would leave any day now.

But we were still there a week later when a caller named Adi brought the conversation back to Mila's wretched father.

"You know," she said, "I looked up that bastard you were talking about, the war criminal."

"Rait Belen," May said.

"You weren't joking—he's accused of some horrific things."

"He is."

"So I was in Battle Hill the other day, and I passed a man who looked exactly like him. And for a moment, I thought I must be going out of my mind, or was just really shook by the fact that I had been reading so much about him and looking at his pictures. But then I remembered—the *reason* I was looking him up to begin with was because you said you thought he might be living in the city."

"Mmm."

"Well, Dispatcher, it's definitely him."

I sat down next to May, taking great care not to make a sound.

"I'm sorry to hear it confirmed," May said.

"And he's just walking around up-island, like it's no big deal." May started to say something, but Adi kept going: "Anyway, I followed him, kind of in a daze because I couldn't believe it. He went into Ricky's Hardware. Then I got a chill. There I was, just following this man who might be responsible for the deaths of thousands of people. What was I thinking? But then I thought, 'To hell with him. What is he going to do? Kill me?' So I waited for him to come out and then I followed him home. Do you know he lives at the Morningside? *The Morningside?*" She sounded absolutely outraged. "That building has been there since before I was born. It's old Island City. Moira Watanabe died in that building. She was my favorite writer. When word got out, you couldn't wade through all the bouquets her mourners had left behind. And now this son of a bitch calls it home. I had a couple of eggs in my ration bag and, Dispatcher, I couldn't help myself. He went in through the gate, and when he turned around to close it behind him I hit him in the face with one of my eggs as hard as I could."

"Jesus, Adi," May said, shooting me an appalled stare. "Your rations."

"It was worth it," Adi said. "You would've done the same thing. And you know what? I hope I'm not the last person to do it."

She certainly wasn't. She knew her fellow up-islanders well. Later that same day, a Zoe Yoon phoned in from the North End to say that she had called out after a man she was pretty sure was Rait Belen. "I just walked behind him and yelled his name until he ducked into a store," she said.

Over the next week, a deluge of neighborhood vigilantes reported similar confrontations. You wouldn't bother calling in about the usual stuff: Rait Belen was the center of life in Battle Hill, if not the entire upper city. He was suddenly on every corner, in every store, taking a blissful afternoon nap on a sunlit bench in every park. "Christ," May said, after one caller detailed following him for blocks, shouting *Murderer,* "you'd think by now he'd give up going outside." It happened so much that May had to remind people that they'd want to be extremely sure the person they were harrying was indeed Rait Belen, and not some unfortunate look-alike. This prompted a rough-voiced man to call in with just such a problem. "Listen," he said. "I am not Rait Belen—my name is Daniel Leigh. In the last week, I've had a lemon and a bunch of tomatoes thrown at me, and I've had enough."

"Stop wasting your rations," May told his listeners. "Do not throw food at strangers."

To make sure they had the right person, a small coalition of lookouts took to camping outside the Morningside to track

Belen's movements and redirect newcomers, who by then were coming up from different neighborhoods to try to get a glimpse of him so that they could have something to call in about.

One day, I recognized Ricky's voice on the line. "I know the man you're talking about," he said. "He comes in to my store all the time. And I've refused him rations twice now."

That prompted a call from the sheriff, who reminded us that merchants were not allowed to refuse rations to someone with a valid card. Ricky called back while the sheriff was still on the air to argue that it was not a valid card, goddamn it, because the name printed on it was Grigor Tozen, and since he knew the bearer to actually be Rait Belen, he was under no obligation to honor the scrip.

All this while, I kept looking at my mother. I wanted to know whether this cannonade of enthusiastic abuse to which Rait Belen was being treated was eroding her fear.

"Did you ever think people would rally like this?" I said. "Isn't it amazing?"

But she was insistent: "Something terrible is going to happen."

And it did.

May returned from a walk with an old neighborhood friend looking like he'd been turned inside out.

"What's wrong?" my mother said, the moment she saw him. "What's the matter?"

Mila had vanished. The news was already old, because the prevailing theory at first had been that she had run away. But now, four wasted days later, it had changed to kidnapping, though no ransom demand had been made public.

Mila had walked the six blocks to Ricky's the morning of her disappearance. Ricky himself had spoken to her—or, rather, if you read between the lines, had fended off a robust challenge

about the price and condition of his batteries, then watched
her storm off down the street, listing in the direction of the
overladen tote on her right arm. She had put the tote down to
rest, according to the nanny who passed her a couple of blocks
later. But she'd never made it home. The tote itself had been
found on Cooper Street two days later and positively identified
by Ricky himself. The batteries and the receipt were still inside.

"God," my mother said. "God, no."

I stood beside her and said nothing, though somewhere in
me a valve released with shattering pressure. Of course. Of
course, Bezi Duras would take Mila. At least now I knew.

May hooked up the TV so we could watch the press confer-
ence that night, the chief of police dwarfed by Mila's father,
who stood beside him, stony-faced, staring too long into the
wrong camera. His eyes looked like they'd been rubbed with
sandpaper, and he recited one platitude after another in a low,
flat voice. "Mila is a very bright girl," he said. "Mila is my only
child."

May was watching my mother. "Are you *positive* it's him?"

"Of course," she said. "It's him."

If her voice wavered, I put it from my mind. During the
question-and-answer session, an unseen reporter from the very
back of the crowd shouted: "Sir, do you think your daughter's
disappearance has anything to do with accusations that have
been recently made against you?"

My mother sat up. "What is she asking?"

"Wait," I said. "Wait."

Mila's father answered flatly: "No."

"No, you don't think it has anything to do with the accusation, sir—or no, you're not Rait Belen?"

"I am not Rait Belen." He leaned over the microphone. "But

I know who has made this accusation against me." The chief of police attempted to bluster in and take the situation in hand, but he didn't manage it before Mila's father held up a picture. It was of my mother's face—the one with her bloodshot eyes, the one you've seen. "This woman is a beneficiary of the Repopulation Program. She and her daughter went missing from our building just before Mila was taken. She is the one who falsely accused me of being this person, this Rait Belen. She is the reason I can no longer leave home without being harassed. She is the reason my child is gone. If you want to find my daughter, you'll start by finding *her*."

While the screen descended into a chaos of camera flashes and waving arms, the three of us went on not looking at one another in the unbearable silence of May's living room. And then, of course, the phone started to ring.

"Well, shit," May finally said.

"We should just go to the police," I said. "We should go to them and explain everything. We should tell them the truth."

"The truth?"

"Yes—that my mother has nothing to do with this. We were here. With you. We have been for a month!"

And here, for the first time, was the truly inconceivable: my mother and May, united in the exact same expression of stupefied amusement.

"Are you crazy?" said May. "Go to the police?"

"Why not?"

"Where do I start?"

MAY TURNED OUT to be fiendishly levelheaded in a crisis. I should have counted on that from the beginning. You couldn't run a pirate radio station on which the entire city relied without keeping your cool. He drove Ena's car to the Marsh and dumped it in a lot teeming with rusted vehicles, then secured hair dye from a contact in the Spur. My mother and I huddled in his tiny bathroom, and we went bleached blond.

The problem was this: even though my mother knew that she had not in fact kidnapped Mila, she more or less agreed with the assessment that she was responsible for her disappearance. If she hadn't told May, and if he hadn't gone on to share what she knew with the entire world, nobody would have given that family on the thirty-second floor another look. Instead, someone had heard the Dispatch and stolen the warlord's child. For revenge, for power over him, for a ransom that had yet to be declared. Did it matter why? She was gone, and every day that passed made it more likely that she was gone for good. Any protestations—that May had been vague, that he hadn't mentioned Mila or her mother at all, that he hadn't specified what neighborhood they lived in, let alone named the building, that all that broad communal knowledge had come from his listeners—evaporated on impact. For weeks my mother's sleepless form drifted between the bedroom and the kitchen, sustaining itself on a diet of water and breaking news. Other developments in the city that blazed up on the Dispatch and would ordinarily have riveted her—the arrest of several crime syndicate lackeys, the burgeoning investigation into financial mismanagement at the Repopulation Program—served now only as a way to pass the time between updates on the Belen case.

May had been able to keep the Dispatch focused on the facts: missing girl or not, the man at the center of the case was undeniably Rait Belen. He had no regrets about pointing this out, and though he disagreed with their methods sometimes, he knew Island City was right to turn on Belen the way it did. But suddenly, excerpts of May's initial broadcast about Rait Belen started cropping up on other stations, other programs, platforms where May had no influence. And then the story went national, every half hour on seemingly every station, regardless even of its political agenda. Repopulation decriers used it as an example of why tighter screenings of incoming refuge seekers were more necessary than ever. Repopulation supporters countered that Rait Belen had not been part of the program, and had only been identified because he had been recognized by a Repopulation awardee. Those caught in the middle theorized about who might be responsible for the kidnapping—and usually pointed the finger at the decriers and the supporters, and then brought on dozens of experts to make their case. "These Repopulation people stick together" was the consensus. "If you want to find the kidnappers, look in the community." So the police did. They questioned Mrs. Sayez, who, to her credit, tearfully defended my mother and me as "such nice people" in several interviews before she had to be hospitalized for her nerves. They questioned Bezi Duras, referring to her in press conferences as "an artist and influential expatriate." None of the interview footage was ever released, even on the Belen case forums, but I bet Bezi had her fun with them.

Popovich was brought in for questioning several times, too, as a person of interest. Beset by news crews on his way out of the police station, looking rumpled and shook, he would always say, "I'm only a businessman. I'm an ordinary businessman." Because nobody had bothered to give my mother her job by proper channels, the trail ended with her Repopulation documents. There was no paperwork to show that she had worked at the Morningside, or for how long. There was a point beyond which any information Popovich provided would actually land him in jail—so all he could do was admit that yes, my mother and I had once lived there.

Meanwhile, my mother's photo continued to circulate. For a while, her face—vandalized in every configuration you can imagine, and some you probably cannot—festooned every forum. Luckily, the picture was old. My mother looked nothing like it. She cut her hair, just in case, and kept it blond until she went gray enough to stop dyeing it. As for me, I got a drastic chop and went through another growth spurt. My face had changed. There wasn't much for us to do but stay out of sight, nothing but two new blondes who kept to themselves and rarely met anyone's eye. My mother took a job with a demolition company that paid her under the table. She never spoke to Fis Sarina or any of the divers who'd pulled her out of the wreckage of the Martinique again. Every so often, raging about the way Popovich had sold us out, and had leased a place to a warlord without thought or warning, and had probably burned all our belongings—everything we had in the world, not to mention all those scrapbooks and pictures of the old house, of Baba, of Ena and Beanie, all of it, gone, gone, gone—she fell into a fugue state, and nothing May nor I did could bring her back.

This was not helped by the way belief about her had aged into certainty. You could see it in the hardening of language: the slow disappearance of words like "alleged" from articles and news stories. The introduction of words like "ill-tempered" and "insubordinate" after residents of the Morningside allowed themselves to be interviewed on condition of anonymity. The surge in conversations that detailed how trauma and poverty might lead women to do horrific things, even against children. "What does this say?" she asked me once, having gotten her hands on a newspaper that featured her in a list headlined MODERN MEDEAS. I tried to give her the overview without dwelling too much on the details: the gist being that whoever had written the article felt that my inscrutable, shifty-eyed, lunatic mother had clearly dispatched Mila, the innocent daughter of a "supposed soldier of fortune."

Sometimes even my mother doubted whether the man to whom she'd brought that star-crossed tea cake was really Rait Belen. Eventually she stopped insisting that it was him, even to us, because every time she said it, it cost her a piece of her own conviction. May and I believed her. The farther out you got from the city, however, the less Rait Belen's identity seemed to matter. National opinion did not deny it but merely relegated the fact that he had been accused of atrocities to the outside loop of factors that were interesting about, rather than fundamental to, Mila's disappearance.

As for me, I kept my hair short and my head down.

And I thought about Mila. Hard as a stone, all the way down.

Experts roped in by the news shows seemed to circle eternally around the question of her death without ever quite managing to land on it. "Mr. Andrews," the host would ask some near-indistinguishable, somber-sounding suit, "in your experience, when kidnappers don't take credit for a kidnapping, and no ransom demand is issued, and months go by, is it typical to expect the victim to be recovered?" It never seemed to be, but the expert would always lift the second half of his sentence to allow for the possibility of being mistaken. They all seemed to think that Mila was dead somewhere in one of the hundreds of thousands of basements in the drowned city. My mother shared this belief. But they didn't know what I knew. And they didn't know her like I did, so I forgave them for not realizing that, had

Mila actually been kidnapped, she would have bullied whoever stole her into letting her go, and would be home by now.

"I don't want you to live in this fiction," my mother said. "That girl is dead."

But Mila wasn't. She was gone, perhaps. Irretrievable. She might never be seen again. She might spend her days as a green-eyed parrot, sitting in an ornamental cage up there in the penthouse tower, or bricked up in a train station, or in some other prison that suited the Vila who had taken her instead of my mother. But she was not dead.

This wasn't belief. It was certainty. She was out there, in one form or another, biding her time. Like a stone, all the way down.

"She's alive," I said, and I left it at that.

I believed this for a year, and then two, and I spread it around school when I was finally admitted into a place on the mainland, under a different name, and well into my late teens I told anybody who brought up the Belen case that the warlord's daughter was still alive. It was none of anybody's business how I knew it. But it was the truth, and I said so whenever the opportunity arose.

Every now and again, I checked the forums that had proliferated as fascination with the case grew. Followers were thorough and obsessive. They argued about whether Rait Belen had insinuated that my mother had kidnapped Mila herself or whether her accusation had merely led to the kidnapping. They posted floorplans of the Morningside and espoused wild theories that grew and spread in incredible ways. They spent hours trawling security camera footage from the neighborhood. They had a pretty good handle on when my mother and I had disappeared, actually: a three-second clip of us driving up the street in that little rattletrap car of Ena's was their foundational text. Even the people who didn't think my mother was responsible agreed that she was somehow involved. Perhaps you're someone who believes this. And maybe, in a way, you're right. If my mother hadn't recognized Rait Belen, who knows what would have happened? But you're also wrong. Because you've never asked yourself what part the blurry passenger in that jolting little vehicle played in all this. And you haven't known, until now, that she asked the Vila to take somebody, anybody, besides her mother.

For years, that moment was the first thing I thought about when I woke, and the last thing I thought about as I lay in the dark. I was certain I would revisit it every day of my life. And for a long time, I did. And then time passed, and eventually I did not. It would suddenly occur to me that a few days had gone by without my thinking about it—which, of course, would break my streak, and I'd feel relieved to find myself unexpectedly plunged back into that room, with its huge painting, and the dogs around it as though they were waiting to be called back into the world from which they had come. But then that got hazy, too. It became the kind of thing I'd tell lovers after deciding they would probably be sticking around. The kind of thing I hoped they'd forget about me when we parted ways.

THE YEAR I TURNED EIGHTEEN, I WROTE TO BEZI Duras. She had come to reside in two entirely separate rooms in my memory: in the more readily accessible one, she was the strange, wealthy woman who had occupied the penthouse of the building in a city that had turned against my mother. In the one I had pushed to the outskirts of my mind, she was the old woman on South Falls Island, the only other soul, besides me, who really knew what happened to Mila. From what I had heard, it seemed reasonable to assume that the woman in the first room was still alive. If she wasn't, news of her death had yet to reach me. "Ms. Duras," I wrote. "I was one of the children present that evening you exhibited your photographs of South Falls Island to the Board of the Repopulation Program at the Morningside, prompting the investigation into fraud and financial malfeasance. You joked that anyone present could turn to you if they had ambitions to leave the city. I have such ambitions now."

To my surprise, Bezi Duras sent two thousand dollars, no questions asked, the banknotes all clipped together in a plain brown envelope. I'd hoped that she might include some acknowledgment, some reference to our encounter in her home that day—even if she could only place me as the nervous-looking adolescent lump who'd stood behind the girl made of stone and put together a couple of sentences in Ours. But I had deliberately avoided mentioning which child from the party I was. Even if she'd remembered me, she would have had no context to connect the memory with the person now writing to her. Included in the envelope was a single sheet of stationery, scrawled with an offhand

Good luck —B. Duras

We split the money three ways, May, my mother, and I, and with my share I bought a car and moved out west.

My mother moved south, to Sebastien. There was a lot of salvage work down there, on both sides of the peninsula. She suddenly became the kind of person who took and sent pictures. A lot of palm trees came my way that year. A lot of wind-blown beaches and electric sunsets. Her care packages came to contain treasure: dried seahorses, bits of bleached coral, fragments of turtle shell.

I wrote her: "It seems like the wildlife there are all died out—why don't you come west to Moraine, where we still have living things?"

But she was afraid of the fires, all that smoke dimming the sky for months at a time, turning the sun into something you could stare at, a red coin, molten when it rose, molten when it set. And besides, she had grown up by the sea, and the sea was where she felt most herself. You could see it in her pictures: always with her little rope-cable arms around the waists of two or three men about her size, all of them sun-darkened save for the broad pale oval where their diving masks sat. Her hair, salt-whitened and dry, heaped on top of her head like another found thing. It helped me to believe that they loved her, this small, dauntless person who could outswim and outdrink them, who could hold her breath longer and shovel her food down faster than they could, a light they felt obliged to tend because they couldn't stand to see it extinguished.

For two summers, May featured prominently in those pictures. Without warning, without explanation, he showed up at her side in a snapshot of a little beach darkened by a purple sunset. They had a thing, I think, my mother and May. Or, at least, I move through the world as though they did, or will. I hope I'm right.

On his fiftieth birthday, May turned a collection of his musings about the city in to the same woman who had published his last book all those years ago. She told him he might have something there—the rook cranes, she said, were the center of a lot of political discourse now, inconducive to study, constantly shifting their rookeries and refusing to settle down in any one given place and let those in the know decide what it meant in the short term, and what it boded for the future. He should follow them around the country, she suggested, and see if he could link their travels to something greater about the state of mind or heart or nation in which we were all presently living. He would ordinarily have balked at the suggestion, but a caller had recently referred to him by name. He started thinking about how long he intended to devote his life to the Dispatch. Another five years? Another ten? What if he wasn't able to change the subject so smoothly the next time his true identity came up? Was he going to keep at it until some patrol broke down his door and confiscated his equipment? Already he was devoting more airtime than he liked to music. On his way home from down-island one day, he looked up and to his amazement saw that someone had spray-painted a speech bubble on the

Regent Grove Dancing Girl. There she was, hand cupped around her mouth, shouting, "Hey Dispatcher!" He stood on the corner, looking up at her, until the streetlamps started coming on. Then he went home and told the city his name. And once people started showing up at his door and stopping him on the street to shake his hand, May came west, too. Part-time only, of course. He had said it was his city, and he had been right—but he hadn't yet figured out how to be its Dispatcher in this new way.

He rented a cabin in a parched clearing about four hundred miles from Moraine, and sat with his binoculars, watching the meadow in front of his window fill with cranes and empty of them. I joined him when I could, and when the cranes moved on to their winter ranges, he made the long drive to my place and we roamed the valleys together, picking up bits of information for Fish and Wildlife, trying to put together stories or evidence of life that wasn't there. Or wasn't there in enough abundance to mean much of anything at all.

May's book sold well. He breathed new life into the Dispatch in a podcast called *Reminiscences*, in which he invited callers to recount their memories of Island City—how it was last year, or ten years ago, or twenty. And people did call, people still on the ground, holding out to the last; and people who had fled long ago but remembered it as the home they wished they'd never left. For the first time, May shared his own memories, too. He talked about how for so long he had failed to understand what it would take to become *of* the city, not simply to live in it. He talked about Benjamin Bowen, and he talked about his time in the Exchequer Street station. Almost nobody ever asked him about Maryam Handak, though he continued to bring her up in the hopes that her mother might hear and reach out. For years, she did not.

May's own mother, Ellen, did come to stay with him one summer. I drove down to finally meet her. She was quite old by then, and movement was burdensome to her, painful and exhausting. She spent most of her time sitting in the cabin window, watching the grasses for signs of life. Shuffling over to the glass whenever a prairie dog reared up in the sage. When she felt sociable, she told us stories of her youth, her time on the Plains before the drought came, her years with May's father on the wind farm. It was odd to hear her refer to May as "Lamb." But that's what he was to her. Lamb Osmond. I tried calling him that once, just to get a feel for it—but it was unwieldy and intrusive, and I never did it again.

When the fires came, Ellen had to cut her trip short because the smoke gave her lungs too much trouble, and she kept insisting that if a burn happened in the woods above May's place, she wouldn't be able to flee. "You'll try and save me," she said, "and end up dying yourselves." There was quite an elaborate cascade of horrors attached to this scenario, so we relented and bought her a ticket on the next train out of Red River.

The night before we drove her to the station, after I had gone to bed, she apparently took May's hand and said, "Ailin Handak wrote me—Maryam's mother." May froze up. "She said, 'Mother to mother, I carry you in my heart. But it's not my place to forgive your son. That's for him and my Maryam to work out between them.' You know?"

WE FINALLY CONVINCED MY MOTHER TO COME VISIT.
She took the train out of Sebastien and traveled for three days
by rail to the Sol Dorado station, where I picked her up this
morning. Standing there with my little sign, and trying to drive
away the urge to let my mind touch the old Polaroid that had
suddenly turned up on the forums, the one of me and her and
Bezi Duras and her boys disappearing up the hill behind us.

My mother stepped off the train. The dread would not leave
me, even when I hugged her, and by then I knew why. It was
because something had shifted out of place. They were all suspended in stasis—Bezi, Mila, Rait Belen, even the versions of
myself and my mother who were in that photograph. Seeing
them in the context of our new lives made it feel like somebody
was digging up our bones.

It was another thousand miles back to Moraine. We drove
past the burned-out ghost towns of the middle prairie, past Can-
see and Sun City, and by that evening were crossing the desert,
stopping so that I could show my mother the way the gradations
of the setting sun lingered in perfect strata in the sky. My mother
had lost the index and middle fingers of her left hand in yet an-

other diving accident, and I had been living in Moraine for almost ten years.

"Moraine," she muttered, when we crossed the state line. "Who in the world would've thought it."

I guessed what she meant was: Who in the world would have thought that you, a child of cities—and not just any cities, but very old ones—would end up belonging to such a distant wilderness. I'd been eager to show it to her: the swales red with willows come fall, and the way those last few elk would glide across the refuge at dawn like mirages. My greatest fear was that she would not be moved.

"It's in the middle of nowhere all right," I said.

But she shook her head. "No. What I mean is: you were born in a place that no longer exists—and now, well. Here you are."

Something about the way she said it felt chastening, even though it was clear that she did not mean it to be. What she meant was that our long journey had somehow rendered my place of birth arbitrary. It had long ago ceased to exist on maps that were being produced, a piece of an older time that had sheared off and crumbled into the sea. And now I belonged far more relevantly to this other place, which, in the days when *she* had been studying maps, had been just as arbitrary, a land-locked point on a distant continent, something she never gave a second thought. Yet here it was, stretching out before us in every direction, empty and treeless.

Around nine, we pulled off the highway, into a little campsite. There were a dozen or so other cars scattered among the low, flat bushes in the shadow of a bluff. We drove around the side and across a cattle guard so we could, in my mother's words, "have nobody at our backs"—but without feeling like we couldn't rejoin the group in the event of trouble. A little light still clung to the sky, and we pumped our water and warmed some beans and spinach on the camp stove and sat in the open hatchback, watching the last pale blue light fade. It was another half hour before all the stars came out, millions of them. By then it was night in earnest, moonless and endless. My mother got out of the hatchback and lay down on the ground. Every few minutes, she waved her little whiskey flask in my direction. After a time, I climbed down and joined her. Someone in the nearby encampment was chasing chords on a guitar.

"It's so bright out," my mother said.

I had to admit it was.

"There are so few places where it's really dark. Where you really can't see anything."

"What's that like?" I asked her, suddenly determined to skip all the hesitant, introductory parts, the part where I asked her whether she knew of any such places, and the part where she said yes and then went quiet again and quickly changed the subject.

She thought about it. "Well, true darkness is cold. Right now, for instance—it's nighttime, and getting cooler every minute. But the places where you see light"—she fanned her three fingers to indicate the heavens and a distant fire in the campground—"give you a feeling of warmth. I guess it's an illusion. None of that warmth's *actually* reaching you. But when you see it, your brain believes a little that maybe it is."

"It must have been bone cold in the Martinique," I said. "Because of the water."

"Well, the wet suit was meaningless after a while. Especially after I took off my gloves. I couldn't see anything at all. Sil, I mean anything. Couldn't tell where I was. A few minutes would pass, and I'd think, 'Oh it's coming clearer now, the light is

coming.' But it was just my brain playing tricks on me, and
when I realized that I'd panic all over again. So I took the gloves
off so I could feel the water, and feel around in front of myself.
Just to give myself some sense of space. To be able to feel ac-
curately if I could see nothing."

"Have you figured out where you were?"

"I guess what had happened was, the pylons fell, and when
the water surged it carried me a couple of rooms over from
where I was working and lodged me in an air trap. The girl who
got me out said it was between two elevator banks. I was afraid
to swim too far, in case the tide pulled me back out through
whatever tunnel I'd been carried in along and pinned me up
against the ceiling. I could tell that the walls were smooth. That
old marble, I think. Eventually—I think at least the first night
had passed—I found a little ledge with a hooked piece of metal
above it, which I guess was where the security camera had once
been. I hung on with one arm for a while, and then the other. I
got the idea to make a kind of sling out of my mask—I let the
strap out as far as it would go, and then I got my arm through
it and sort of hung there. It kept me from having to kick, so I
didn't get as tired—but then I was colder, of course. Whenever
one arm went numb, I'd switch to the other one. A couple of
times I fell asleep and dropped out of the sling."

"God." I wanted to squeeze her hand, but I was worried that
she'd had to fall away from me to talk about this, that touching
her would bring her back and silence her. I couldn't believe
that I was finally getting the facts. And here I'd been thinking I
would have to make them up for the rest of my life.

"I could hear the water sliding against the walls. I didn't
worry that anything was in there with me until I started imagining things—that something had brushed up against me, or the
sound of a distant splash. That would put me in a panic, be-

cause there was nothing to see, and so no way to reassure myself that it was all in my head. So all the singing I was doing to keep myself awake kind of died out because I got afraid that if something really *was* in there with me, I wouldn't hear it coming closer."

She went silent for a while, and I thought that must be the end of it. Until: "You know, there was a brief moment at the very start where I was afraid of dying. But then the darkness and the cold—I felt pretty sure that if I died, I wouldn't know it. And that would be all right. But the real fear came, I guess, sometime the second morning. Or—no. How long was I down there?"

"Seventy-eight hours and twenty-two minutes," I said.

"Well. The real fear came when I started thinking about you. I'd lost all sense of time. And the more I tried to get it back, the more I started to feel that years had passed. I knew they hadn't, of course—I knew it was only hours, maybe a day or so. But the not seeing and the not knowing disoriented me. And a little part of my brain started saying: *It's been years.* And I couldn't do anything to shut it up. Forget singing, or multiplying, or thinking about all the animal facts I knew. And the more I thought that years had passed, the more I started to wonder where you were. How the hell was I going to find you? And this all led to the conviction that it wasn't me who was going to die. It was you. Maybe you were already dead. I pictured a thousand different ways that it could happen to you, up alone in the Morningside." She clapped a hand against her face.

"That's why you said that." I suddenly understood. "When they got you out."

"What did I say?"

"You don't remember? You said, 'Please help my daughter—she's dead.'"

She shuddered.

"It was a horrible thing to hear."

"Yes."

"The strangest thing was—I could see you," I said. "I was up there on the thirty-second floor, with Mila. The choppers were out and all the lights on the building. I could see the whole site. And all I could think about was that I was looking at you. You were right *there,* and I didn't have a way to see you. But if I just kept looking for long enough, maybe that would change. Like a Magic Eye picture or something."

"When I think about that poor girl. Mila. That poor mother. Dead now—and without a single answer about what happened to her."

It seemed necessary to tell my mother that it wasn't her fault—but what good would that have done, really? She knew that, even if she couldn't allow herself to believe it. "What about Rait Belen? Is he dead?"

"I don't know—I heard he returned to some village Back Home. But I don't know if he's still alive."

"He'll outlive us all."

"I still can't believe Popovich. Knowing who that man was, everything he'd done, and still offering him a home. I guess he thought nobody knew."

"Bezi Duras knew," I said.

"Did she?"

"Yes. She was always suspicious of Mila. Always trying to get Mila to speak to her in Ours. She didn't have much language herself after so many years abroad, but she could tell Mila was keeping something back. And she could tell there was something about Mila worth puzzling out."

"That girl had razor wire around her—and who could blame her? Imagine being steeled all your life for the inevitability that your father was going to be accused of horrors you couldn't even fathom, and then having to believe that no matter what you hear, none of it is true. That your father is a good man. A hero. That everyone else is wrong, and you are right."

"She had the right temperament for it."

"You always believed she'd be found."

"I believed she wasn't dead. I still believe it."

"Foolish girl. Why?"

"Because—Bezi Duras once told her she was stone all the way down. And it was true. And people like that, they don't just die. They crawl out from under bridges after a thousand years of entombment with their teeth gritted and keep right on living. But they don't just die."

"What the hell are you talking about?"

I let myself think. "Remember when I was so sick and quiet that fall we first moved in with Ena? Well, I saw Bezi Duras's mastectomy scars, and I thought it meant something about her."

"Like what?"

"I don't know. But I told Ena about it before she died and she told me that Bezi Duras's dogs were actually human men, transformed."

"Oh, Ena." My mother put her hands over her face. "Always spinning nonsense for you—it drove me crazy. Rest her soul."

"Well, I not only believed it, but I spent the whole of that year trying to prove it. I wanted to be able to tell you it was true. That night I went missing? We were following Bezi and the dogs out onto South Falls Island."

My mother sat up and looked at me. "I could've killed you. I came home and you weren't there. I called the police, and they told me you'd be home when you got hungry."

"Well. Now you know. That's where we were."

"God. How crazy. I could strangle Ena for that. I wish you'd been out doing something normal—sneaking into a party or something. Following Bezi Duras to South Falls Island because you thought her dogs were human men. God in heaven." She was still staring at me. "Did she know you were following her?"

"I don't think so." Then I told the truth: "I don't know."

"So if something had gone wrong—if someone had stolen you, or worse. Not a soul in the world would have known what happened to you." I looked into this abyss with my mother. It was the worst thing she could think of, and suddenly it was the worst thing I could think of, too.

"I wasn't afraid enough of the city, I guess."

"No, that's not it. I didn't grow up afraid, either. But I think when you have that mindset that Ena kept trying to shove you toward—that magic nonsense. You don't have a sense of true consequences. Everything comes out okay somehow, because somebody has to be left standing at the end. But people aren't left standing. Thousands, hundreds of thousands, have died and nobody knows about them. They're buried God knows where. Like that poor girl."

"She's not dead."

"See? That's Ena talking. That's Ena's belief."

"It's not belief. It's certainty." Here was the door, and I walked right through it. "When you went missing, I asked Bezi Duras to take Mila instead of you."

My mother went still. "What are you talking about? What do you mean, *take*?"

"I didn't want you to die. I thought she could help. So I asked her." She was quiet long enough for me to believe I had an opening. "You've thought it was your fault this whole time. But you see, it was actually mine."

She laughed. "God forbid—hush now with that nonsense." I
felt her hand on mine in the dark. And that was all, really. After
all this time, that was all. My mother said, "I never wanted you
in the grip of that folksy stuff."

"But you were raised with it, too. The folksy stuff."

"Yes, but—but that's not what Back Home was like. Ena
wanted you to think it was all forests and toadstools and magic
violins, but it wasn't like that at all."

"It *was* for Ena."

"But not for me. My youth was the stuff of life. So was hers,
until the world turned vicious and broke her heart. We'd ride
our bikes up the coast in the morning. Her and me and all the
neighborhood young people. Backpack on and a little jacket
rolled up for later, and some money in case you wanted to buy
something, though we almost never did. Just a line of us pedal-
ing up the highway and the cars all beeping gently to let us
know if one of us strayed into the road. This vendor at the halfway point who always had apricots to give us—for free, because
we were just kids, and she knew our mothers, and it made her
happy to see us go by, it gave her a sense of safety to know that
we were always coming up on a Saturday, and we always would.
We'd ride right into the city and leave the bikes in a big heap by
the fountain and then wander around, getting ice cream, peering into the bookshops. The musicians were always there, so
the air was filled with music—all different kinds, a violin on this
corner, a soprano on that one, boys rapping and handing out
their clips as you walked by. Café after café full of life, people,
conversation. And the beautiful city girls with their loose hair
and bare arms. Your aunt Ena, she lived those things—but they
didn't mean the same thing to her. When she was young, in the
time when she was most herself, when she wanted to burst out
of the stitching that held her together, she wasn't allowed to be

part of it the way I was. She didn't feel safe in it. So what she carried with her was that old stuff, death and enchantment. But my life was very different."

"I wish I'd known about your life," I said. "Why didn't you ever talk about it?"

"Because it was gone, Sil. And I didn't want to get all tangled up missing it."

"I'm sorry I never got to see it."

"I'm sorrier. I wanted that for you—that life I had. I wanted to tell you: *Here is how I grew up, how Baba kept me safe, and that's how you'll grow up, and how I'll keep you safe.* But by the time you were born, it was gone. And I thought: 'Well then, we'll just head someplace else and find it.' But it was gone everywhere, everywhere, everywhere. They kept telling us it wasn't, but it was. And my heart just broke and broke and broke every time we staked up someplace new and found more of the same. The same confusion and uncertainty. And I realized that I'd brought you into life at a time when everyone else's debts had come due. Only, the debtors weren't around anymore to pay up. So it'd be you doing the paying. And the life you were going to live would be nothing like mine. You couldn't plan for it. I couldn't even see two years down the road, let alone five or ten. All I could do was keep you in one piece so that you could live to see what it would eventually become. If you'd told me, when I was that young girl sitting under an umbrella in the town square, *She'll have none of this, your kid. She won't know a year that was safer or calmer than the one before it. She won't live in a time when she can expect anything. Nothing you know will be useful to her,* I would never have believed you. But you know something?" She reached out and squeezed my temples. "Your kids won't find peace or happiness in the things you had, either. The things you had, the things you saw will probably be gone by the time they're born. You'll find yourself telling them about your youth and they'll look at you like you're crazy, and it'll hit you that you have to explain how elevators worked. Or trains or something. And that's all right. They'll be all right, just as you've been. Here or back in Paraiso—or on the moon, hell, I don't know. The past is immense. But it means less and less. So we go on without. And that's fine, Sil. It's fine."

THIS MORNING, WE ATE COLD BEANS AND WATCHED the other cars pull out of the campsite one by one, until we were the only people left on the flat. We lingered to watch a pair of antelope in the distance, so we were late leaving. May called around noon to check in on us. "How you girls doing, Snoopy?"

"Almost home," I said. "Dinnertime at the latest."

"Call when you're an hour out, then. I caught a couple trout down in Greys this morning—I'll throw them on the fire."

"That sounds lovely."

He seemed oddly quiet, even for the way he was getting these days. I asked him what the matter was. "I had a caller today who said—well. Something's happened. Or at least, I think it has. You won't believe it. I'm not sure I do."

"What is it?"

"Better listen to it yourself. Do you have signal?"

"Some."

"I'll send it through."

We were in a long, aspen-brightened valley, weaving in and out of signal, but the urgency of his voice made me speed into the curves. We drove up a steep hillside overlooking a pale blue lake—which my mother said she recognized. "I know this place," she said. I figured she had seen it in a brochure or maybe one of those photo arrays at the train station. "No," she said. "I *know* this place."

So we had to linger while she tried to remember why. We went down to the beach and walked among the nodding heads of abandoned umbrellas. My mother sat down on a deck chair and began unlacing her shoes.

"Oh, I don't know, Mama," I said. "I don't know about that water."

"It's safe," she said, and went down to the shore and dipped her feet in. I took my shoes off and joined her. It was a little slimy but otherwise cool and fine.

About twenty miles from there, we found a little shack boasting that it served THE BEST RASPBERRY MILKSHAKES IN THE WORLD, and we sat around the parking lot, waiting to see if anyone would return and open up. Only a couple in a little van rolled through—and the four of us caravanned out of there after a while, apparently doomed to enjoy only the second-best raspberry milkshakes in the world from then on.

I didn't remember May's caller until my mother was back at the wheel in the late afternoon. The episode loaded slowly, stalling out every few minutes in the middle of the usual stuff: a story from a young woman who'd spent her late childhood in a street gang collecting rook crane eggs for money; a story from a water-taxi driver who fondly remembered the way people would ask him to take the long way through their old, submerged neighborhoods. Nothing particularly unusual, but it was nice to sit back with May's voice all around us in the car. The last caller was a person named Tida.

"Hey there, Tida, what city reminiscence do you have for us today?"

"So, this is one of those truly weird things that happened in my neighborhood about two years ago."

"And what neighborhood are we talking about, Tida?"

"Battle Hill."

"I used to live in Battle Hill."

"Then you'll really appreciate this, Dispatcher."

"Go ahead and tell me."

"Well. So a few years back, there was this painter of some renown who lived in an old luxury tower up the street, and she died. Everybody in Battle Hill knew her by sight, but didn't know much about her except that she was old and had a habit of walking her dogs late in the evenings. And the dogs were absolutely massive. Wolfhounds or something. Nobody could believe that a solitary person could have a handle on them. And sure enough, when she died, the coroner couldn't get up there to retrieve her body because these hounds didn't want to let her go, and they were starving now that she was gone and would go crazy if anyone so much as touched the door. Experts from all over the city come in, but nobody can find a way to talk to the dogs, or a command to subdue them. And these dogs are like tanks, Dispatcher. I'm telling you. So the police chief decides that the dogs need to be shot, and a sniper is sent up to the thirty-third floor to do the deed. We're all below, protesting, because it seems cruel and why not just wait to see if the old woman has kin, or if someone else in the building will take them, you know? Anyway, the sniper finds a good vantage point, sets up his equipment. But when he peers inside, there's no sign of the dogs. He sees only the lifeless old woman, lying in this room full of paintings. What exactly is he supposed to shoot? He keeps radioing down, 'There's really nothing for me to do here.' He waits around a while for the dogs to drift into the room, but they never do. After he packs up, the police try the door again; and sure enough the dogs come roaring back.

"Finally, after a couple of days of this back-and-forth, this young woman shows up at the police station. And she says, you know: 'I grew up in that building. I know those dogs. I can help.' I was there the day she came by, and I can tell you: she was a tiny little thing. Rail thin, with these huge green eyes. Rude as hell, too—we heard she was so rude to the attending officer that he nearly threw her out of the car on the way up-island. Anyway. The girl comes in. She doesn't say a word to any of us. Against the protestations of every person there, she rides up in the elevator, opens the apartment door, and just goes inside. Soon afterward, she comes out with the dogs behind her and goes back downstairs. Everyone is so preoccupied with getting the body out, they fail to keep track of her. And by the time we look around for her again, she and the dogs are gone."

"And—what?" my mother said, after we'd listened to the account a second time. At the first mention of the dogs, she had pulled over onto the gravel shoulder somewhere at the top of a pass. It was gray out now, and promising a bit of rain. "What?" she said again.

"I don't know."

"Well, what does May mean? Why did he send you this?"

I could picture May sitting by his phone, waiting to hear back from me about the caller, and I kicked myself for having taken so long to listen to the clip. Perhaps he'd already tried me to see if we'd had a chance to listen. Or perhaps he'd resigned himself to waiting to talk about it until my mother and I got back. In any case, he would be indoors now, fussing over the little potbellied stove to get a fire going—for my mother, who hated the cold. When we finally got in that night, he would embrace her the way he usually did: with one arm, lifting her up off the ground. It would turn out that he had set the table—potatoes, greens. Three trout from his expedition that morning would be sitting on the butcher's block in the kitchen, salted and oiled, stuffed with lemons, amid scattered votives and wine corks, and the little mismatched gilded glasses we had bought at a flea-market sale, and streamers he'd found God knows where, while he sat in his chair listening for our tires on the drive. He'd have spread everything out as if thirty people were coming. Music would be playing. By the end of the night, my mother would dance with a lamp.

Before all that, though, she leaned in to look at me. "What does this mean?" she asked again.

"I think he might believe this girl was Mila." Mila, who climbed out of her cage one wild evening with her captor dead and what was left of the city gathered in the courtyard below; Mila, who stood outside the door, whispering endearments of some bygone age, of some place that no longer existed, in that language Bezi Duras had always known she understood, until she heard the dogs move back from the door, and she turned the knob, saying, *Don't worry, boys, I'm here, it's all right, it's all right, it's all right.*

"That's absurd," my mother said.

"I know."

"But don't you see how absurd it is?"

"I do."

An hour later, as we were entering the Greys River canyon, with thirty miles still to go and a wall of pines darkening before us, some coolness I'd never known came in and sat with, not between, us. My mother touched my arm again. "What if it *was* Mila? What if it was her?"

"What if?" I said, and so it was.

Acknowledgments

Most of this book—the parts of it that made it into the final draft, anyway—was written in the hazy half-dream of pregnancy and early motherhood. It would not exist without the love and support of family and friends, especially Dan, Caroline, Rachel S., Rachel A., Parini, Jill, Shima, Steph, Emily, Cathy, Jared, Maria, Nana, Greg, and Lucas.

It would also not exist without the sanctuary and solace provided by the Teton County Library.

I have been fortunate to travel this road for many years with a brilliant and passionate publishing family. These are strange and frightening times for books. Seth, Andrea, Rebecca, Will, Caspian, Maria, Melissa—thank you for tending the flame.

And finally, I am grateful to my students—some of the smartest, fiercest, kindest, most talented and resilient people I have ever met. How lucky I am to know you.

The Morningside

Téa Obreht

Random House Book Club

Because Stories Are Better Shared ™

A Book Club Guide

A Letter from the Author

Dear reader,

The germ of an idea for a book can be a difficult thing for a writer to pin down. You retrace your steps through years of work and life. You try to track down the first draft, the first line, the first note you scribbled on the back of a takeout menu. In some cases, you arrive at the beginning and find a single moment: a sighting or interaction when you became instantly obsessed. In others, you realize that a series of impressions moved into your mind and heart and lived with you for years without you even realizing it.

For me, in the case of *The Morningside*, it was a bit of both. My husband and I had moved to Wyoming after many years of living in New York, and I was feeling unexpected nostalgia for the city. I had struggled, while living there, with the sense that I didn't really—or perhaps *couldn't* really—know New York. It was a maze of history and narrative, and it guarded its secrets closely, as all cities do. Away from it, I began to realize that my knowledge of it was made up of singular, intimate moments I had taken for granted: The sight of a tiny, frail, elderly woman walking three Rottweilers along Amsterdam Avenue. How the huge new luxury tower that had replaced a historic building two doors down had changed the quality and movement of sunlight on our little street. It was early in the pandemic. I was trying to write and was feeling drawn again to the dark woodland folktales of Yugoslavia, where I had been born, and which

I had left just a few years before it ceased to exist. I was thinking, too, about my family, their heartbreak and displacement and lifelong struggle to belong. All these things coalesced one afternoon into a single scene: a mother and daughter walking down the street toward a massive empty tower in a city ravaged by the rising tide. Who were they, this mother and daughter? Where had they come from? How had they ended up living in this tower? What was waiting for them there?

It took me years to write my way to the answers to these questions. Thank you with all my heart for joining me here, and I hope you enjoy getting to know Sil and the women that shape her life: her mother, her aunt Ena, her friend Mila, and her upstairs neighbor, the elusive and mysterious Bezi Duras.

Thank you for joining me in *The Morningside*.

Yours,
Téa Obreht

The Vila in Slavic Folklore

The Vila was a spirit of the mountain. Not every mountain had a Vila; but every Vila had a mountain, some high place from which she could observe her lands and tend her gardens without interference.

The Vila (plural: Víly or Vile) is a type of mythological creature bearing roots in Slavic folklore. Slavic mythology ties their origin to pre-Christian times, with the story spreading across various Slavic nations, each with slightly different depictions of these mystical beings. The tale of the Víly is steeped in the culture of these areas, emphasizing both fear and reverence for the supernatural, which were common sentiments in ancient Slavic societies. As is the case with most mythological creatures, the Vila's characteristics and lore diversified over time as its story grew with the expansion of Slavic culture.

Víly are typically portrayed as stunningly beautiful young women with ethereal qualities, similar to nymphs or fairies in other cultures. They are endowed with magical abilities and can shapeshift, often transforming into swans, horses, falcons, or wolves. Known to be fiercely independent, they reside in natural landscapes such as forests, mountains, meadows, or clouds. They're sometimes believed to be the spirits of women or girls who died prematurely or in tragedy. The Víly's interaction with humans varies in different stories; however, they are typically seen as both beneficial and dangerous, rewarding those who treat them well and punishing those who disrespect them.

Questions and Topics for Discussion

1. Describe the setting of *The Morningside*. What did you think of Island City as you came to understand it? Did your feelings change as you delved deeper into the world?

2. What similarities, if any, did you see between the world of the novel and our own?

3. What does Bezi Duras represent for Silvia?

4. "There's a world underneath the world," Ena tells Silvia. "You can't ask and ask and ask to see it. Otherwise, these glimpses of it, they turn bad" (50). What do you think she means by this?

5. "Her version of things became the only one," Silvia says of Ena. "She could change the reality of something you thought you'd known all your life" (32). What does Ena become for Silvia? What does Silvia lose when she loses Ena?

6. What did you make of the story of the Vila?

7. What role does the Dispatch serve for Island City's residents?

8. In what ways does *The Morningside* feel like a folktale? What characteristics does it share with other stories in that tradition?

9. Why does Silvia's mother forbid her from mentioning Back Home or speaking Ours? Do you think she was right to make these rules, given the events of the novel?

10. Ena, Silvia, and Silvia's mother all have different memories and ideas of what Back Home was like. How do these recollections differ? Have you ever found that your memories of a time, place, or person differ drastically from someone else's?

11. What did you make of May's career trajectory? His mistakes? Do you think he deserves forgiveness?

12. Discuss the Dancing Girl billboards and their slogan, "We're nearly there" (24). Do you think Island City will ever return to its former glory? What do you envision for the city's future?

13. What did you think of Mila's father when he first appeared on the page? How did your feelings evolve as you learned more about him?

14. If you could create a protection in your life, what three objects would you use? Why are these objects meaningful to you?

15. Do you believe Bezi Duras is a Vila? Does it matter? Discuss.

© ILAN HAREL

TÉA OBREHT is the internationally bestselling author of *The Tiger's Wife*, which won the 2011 Orange Prize for Fiction and was a finalist for the National Book Award. Her second novel, *Inland*, was an instant bestseller, won the Southwest Book Award, and was a finalist for the Dylan Thomas Prize. Her work has appeared in *The Best American Short Stories*, *The New Yorker*, *The Atlantic*, *Harper's*, and *Zoetrope: All-Story*, among many other publications. Originally from the former Yugoslavia, Obreht now lives in Wyoming.

teaobreht.com
Instagram: @teaobreht

About the Type

This book was set in Caledonia, a typeface designed in 1939 by W. A. Dwiggins (1880–1956) for the Merganthaler Linotype Company. Its name is the ancient Roman term for Scotland, because the face was intended to have a Scottish-Roman flavor. Caledonia is considered to be a well-proportioned, businesslike face with little contrast between its thick and thin lines.

RANDOM HOUSE BOOK CLUB

Because Stories Are Better Shared

Discover
Exciting new books that spark conversation every week.

Connect
With authors on tour—or in your living room. (Request an Author Chat for your book club!)

Discuss
Stories that move you with fellow book lovers on Facebook, on Goodreads, or at in-person meet-ups.

Enhance
Your reading experience with discussion prompts, digital book club kits, and more, available on our website.

Join our online book club community!
 randomhousebookclub.com

RANDOM HOUSE